# A CHIP ON HER SHOULDER

## A Magical Romantic Comedy (With a Body Count)

### R.J. BLAIN

A CHIP ON HER SHOULDER
A MAGICAL ROMANTIC COMEDY (WITH A BODY COUNT)
BY R.J. BLAIN

After a deal with loan sharks sours, Darlene's brother is permanently transformed into a chipmunk. Not one to accept impossibility as a good excuse for failure, she's determined to rescue her brother and secure revenge against those who'd poisoned him with grade-a transformatives.

If she wants to perform a miracle, she'll need to join forces with a divine, but the man upstairs and his angels refuse to help.

None of the other so-called benevolent divines are willing to help her, either.

Running out of time and options, Darlene prepares to storm the gates of hell for her brother.

She never expected to fall in love with the Devil.

Warning: this novel contains a woman with a chip on her shoulder, humor, and one hell of a hero. Proceed with caution.

information storage and retrieval systems, without written permission from the author, except for the use of brief quotations in a book review.

Cover design by Rebecca Frank of Bewitching Book Covers by Rebecca Frank.

# ONE

My brother had lost his human life
for five thousand dollars.

RATHER THAN TRY to talk my brother out of
the money he rightfully owed them, the local
mafia's loan sharks opted for a more permanent solution to their problem. They transformed my asshole brother, Jonas, into a
chipmunk and saddled me with the bill.

My brother had lost his human life for
five thousand dollars.

What a waste.

Since that wasn't bad enough, the goons
my brother had pissed off forced me to watch
the entire process, which involved forcing
him to drink a vial of clear fluid. The transformation took a matter of minutes, and he
started screaming within seconds of consuming their concoction.

It took until he'd shrunk to half his true
size to stop screaming, and he squealed
instead.

Shapeshifting hurt like hell; I went
through the gruesome process every few

days, when my thin, human skin drove me to the brink of madness. Some days, I took on my more hybrid form, sporting a tail and my feline ears. Sometimes, I tossed in a light coat of spotted fur to ease my discomfort. Sometimes, I kept the thin, human skin to pretend I fit in with the rest of the neighborhood, hiding my tail and ears beneath my clothes. One day I'd give up on hiding my true nature. Every rare now and again, my hybrid transformation came with a full coat of fur, my ears, and my beautiful tail, something I loved.

My light coat was a mockery of my full glory, and one day, I'd master my magic so I decided which parts of me had light fur, no fur, or a thick coat best suited for wintry mountains.

My spots were my best assets, and I loved each and every one of them. Life would be so much better when I could wear my spots whenever I wanted.

When the mood struck me, the night was young, and the weather was cool, I ran as a snow leopard, displaying every one of my spots and hunting through suburbia for prey, typically one of the more annoying squirrels or rabbits to menace my garden.

I'd be hunting for bigger prey soon enough, and I kept my expression cold and calm. Warning my prey I would be coming for them wouldn't do.

A wise huntress gave no warning before the ambush, and I would use every opportunity to crush the entire mafia. Unlike the local law enforcement, who played by civilized rules, there would be nothing civilized about me.

They had destroyed my family, so I would destroy their family. No, I would do far worse than merely destroy their family. I would destroy their ambition while I was at it. When I finished with them, ruin and suffering would be all I left in my wake.

Sometimes, I was not a very good person. Actually, no. Most of the time I was not a very good person.

I'd learned early on being good left me taken advantage of, alone, and miserable. When I did good, I did it because I wanted to, expecting nothing in return, for I'd learned that lesson well enough.

What went around rarely came around, and I'd gained nothing from any of the good I'd done in my life.

I kept my breaths slow and even, waiting while doing my best to detach myself from the reality of my situation. Panic would win me nothing, neither would fear. Patience might win me a lot, depending on what I learned in the next few minutes.

One of the thugs, someone who'd gotten into a fight with a fire and lost, held a rather nasty gun to my head to make sure I behaved.

I behaved, but only because we had one rule in our household of two: survival came first. Once I survived my current mess, I would add a new rule to our household of one and a rodent: revenge would come eventually.

I couldn't win against eight men who'd cut their teeth on violence, not even if I transformed and put my sharp claws to good use. Not yet. I'd keep my claws a secret for a little while longer, and when I brought them out, I would shred their entire outfit.

Revenge would be mine, and I would enjoy obtaining it.

Revenge wouldn't save my brother. If I had fought against the mafia he'd tangoed with, I couldn't have saved him anyway. They likely would have killed us both. I'd find some way to do the impossible and restore my brother somehow. The man my brother had been was gone, replaced by a chipmunk with a rodent's puny little brain.

No, he was still my brother, but he possessed a rodent's puny little brain. He might remember me. He might even be able to understand English and allow me to keep him outside of a cage.

Maybe.

That stung.

My brother was an asshole. He probably deserved some form of punishment at the hands of the mafia, but he was my asshole brother, and nobody beat him other than me.

I would make that our third household rule, and I would adhere to it.

I took my time memorizing the faces of

those who'd pay for their crimes. Their scars would make them easy to identify. I wouldn't forget their scars, I wouldn't forget their faces, and I gave it a week for me to learn their names.

Then the fun would truly begin.

They weren't the only ones who could get their hands on transformative drugs. It just cost a little money or having the right ingredients available. I could get the money, and I could go where the rare ingredients grew.

So hellbent on revenge, I barely remembered the conversation leading up to my brother's transformation into a rather small rodent. I remembered the part about the money, where they wanted me to bring it and when, but the rest remained a blur.

I needed to memorize their scarred faces so I could do what an Esmaranda woman did when she got mad.

I'd get even, and I'd charge interest.

My mother, may her soul rest in peace, had taught me that from the day I'd busted out of maternal prison and escaped her womb.

Picking my brother up by his furry little tail, the lead asshole, who had a rather ugly scar over his nose where someone had failed to slice his skull in half, tossed him my way. I forgot about the gun pointed at me, scrambling to catch my brother so he wouldn't escape. He squealed and squeaked protests before biting the hell out of my hand.

What an utter asshole. I prevented him from running away and losing all chance of becoming human again, and he bit me? When I refused to let my brother go, he took another chomp out of the fleshy part of my hand connecting my index finger and thumb.

I bled.

The mafia goons laughed, and then they left.

They'd pay for that, too.

Come hell or high water, they'd pay.

AS THERE WAS no way in hell I could afford my brother's debts without selling off the shit he'd spent borrowed money to buy, I stuffed the asshole into a shoebox until I could get him into a chipmunk-proof cage. Earning the money back would take a few days, and I'd have to play the game just right.

To get revenge would require I play dumb and act like I didn't have all the money, but some of it; I'd need to give them enough of it for them to lure me into the cycle. They'd then charge me extra interest to profit on the situation.

I'd gather information, and once I was ready, I would destroy them.

Jonas squeaked and scraped his tiny claws against the cardboard, which warned me I'd have a limited amount of time to get a cage before I would need to find some other container for him.

"You're a pain in my ass," I complained, taping the box closed before I transformed my hand enough I could stab holes into the lid with my claws. Jonas squeaked. "Oh, shut up. I didn't hurt you."

While my brother was a pain in the ass, I'd never hurt him. Well, permanently. If he ever became human again, I'd be beating common sense into his thick skull so he'd never cut a deal with the mafia ever again.

He deserved a sound beating, one that'd teach him not to be so infernally stupid.

Spewing curses that would've had my mother either beating the sin out of me or laughing at my creativity, I grabbed my purse, which contained the spare keys to my brother's car. I marched for the street, where the source of my brother's misfortune waited. The mafia could've taken the sporty vehicle and gotten more than they'd ordered me to give them without an issue, but no. That would've been too easy.

That wouldn't have sent any messages to anyone. It wouldn't have forced me to play their game.

Thugs like them, pasty white trash who thrived on suffering, never wanted the easy way out. They liked the hunt.

Well, they picked on the wrong woman. Not only did I get mad, I would get even, and

I would bring ruin to their empire in so violent a fashion even the Devil would fear me.

My brother was damned lucky I loved him. "I swear, once you're back to human, you're going to be licking my feet and begging for my forgiveness, you furry little shit."

Jonas squeaked a protest and pawed at the thin walls of his shoebox prison.

"Break out of there, and I might just eat you. You're dumber than a fucking stump. You're lucky I'm spending a single penny on you. Tonight, I'm spending at least an hour tearing into you over this bullshit, and you will sit there and take it like a man even though you're a rodent-brained moron now." I growled, and when that didn't satisfy my flaring temper, I hissed. "And the first thing I'm doing is selling this piece of shit car of yours so I can play their game. That'll teach you, because yes, you asshole, you had to have my name on the title because you're so shit at money no sane dealership would sell you a car otherwise. I'll make those goons think they've won, and then I'll show them the true meaning of fear."

Making the Devil cringe in sympathy would be my gold standard.

As I couldn't sell his car if I damaged it, I took care with driving to the pet store. Once there, I tucked the shoebox containing my brother under my arm and strolled inside, heading for the rodent section to pick his new home. A bored employee wandered over. "Need something?"

Any other day, the country bumpkin accent might've amused me. The kid likely spent more on gas than he earned getting to work if one of his parents didn't work nearby. A lot of folks with some money and little sense spent two or three hours out of their day driving to jobs that barely paid their bills.

We had an unofficial rule in our household; if we couldn't make it to work by public transit or within thirty minutes, we moved. If we couldn't afford the rent, we didn't take the job.

Since we owned our house, we never moved, and we took jobs close to home to pay the property tax and keep the place from falling down around our ears.

Considering the supplies, I sighed, bit the bullet, and replied, "Actually, yes. I have a rescued pet chipmunk that can't be released into the wild, and he needs a house. It needs to be a nice house, and I need everything for him."

"A chipmunk?" He asked, and according to his expression, I'd said the best thing he'd ever heard in his life.

"Yes, a chipmunk." I patted the box under my arm. "I'll need a good travel container for him, too. He'll be coming places with me often."

"That's so cool!"

Great. Not only did he likely spend more

on gas than he earned, he loved animals enough he wouldn't complain about the drive or the wasted money. Oh, well. I'd benefit from his enthusiasm even if he tired me out. "Pick out the best stuff for him, and I'll need food, treats, and toys, too."

The kid started grabbing stuff off the shelf and adding them to my cart after asking if I liked his choices. As arguing would only extend the pain, I approved everything, expecting to wipe out most of my bank account caring for my idiot brother.

After I got his furry ass back to human, proving the impossible could be possible in the process, I'd make him pay me back tenfold, and I'd make him quake in fear of my wrath if he screwed around again.

In some ways, I envied the kid and his carefree delight in helping me shop. I worked as a slave at the neighborhood grocery store, stocking shelves because the boss didn't trust me with the customers. He'd caught me on the street with my ears and tail, and he'd brought the CDC into it, but their fancy meters hadn't registered any diseases, barring me from being fired as I hadn't done anything wrong.

To keep my job, the CDC sent a damned bureaucrat over to steal some of my blood to feed to their demonic meter, confirming I wasn't infected with lycanthropy or some other nasty disease someone might catch from coming in contact with me. Usually, they sent some doe-eyed girl to play to my nicer side, the one who wouldn't punch her in the face for annoying me.

The first and last time they'd sent over some damned baby devil who owed someone a favor, I'd socked him in the nose and told him to fuck off and tell his master hello. The devil had stuck around long enough to steal a drop of my blood for the meter, but I'd made him pay for it tit-for-tat with interest.

Devils pissed me off.

They reminded me of the mafia, and they worked for an even nastier boss.

"There are better chews for rodents at the cash register, but if you can give me a few minutes, I'll ask my manager if I can use the office computer to check which diet is best for a chipmunk."

"I don't mind paying twice, but I'd like to get him into the carry case while you do that. Help on what to feed him would be great."

I lied in more ways than one, as until I got a chance to vent out my anger over Jonas's stupidity, I couldn't care less what the fucker ate, I did mind paying twice, and I only wanted to put him in a better carry case so I wouldn't have to hunt for his ungrateful, selfish ass if he escaped me.

I did have to give the kid credit; he was as efficient as he was enthusiastic, and while I did have to ring up my order twice, it took him less than five minutes to get the information on what my rodent brother needed to eat. Jonas squeaked his protests and beat on the smooth plastic of his new carry cage, balling his little paws into fists.

I lifted him up, stared him in his beady little eyes, and whispered, "Well, it's your own damned fault you're like that, so you just sit your furry ass down and be grateful I didn't toss you out on the lawn to fend for yourself."

My brother sat his furry ass down, which offered some hope Jonas was still in his chipmunk body somewhere—or at least understood some English.

Almost two hundred dollars later but with enough toys, treats, and chews to keep my brother fed for six months, I left the pet store, loaded my brother's car with his new habitat, and returned home.

One of the mafia goons waited for me on my doorstep, and I considered digging out the pistol hidden in my brother's glove box. Narrowing my eyes, I leaned over, popped it open, and grabbed the weapon, checking that the magazine had been properly loaded with bullets and making certain a round was in the chamber and ready for duty.

I got out with my purse slung over my shoulder, my brother's gun in one hand and my brother's cage in the other. "You sent your invitation already, so you get the fuck off my lawn, or I'll send you back to your family with a new hole. If you're lucky, I'll patch it before tossing you into the street so you don't make a mess on my grass."

As I'd expected my brother to get me into shit one way or another, I stepped so I presented as small a target as possible, extended the firearm, and waited.

The shock on his face amused me.

Revenge would be far more fun if they offered me a little challenge while I destroyed them. After all, I needed to achieve my gold standard and make the Devil cringe.

I smiled for my unwanted guest. "Did you really expect me to go unarmed after I had a gun held to my head once already today? Obviously, since you're on my doorstep probably trying to deliver some new threat. Deliver it, then you get your ass the fuck off my property. You've finished your business with my brother, you've issued your threats, and while my brother may have broken the law, I haven't, this is my house, and I will call the cops."

"You'll call the cops?"

"A bunch of men broke into my house, turned my brother into a chipmunk, and threatened me. Unlike my idiot brother here, I have a clean record and no association with you cockwombles. So, yes. I fully intend to call the cops, and if I have to shoot you first for being on my lawn and trespassing, well, that's a pity, isn't it?"

"How did an ass like him have a sister like you?"

"I'd say ask our ma, but she abandoned ship." That was better than saying she'd died and left me the house since she hadn't trusted my brother. The way I figured it, she'd been one hell of a smart woman, and I hoped she was taking over heaven along with our pa.

Nobody believed our pa had been a well-respected pastor.

He hadn't taken the emergence well, growing up with his religious beliefs challenged by the strange and stranger. Some days, I wished the angel hadn't come calling. My pa might've lived a little longer that way.

Then again, maybe not. His heart would've given out on him eventually.

While I usually practiced good trigger discipline, I eased my finger onto the trigger to make it clear I'd shoot if given a single excuse. "Well, what'll it be? You going to leave peacefully, or will I be shooting you before I call the cops?"

"We don't need to bring the cops into this."

"You're a lot dumber than you look. You used a transformative on him. That's permanent. Law says I've gotta report his new status as a chipmunk. If you braindead morons wanted to keep the cops out of it, you should've done something else."

"You're one of those law-abiding goody-goodies?"

"I get a paycheck for becoming my brother's caretaker, and they might be able to help me restore him back to human. If you didn't want me calling the cops, you should have picked a different plan. Now get the fuck off my property. The safety is off, a round is chambered, and what's one less of you thugs out to bother people?"

"I have a message for you."

"Deliver it by mail, then, and don't you even think about making me pay postage."

"But—"

"I'm about three seconds from shooting you, and I really don't give a fuck if I put the round through your forehead. You got me? If you haven't figured out I mean business, look really carefully where my finger is resting."

He checked, and he had enough sense to blanch. "I'll be telling the boss about this, little girl."

"Tell him if he wants any money out of my brother, well, you idiots should've left him in a form he's capable of paying in. Leave. Now."

He did, and he got into a black car. I made a show of clearing the chamber, popping out the magazine, replacing the round, and restoring the firearm to working order before gesturing with the weapon for him to leave.

While shooting out one of his tires would've appeased my temper, I let him go.

I had enough troubles without doing more than informing the assholes I wouldn't go down without a fight.

## TWO

Rule one: angels did not like when
people reacted to their lack of a
head.

TAKING my brother to the police station
earned me a lot of odd looks, and while I
waited for my turn to speak with the lady behind the plexiglass shield, I wondered why
the cops bothered with such flimsy protection. Ever since magic had come flooding
into the world, guns had made way for
fancier ways of killing people, and the shields
they favored might stop a bullet, but it did
little good against a practitioner with a
grudge.

The guy in front of me left with a slip of
paper, and I went up to the counter, set my
brother onto the ledge, and said, "Some mafia
thugs turned my brother into this chipmunk,
and they told me to pay them. I have a clean
record, and I request an audience with a
divine."

A divine might help. I'd get an angel; the
police worked with angels all the time, and

they tended to like humans to a certain degree. I'd also get the truth and nothing but the truth out of an angel. If an angel couldn't help me, I could ask if they could put me in touch with another divine who might be able to undo what the mafia had done to my brother.

"Name?"

"His or mine?"

"Start with his, then give me yours, please."

"Jonas Esmaranda. He has a record, mostly misdemeanors. I'm Darlene Esmaranda." I pointed in the direction of our house and told her where I lived. Then, because I bet one of the scarred assholes had a record, I described each and every last one of the cockwombles who'd poisoned my brother with a transformative.

The cop dutifully wrote down my report, and she pointed to one of the hard plastic and metal chairs bolted to the floor along the wall. "Sit there, and I'll pass along your request for a divine to verify Mr. Esmaranda's condition and listen to your statement."

"Thank you." I sat down where directed, put my brother on my lap, and settled in to wait. I'd never made use of an angel before, but after running with my brother and his crowd, I'd heard stories about them.

Rule one: angels did not like when people reacted to their lack of a head.

Rule two: angels really didn't like when people cursed too much, but a little cursing was okay as long as you didn't commit some act of blasphemy.

Rule three: definitely don't mention anything about Jesus Christ doing anything on any crackers.

I thought the rules were a little weird, but I could understand the first rule. Of course, the only frame of reference I had was watching people stuck in wheelchairs reacting to the thoughtless reactions of others.

I'd learned early on the best way to handle those in wheelchairs was to smile, offer to help them with pesky doors, and push them up ramps as needed. Once, a little old lady stuck in her chair had needed to go up three steps, so I'd put down my bag and shoved her whole chair up the steps to get her in the store, and because I figured other humans were garbage, I'd waited for her to finish her shopping before helping her down the steps again.

I'd been right about nobody else wanting to help her. Most folks averted their eyes, as though being old and unable to walk was somehow contagious.

Fuckers.

I'd learned early on if I couldn't be bothered to do the right thing, I sure as hell couldn't trust someone else to do it. That got me in trouble, although my kind of trouble tended to involve me losing friends and pissing my brother off because I tended to speak my opinion at precisely the wrong time.

Too bad, so sad.

Not.

My brother sulked in his cage, and I cracked open the lid and slipped my hand inside. "Don't you dare bite me again, you little shit."

Jonas kept his teeth to himself, and I pet his head. While rodents weren't my thing unless I was hunting and wanted a crunchy snack, he had a decent coat, although he'd never match my pristine spots. If he'd been a little more like me rather than like Mom and Dad, the transformative wouldn't have been a big deal. I could shake them off through shifting to one of my other forms. My strange magic broke some of the CDC's precious rules, just like they couldn't figure out why I could shapeshift without the lycanthropy virus.

The CDC really didn't like when people broke their precious rules. I really didn't like that an organization best known for questionable containment of infectious diseases had full reign over all things magical, including regulations on the one damned recreational drug I could use without wanting to kill somebody when the high wore off.

Yeah, I'd have one hell of a record if the coppers ever figured out I wasn't shy about experimenting with things I shouldn't. Pixie dust would remain my favorite hit, as who didn't like a great high with no downer?

My wallet hated the price of pixie dust, so I went without more often than not. When I ran as a snow leopard, I went for my second-favorite substance, although I would never admit to anyone I liked catnip more than pixie dust.

Pixie dust couldn't beat a catnip-induced nap.

A cop emerged through the steel door barring the station entry from the rest of place, and I sighed my resignation. As nobody else was in the waiting area, he was likely about to make more of a mess of my day. Old, tired men didn't like dealing with crazy young chicks who lived in a questionable part of town, especially when they happened to have a sibling with a rap sheet.

Jonas drove me nuts sometimes.

"Miss Esmaranda?"

I gave my brother a final pat and removed my hand from his container, secured the lid, and rose from my seat. "I'm Miss Esmaranda."

"Come with me."

Lovely. Not only did I have the old, grumpy white dude, he'd left his manners at home. Why did I always get the jerks?

Then again, to be fair, my request for divine intervention led to a lot of expense and paperwork—and once the angel verified my brother had been forced to consume a transformative, I wouldn't be the one saddled with the bill.

Victims didn't pay the bills for the angels. The bills became the problem of the guilty, something I wasn't. My brother held responsibility for his fair share of crimes, but I'd had a gun held to my head and been forced to watch him pay the piper.

Angels considered things like that when issuing their verdicts, or so I'd been told.

Stirring the cop's ire would land me into trouble, so I went along with him without a peep. A woman won wars by picking her battles, and if I wanted to tango with the cop, I'd have to bide my time, mince words, and otherwise avoid giving him a reason to give me a hard time.

He led me through a maze of corridors, through a cubicle farm loaded with coppers, and into a small room with the kind of dinky chairs that would make my ass go numb within five minutes. He gestured to one, and aware they made the damned things as uncomfortable as possible to encourage people to tell them the truth faster, I checked it for thumb tacks or other painful things before easing my weight onto it.

Yep, I gave it five minutes before I'd regret coming to the station at all.

"I was told your brother has been transformed into a chipmunk?"

I plunked my brother onto the steel table. He squeaked a protest and waved a furry little fist at me. "This is Jonas. He's my brother, at least when he's not a pint-sized pest out to chew up everything we own. He seems to still understand English. I don't speak chipmunk, but if he bites the shit out of my hand again, I'm spanking the little fucker." I showed the cop where he'd gotten a hold of me. "At least it stopped bleeding."

Well, for the most part.

"Please start from the very beginning, ma'am. What happened, and why do you believe your brother is now a chipmunk?"

"He took out a loan from a mafia shark, and I guess he didn't pay it back. The sharks came over to the house, put a gun to my head, and shoved a vial of liquid down Jonas's throat. He became a chipmunk. This chipmunk, to be specific. Those damned goons threw him at me, and that's when I discovered he was able and willing to bite the shit out of me. I shoved him into a shoebox, took him to the nearby pet store, got him a cage, and then came here. One of the sharks came back to my property, but I've got a concealed carry permit, so I told him to get the hell off my lawn before I fed him to my grass. He wisely left."

"You pulled a gun on someone?"

"After him and his buddies broke into my house and held a gun to my head, you better fucking believe I pulled a gun on someone. He was on my property, and his cockwomble, asshole friends just turned my brother into a fucking chipmunk. What was I supposed to do? Gasp, put my hand to my mouth, and bless their fucking hearts? Men like that don't come to a house like mine without bringing more trouble. I've had enough trouble for one day."

"She speaks the truth," a masculine voice announced from behind me.

"Jesus fucking Christ on a goddamned cracker!" I screeched, jumping to my feet and whirling around. The angel's lack of a head bothered me far less than his nudity, lack of clothes, and rather noticeable lack of genitalia of any sort. His wings, white banded with blue, added a splash of color to his otherwise pale countenance. "At least put some nipples on if you're just going to leave your chest out like that!"

Why did the angel have no nipples? What had happened to his head? What had happened to his poor dick?

Over the years, I'd learned to recognize stunned silence when I heard it, and I realized I'd rendered an angel speechless right along with the cop.

Oh, right. The rules.

I reviewed each one in my head, determined I'd broken all three of them in one fell swoop, and shrugged. "Well, I guess that blows any chance of you helping my brother, doesn't it?"

Maybe I could carve nipples onto the angel, since I'd already gone straight over the line of decency into pure blasphemy.

"Please do not carve nipples onto my chest, Miss Esmaranda. As for your other thoughts, it is not a matter of chance. It is not something we are permitted to do. Your brother is as he is, for he is paying a consequence for his actions. While there is power in prayer, this would be an unanswered prayer. I cannot help you with that request."

Well, shit. "Can you at least tell the cops I'm not lying about those assholes showing up at my house, putting a gun to my head, and forcing me to watch my brother get turned into a rodent?"

"You speak the truth. The chipmunk in your possession is your brother, and you witnessed his transformation."

"Can you tell me what was used?"

"You humans classify it as a top grade transformative. Unlike the lower grades, it will not reverse with time. It would take divine intervention to restore him to even a humanoid form."

"Can't I just give him another dose of transformative? Won't that change him back?"

"I am afraid not, Miss Esmaranda. That is not how these substances work in humans. It would have no effect on him. That is as much of a blessing as it is a curse. You would need the assistance of a divine. *He* will not help you, and as such, *His* angelic host cannot help you. It is not that we do not feel for your plight, but that it is a rule which we must obey."

Well, shit. Since angelic help would be a bust, maybe I could recruit assistance from some other divine. "How about one of those Greek divines? Would one of them help?"

"I fear not. They have no interest in mortal affairs, and many of them still slumber. The ones awake would have no desire to aide you, nor would you be able to pay the price they would ask of you, should they be willing to help."

Fuck. "Egyptians?"

"They are busy with more important matters, although you might be able to do a favor for one for information. I am willing to broker such an agreement with you, to serve as a relay. The Egyptians are keeping their activities modest on the mortal coil for the moment."

"I'm listening."

"Sir, if you might excuse us for a few minutes? This is a matter that should be discussed in private. There will be no point in recording what I speak with her about. Your machines will not cooperate with your wishes."

The cop sighed. "How long do you need?"

"No longer than an hour."

After the officer left the interrogation room, the angel sat on the edge of the metal table. "The work you would do is small now but significant later. You will be meddling on behalf of the Egyptian pantheon to ensure a future outcome, one with potentially dire consequences later. I was made aware of this situation before coming here."

"Who made you aware of this situation?"

"*He* did."

The God Almighty, the head honcho of the Christian faith, involved himself with me? No, with my brother, who made a pretty good candidate for a long-term stay in hell? My mouth dropped open. "Seriously?"

"*He* works in mysterious ways. *He* asked me to take on this task. It is both simple and difficult."

"Okay. I'm listening. What do I need to do for the Egyptian pantheon? Who, I presume, has *His* permission, as you're here negotiating with me to be the plaything of divines."

The angel's laughter chimed, and something deep in my chest relaxed, as though I'd sipped sweet, cool water on a scalding hot day. "You are right in more ways than you can possibly know. This has been in motion for some time. Two months ago, a newborn infant was abandoned and placed upon a ship coming here. The ship docks this evening. There is no one to retrieve the child. You will take the baby to a government building, which I will give you the address for. You will apply for her citizenship and birth certificate. You will name her, for the one who will become her guardian will not be kind in the choosing of it, for she is a black mark upon her family. In their eyes, that is. She is anything but. Once you have named her and secured her citizenship and birth certificate, which will only be a matter of a few hours of your time, you will have her delivered to her guardian. This is where things will become difficult for you."

"Explain."

"You must choose to love this child unconditionally, for you will be the only nurturing hand she will see for many years. You must teach her kindness, for she has never seen kindness before. It is only for a few hours, so this task shouldn't burden you much."

"Nobody has ever been nice to this baby?" I blurted. "But she's a baby."

"Correct. She has had a difficult journey. She was cared for and provided with milk, and she has been kept healthy, but that is the limits of their kindness. She is an unwanted child."

Poor kid. "That's so sad."

"It is. She will have better days, and you will be part of why she will enjoy them."

"Okay. I'll bite. How am I going to be a part of that?"

"Do your part of this bargain, and you will see."

"Angels bargain? I thought that was more of the Devil's thing."

The angel laughed again. "I am doing

something for you, you are doing something for the Egyptian divines, who have requested me to speak with you on the matter. It is, in its way, a bargain."

"All right. So, I just go pick up this kid, cuddle with her a bit, make sure she's been fed, change her diaper, play with her a little, and take her to get her citizenship and paperwork? Then I make sure she's delivered to some asshole who'll abuse her? See, I have a problem with that part."

"It is not quite your time to be a mother, Darlene. You will have your chance down the road. The hard part for you will be letting her go, knowing she will have a difficult life for a while. But because her life will be difficult, she will have the strength needed for greater things later. You will, in exchange, get the information you need to help your brother."

"Does that information also help me get some payback while I'm at it?'

"Perhaps, although I do not believe you need any help with that. You are more than capable of acquiring any payback without divine intervention. I would suggest you temper justice with mercy, but there is no mercy for the merciless, and those you wish to war against have no capacity for mercy in their souls."

"Well, that's good to know. I won't feel much guilt for giving them a serious case of just desserts."

"Desserts?" the angel asked. "Do you not

mean deserts instead? You think of..." He sighed, and I could easily believe he shook his head if he had one. "Pie. You think of pie. Apple, specifically."

"That's right. Desserts. It's delicious, just like a nice piece of pie. Whomever said it was just deserts is wrong."

The angel thought about that. "May your just desserts be appropriately sweet, then."

"I'm so glad we could agree on this matter. I'd say eye-to-eye, but eye-to-eyeless is a little weird."

"I stress you, don't I?"

"You have no head and you left your nipples somewhere. Any sane sentient would be concerned about that."

"Would nipples make you more comfortable?"

"A nice pair of nipples makes man-chests worth admiring."

"You are a wonderfully terrible human." The angel snapped a finger, and the requested pair of nipples appeared in the appropriate places. "Is that better?"

"Absolutely. Your chest is just divine."

"You are a most wonderfully terrible human."

"Thank you for noticing. How will I receive the information I'll be earning tonight?"

"You will be paid in advance for your service."

Huh. "You all are trusting me with this, paid in advance?"

"I have seen your heart and understand its worth. For this night's task, you will be a bright light in the darkness. For those who have taken your brother's mortal life? You will be the darkness capable of swallowing all light. Frankly spoken, Miss Esmaranda, you have anger issues at times."

"No shit."

The angel sighed.

"What? If you wanted an angel, you wouldn't be talking to me right now. You'd be talking to one of your brethren, probably sipping tea. I'll admit, threatening to shoot that asshole on my lawn felt damned good. I would've done it, too."

"I am aware, and they are beginning to become aware of this. Fortunately for you, they find women like you to be rather attractive, so do not be surprised if you find yourself courted by all sorts of unsavory beings."

"There's a special place in hell for rapists, and I mean to direct them there violently. So there are no misunderstandings. I'll join them in hell rather happily after helping them get to their final destination. Does that make my stance on this clear?"

"That was not the form of unsavory I referenced, but while they are not planning to engage in that sort of activity with you, they have other methods they will engage in order to win your cooperation."

"Lovely."

"You are an exotic human, and men like those appreciate exotic women."

"I don't suppose we can just jump to the chase and you tell me what the best name to give that little girl is? I'm no good at things like that, and I don't want to give her something utterly stupid as a name. I mean, a little stupid but pretty might do—at least that way, her asshole guardian won't try to change it."

The angel stayed quiet for a while. "I can offer, perhaps, some guidance on what name you should bestow upon the child."

"Okay. I'm listening, Mr. Angel."

"Michael."

Jesus fucking Christ on a cracker. "I've been mouthing off to an archangel?"

"Indeed. As you say, you have been mouthing off to an archangel."

"And you're just serving as the middleman between me and some Egyptian divines?"

"We have an amicable enough relationship."

"Huh. I'm going to hell for this, aren't I?"

"Very probably."

"Well, that's a bummer. I better at least earn my stay. Where do you recommend I begin?"

"You will not need much help to get to where you are going."

"Well, isn't that just grand. Okay, since I'll be going to hell, I may as well get around to earning it. How can I earn a few points towards my trip to hell when it comes to this little girl?"

"She is Egyptian, although her heritage is somewhat mixed. But her name should be of Egyptian heritage."

"I don't know a single damned word of Egyptian, so I'm going to need a little help with this, Michael."

"She is darker of skin than you, although not as dark as her mother, who is of Egyptian heritage. Her hair is pitch black, a gift from her father."

"It's actually black? It's not a dark brown?"

"Her hair is truly black. It will be quite striking against her skin, and while she will not be a traditional beauty, she will still be quite beautiful in her own right."

"What's the word for black in Egyptian?"

"There are two words for black in Egyptian. Kem is the black of the Nile's silt, and is often used for the color. For a little girl's name, you would use Kanika."

"That's really pretty."

"For you, yes. For her, it will be somewhat of a nuisance. However, because of that, her guardian will not change it. That is a good thing. The name that would be picked would not be pleasant."

"What would this guardian call her?"

"It is better I do not tell you. You will have a chance to bring ruin to that household in due order."

"That sounds promising. Motivate me."

"She would be named as a plague upon their household."

Wow. I'd seen more than a few cases of bad parents in my day, but to name a child after a plague? "That's horrible."

"It truly is."

"Isn't there anything I can do for her?"

"Taking care of that pesky human paperwork will be a significant help to her later. It will give her something invaluable."

"What?"

"Her freedom."

I twitched. "Remember those anger issues you claim I have?"

"I do."

"I'm getting a little angry." Informing the archangel I had issues helped a little, although nothing short of giving any asshole who'd hurt a baby a beating would do.

I had lines. Hurting little kids crossed it.

"You will have your chance to arrange things to your liking later, never fear. Just remember to be subtle. You know how to be subtle already. Just remember it will serve you well to be particularly subtle later. You will understand in the right moment. That is the price you must pay for help with your brother."

"Okay. Fine. I'll make sure she has the right paperwork. Is there anything else I can do?"

"Learn to wait patiently for your turn."

"That's so rude. I know how to wait patiently." After some consideration, I came to the conclusion it was a good thing angels lacked heads, as I had no doubt I would have been subjected to a rather unpleasant glare. "Somewhat patiently."

"Very well. The information you need comes in several parts. I expect you will test the truth of my words because that is your nature, but there is only one divine who would be willing to help you do what you require. The others will not help you. There are many reasons why, but most of them involve the universal laws. Transformatives have a special place in the universal laws, and these substances already verge on breaking them. They turn someone into something they were never meant to be. The lower grades reverse over time. The ones that do not reverse are a punishment for toying with magic beyond the natural order."

"But I'm a shapeshifter. I break that rule, don't I?"

"Of course not. You were born that way. It is a natural part of you."

"But I'm the only one in my family."

"That does not mean it is not a natural part of who you are. Your shapeshifting is a blessing. Consider it a gift from the universe, if you will. Just because your parents, their parents, or their parents before them lack your magic does not mean your magic is not natural."

"But if he had this, he'd be okay right now."

"No, Darlene. He would be dead. He is alive right now because he is what he is."

Well, I supposed life as a chipmunk beat no life at all.

"That is a better frame of mind for you. But that does not change much for you, does it? Do not feel you must answer that. There is only one divine who will help you, but such help would come at a price."

"Doesn't everything?"

"Yes."

In some ways, that made me feel better. "Okay. So, the Egyptians are willing to tell me the identity of the divine who can help me, assuming I'm willing to pay the required price. I don't suppose they'd be willing to help me find this divine?"

"Yes. That is part of the price for you to handle the matter for this child. You will be given a way to reach the divine who can help your brother. They have reason to believe you will be able to convince him, but it will not be easy. They cannot help you with that. Their relationship with him is rocky although somewhat tolerable."

"Doesn't that describe the relationships of most divines from differing pantheons?"

"I do not believe you understand just how much truth you speak."

"That's okay. I don't need to understand. I

just need to beat this divine until he gives me what I want."

"In most cases, I would not recommend that course of action when dealing with a divine, but there is the potential that might work with him."

"Seriously?"

"I am quite serious. As the divine in question does not surface often, you will need the appropriate power in order to survive where you need to go. One of the Egyptian divines will be providing that for you, although I have been asked to bestow that gift for you with a little help from *Him*."

"*He* is willing to step in? For this?"

"Debts are important for *Him*, and *He* has a vested interest in this child's life. One day, you will understand. As I am the relay for this agreement, it is in *His* interest to ensure all goes well."

"Okay. This won't kill me or anything, will it?"

"You will find it will have the exact opposite result."

"Well, as I like living, please tell them I'm very appreciative of that."

"I shall do so."

"The divine. Which one is it? It seems rude to show up and just make demands."

"Lucifer is the one who can help you."

Shit. "You are a feathered freak. You told me I was going to hell because you knew the

Devil is the only one who might be able to help me."

"Yes. I certainly did."

For a long moment, all I could do was stare in utter awe that someone with such a good, benevolent reputation could be that much of an asshole. "I think I could love you."

Michael laughed. "I appreciate that, Darlene, but my good nature would inevitably drive you insane within a few hours of keeping company with me. I am pleased to help you with this task, as my fallen brother deserves everything you will do to him on your quest to restore your brother to a more appropriate form."

"He'd like if I beat on him, wouldn't he?"

"He is not called the Lord of Hugs. There is a reason for this. He is the Lord of Sin, the Lord of Lies, and the Warden of the Hells. You will find his sense of humor twisted at best. That is what an eternity of being the gatekeeper does to a soul. The Egyptians did not even whisper the hint of a lie on this matter. You have all of the tools in your possession to get what you want, with the exception of being able to fully survive in my brother's many hells. *He* will help you with that on behalf of the Egyptians. After all, only *He* truly understands my brother's full powers, and the Egyptians would not repay you for your help with your death."

"Dying would not help my cause."

"Precisely."

"What time does this ship arrive?"

"It will reach the harbor in an hour, but it will be another two hours after that for someone to remember the child."

I wasn't sure who I hated more at that moment, the monsters who'd turned my brother into a chipmunk or the ones responsible for a baby's misery. "And if I show up early to remind them?"

"That would lead to her being in your hands sooner, yes."

Fuck it. "Get the cops off my back. I'll go get the kid."

"While I can do this, it would result in some of your brother's crimes coming to light."

"What are they going to do to a chipmunk? He's already caged. It's like a rodent prison."

"This is a sad truth. I will remind them of this and appeal to their better natures. It does not mean he may not need to pay for his crimes, but he may not need to pay for them quite yet."

"I can work with that. Just tell them I'm rescuing a baby or something."

"I will do this for you. Please sit still for a moment. This may sting. I would also be wary of thinking too much about fire for a while, else you may find yourself using magic you do not wish to. Use this fire with a purpose. Accidental incinerations would be distressing for you."

"You're trusting me with fire?"

"You certainly can't wander into my brother's many hells without protections. I will likewise safeguard your brother, although he will find he will not be able to summon any actual flames like you will be able to."

"But a fire-breathing chipmunk would be so cool, Michael."

"No."

Oh, well. "Sorry, Jonas. I tried."

My brother squeaked in his travel-sized prison and sulked in the bedding I'd given him.

Michael chuckled. "I will do my best to be gentle with you, but this sort of magic tends to be hard on humans. It will hurt, and you will be stunned for a few minutes. You will come to no lasting harm, however. That much I can promise."

"Do your worst," I invited.

He did.

Over the years, I'd gotten into my fair share of fights, and while having my clock cleaned hurt, not a single one of the punches I'd intercepted with my face came close to comparing. I burned from within, and by the time the pain settled to something closer to tolerable, I'd sprouted tails, ears, and a full coat of fur. I hissed at him, flexing my hands. My claws had grown in, too, a sign my body had gone into full defensive mode.

"I would apologize, except I had tried to warn you."

"So you had."

"I helped your clothes better fit your current form. I recommend you pick the child up as you are. It will comfort her."

"It will?"

"She loves cats."

"But she's just a baby."

Something about Michael's body language made me believe the archangel smiled. "Cats are special to Egyptians. It will make her happy."

Well, if something so little would make the baby happy, I'd play along. "That leaves my last problem. How, precisely, does one storm the gates of hell?"

"Your first thought is to storm the gates of hell?"

"Well, yes. How else would I gain audience with the Devil?"

"I have not been this entertained yet in this emergence. There are many ways to gain an audience with my brother, but I doubt any of them would be quite as interesting as you choosing to storm the gates of hell. Should your efforts to gain entrance to his many hells fail to go to plan, I will give you his phone number."

"Excuse me, but did you just say the Devil has a phone number?"

"Yes."

"They have phone service in hell?"

"He enjoys electricity, too. He is the Devil, Darlene. He is also quite spoiled and requires his luxuries. You will find his domain comfortable—assuming you win an invitation into his actual domain rather than a lengthy visit to his dungeons."

"I'm receiving mixed signals about him, Michael."

"I did not say anything positive about him there, Darlene."

"I like electricity, I want to be spoiled, and I wish I could require luxuries to get through the day. A comfortable domain is important. And he has a dungeon." I smiled at the thought of what I could do to the assholes who'd transformed my brother with an entire dungeon to work with. "Nope. I'm not seeing a problem with this. Anything else I should know about? I don't want to get offed by some angry woman thinking I'm edging in on her turf."

"My brother is an eternal bachelor. His succubi are convinced should they be chosen to be his bride, they will find themselves in holy monogamous matrimony until the End of Days. They are not wrong. Some parts of his angelic nature remain. Frankly spoken, he has no loyalty at the moment, but should he give his loyalty, it will be for all eternity."

"Why does that sound like a warning?"

"Because it is."

"I'm going down there to browbeat him into helping my brother, not join any succubi in seducing him. I've heard incubi are a good time, though." As I doubted angels had much conception about humans and their preferences, I added, "I'm not into other women."

"What makes you think my brother lacks the abilities of an incubus?" The amusement in Michael's tone annoyed me into scowling.

I took a few minutes to think about that. "I really don't have the time for commitment right now, but hey, I'll seduce the bastard if it means he'll hurry up and make with the magic to fix my brother. I'm not above using my feminine charms." I stood up, took hold of my beautiful tail, and showed it to the archangel. "Look at this beautiful fur. This tail is worth at least one brotherly transformation."

"If you say so."

## THREE

What sort of asshole names a cargo
ship the Attack Goose?

ACCORDING to the address Michael gave me, some asshole had shipped a child on a fucking industrial cargo ship. My tail puffed, and nothing I did convinced my fur to lie flat. It would have to do, as I couldn't afford to take the time to go home, take a cold shower, and brush my coat to restore it to order. Unfortunately for me, the address was in a rather secure complex, which would make getting to the little girl interesting.

I'd start with the security gate, and if they gave me a hard time, I'd gain access another way.

With my tail still puffed out and my ears lying flat, I approached the closed steel monstrosity of a gate with its guard post. "Excuse me, but I was given this address. I've been tasked with picking up some very important cargo from a ship." I referred to the slip of paper. "The ship is the..." I stared at the name scribbled on the sheet, blinked, and read, "*Attack Goose.*"

The guard snickered.

I glared at the paper. "What sort of asshole names a cargo ship the *Attack Goose*? Come on. Is that even the ship's name?"

"It is. It's a privately owned ship out of Canada, and the owner hates geese. The ship is real, and she just arrived. Do you have the docking number for your cargo?"

That explained the long string of numbers and letters on the bottom of my paper, which I handed over to the security guard. He picked up a phone, relayed the number, and after a moment, he hung up. I waited, my ears perking forward as the guard hadn't turned me away while laughing.

"Okay. Do you have a vehicle?"

My brother's car, with my idiot rodent brother trapped inside, waited at the street, as I hadn't been brave enough to drive it to the security gate. I pointed at it. "The sporty one over there."

"Drive it on in. You're going to go straight in, go to the third stop sign, and turn left. Follow that street until you see Pier A. Turn right and park wherever your find a spot. Give one of the cargo hands your docking number. They'll bring you your cargo. You'll sign off, and then you can come out the same way you came in, and I'll let you out of the gate."

"Thanks, man. I really appreciate it."

"Expected trouble?"

"Well, yes."

"Don't worry about it. We usually get a few small item pickups every time a ship comes into port. The owner of the vessel often opens his ships up to smaller freight."

I opted against notifying the man the cargo was a living, breathing human. As far as I was concerned, taking the little girl to the CDC would put an end to any possibilities of human trafficking, which I appreciated.

It wouldn't make her life any easier, but I would cross that bridge again later, and if I really didn't like what the archangel had set up, I'd insert my foot in his ass.

Kicking an archangel's ass seemed like a pretty good way to go if I were to make an unexpected exit from life. The headline would be amazing.

I retrieved my brother's car, discovering Jonas had made himself a nest and indulged in a nap in the short time I'd been speaking to the guard. As promised, the guard opened the gate for me, and I followed his directions to Pier A, where a frenzy of activity surrounded a massive cargo ship with Attack Goose proudly painted on her side.

I supposed if the owner could afford such a huge vessel, he could name it whatever he wanted. After a few minutes of figuring out where to park, I moved my brother to the backseat, earning a disgruntled squeak before he returned to his sleep. Armed with my slip of paper and docking number, I found an employee. It took several tries before I found someone who could help me, and he took my paper out of my hand, boarded the ship, and left me waiting like an idiot. I stayed out of the way of the people scurrying around, waiting to unload the freight containers, the kind I expected to be on a train.

The man brought me a box and handed it over. "Good luck. She's a screamer."

"Don't I need to sign for her?"

"No." He left me with the box, and I peeked inside, torn between furious anyone would just dump a baby in a box and hand her over to some strange cat lady and pleased I wouldn't have to deal with more paperwork.

I took her to the car, buckled the box in, and pulled away the pale yellow blanket. A baby with tufts of curly black hair slept, and while she'd been dumped in a box, someone had made an effort to make a nest for her. Several diapers were crammed into the box at her feet along with a baby bottle and a jar filled with cream-colored powder.

I'd have to sort that mess out if I needed to feed her before handing her over, but I figured the CDC would be able to help me take care of the little girl as needed.

People sucked. At least Michael had foreseen the loss of my first scrap of paper, giving me the address for the CDC headquarters on a full page along with a statement relaying everything he'd told me.

The archangel's signature shimmered on the page and glowed with a soft, gentle light.

It took me almost an hour to reach the CDC's headquarters, where I parked in the public lot. The baby continued to sleep quietly. Unable to tolerate the thought of carrying her into the building in a fucking box, I put her diapers, bottle, and jar into my oversized purse along with my idiot brother, who squeaked his protests over being treated like cargo.

"Deal with it, Jonas. If you hadn't been an idiot, you wouldn't be in a tiny cage right now. We'll talk after I handle this."

I eased the baby out of the box, and aware she needed to have her head supported, I cradled her in my arms, cooing at her in case she woke.

She did, and she stared at me with dark eyes. She inhaled, and I braced for her screaming, but she cooed back at me instead.

I stroked her hair, startled at how soft and thick it was. "There's a good little girl. Don't you worry. I'll make sure you have everything you need."

I hated I'd have to let her go, hated the lies I knew I told, and wondered how much trouble I'd get into if I just ran with her. I understood the basics.

The reality of my situation squished any hope of keeping her. With an entire mafia out for my brother's blood, my need to deal with the Devil, and everything else life insisted on throwing at me, I wouldn't be able to guarantee her next meal or clean diapers.

That wasn't fair to her.

Damn it.

I didn't even like babies. Babies weren't cute—except she was, with her big dark eyes, her chubby little cheeks, and her whisper-soft coo and pudgy, reaching hands. She kicked at the blanket, wiggling in my arms.

With my free hand, I offered her my fingers as a toy. With surprising strength, she grabbed hold onto my fur, brought my palm to her face, and rubbed.

Why couldn't I take her home with me? Disgusted with everything about the situation, I forced a smile, pretended I didn't want to cry, and kissed her forehead. "It'll be okay, little baby."

One day.

Maybe I'd make a second deal with the Devil, going behind the archangel's back and making certain someone took care of her later in life. Maybe I could make the Devil go deal with the assholes who'd abandoned her.

I could work with that. What was one extra demand added to my list? If I could get the Devil to do the impossible with my brother, how much more could he possibly charge me for a good deed destined to ruin his reputation if anyone found out about it?

Storming the gates of hell and taking over seemed like my best and only option, because the Devil wouldn't do a bunch of nice things without a damned good reason. Ruling over the Devil's hells would be annoying, but I didn't have to keep the place for all that long. He could have it back once I was done with it.

Of course, I might need it long enough to make a very warm reception for any assholes who hurt the little girl I held. Ruling hell for a minimum of eighteen years would annoy me, but some sacrifices were worth making.

The Devil would just have to live with being my minion until I finished my work and claimed her all for myself. With the baby drinking up attention, I spared the few extra minutes for her to satisfy her desire to try to mark my hand as her territory. Rather than cry, for either food or a diaper change like I expected from an infant, she yawned, gave a final kick or two, and resumed her nap.

The anger and resentment over my lot in life roiled to the surface, but I refused to frighten the baby. As always, I bottled everything inside, settled my purse over my shoulder, and carried her into the headquarters armed with the letter an archangel had written to make sure she got to where she needed to go without incident.

The security guard took one look at the note, paled, and asked me to sit and wait until someone came for me.

Within five minutes, an older gentleman in a pristine black suit with a red tie strolled over. I appreciated his lack of a smile; it somehow seemed more honest to me.

"I'm Francis Lemon. I have read the letter written on your behalf, and I've called to verify its authenticity. I've prepared the basic documentation, and as you're her current guardian, you will need to sign them. With an archangel vouching for the situation and de-termining she is at risk without United States citizenship, the government has opted to nat-uralize her despite her lack of American an-cestry. You will need to verify under oath that you retrieved her from the vessel, she had no one with her, and all of her possessions."

"Are we counting some diapers and for-mula as possessions?"

"No."

"She doesn't have anything, then."

Mr. Lemon scowled. "While we are aware that the household she is intended for has blood ties, we would like to take a few pre-cautions to ensure she does not become a vic-tim. With an archangel expressing concern, we have cause. However, it requires some pa-perwork, and there are some fees for the han-dling of the situation."

The fees would be a problem, but I had my brother's annoying car, and I already planned to make the mafia he'd tangled with kiss my pretty spotted ass. "How much?"

"A hundred a year."

"That's it?"

"That's it. It mostly consists of a legal re-quirement for an agent to verify the whereabouts of the child until the age of sixteen, at which point she will be considered old enough to handle most matters on her own. It will require any future guardians to meet with the agent, with her in attendance, to ensure she has not been unlawfully sold. The penalties for violating this are quite severe. Considering the circumstances, it would be wise."

"I'll pay that. Can I pay the entire amount in advance?"

"Yes, you can do that. The payment will be due in thirty days."

I did the mental math. If I scraped together every penny I had from every account I had, I would have enough—barely. I'd be stuck on paying for anything else, but I could make the payment on time. "Okay. That's good. Where will I need to pay?"

Mr. Lemon pulled out a slip of paper and offered it to me, and I discovered it was a printed invoice for the first year of the service, a list of what the government would do in exchange for payment, and a file number. "Call the number on this invoice, and they will direct you on how to make a payment. If you're paying by check or cash, you can bring it to any CDC or FBI building. Either agency can handle the payments for this. You may also take your payment to any United States courthouse for processing. If you'll follow me, we'll handle the signing of the paperwork, issue her passport, and take care of everything else she needs to ensure her general protection."

"May I ask a question?"

"Yes, of course."

"Isn't this a little excessive? I mean, I tried to get my passport once. It was not easy."

"You don't have your passport?"

I shook my head. "My original birth certificate isn't readily available, and I was a minor at the time I requested it. Seventeen. They needed a parental signature."

"Estranged?"

"Orphaned."

"What's one additional passport being processed tonight? We have the ability to pull up vital records as necessary, so we'll take care of that upstairs. We have angelic verification of your identity, so you won't need a parental signature or supporting documentation. There will be a small fee to process the passport, but as there's an angel involved, you'll get to skip the expedition fees."

Huh. For the first time in my life, was I actually experiencing the reward of having done a good deed? If I ever crossed paths with Michael again, I'd have to ask him about that. Aware of the archangel's claims about the baby's treatment, I kissed her head and rocked her. "Can I ask a possibly strange question?"

"Of course."

"Is it possible to pay for more frequent checks on her? I don't know the household she's going to, but I don't trust them." I hesitated, but as I toed lines anyway, I added, "Michael gave me reason to believe there will be problems. But I can't keep her."

I wanted to.

I didn't even understand why.

Mr. Lemon's expression darkened. "Normally, I would say it's not, but I will make an exception. The fee may be higher, but we have learned to trust the word of angels—and archangels. And archangels do not interferc with mortal affairs without good reason. How often would you like her to be checked on?"

"I would pay to have it done once a month if I could."

If anything, only to make certain her future guardian walked a narrow line.

If something happened to her, I wanted to know—and I wanted to know immediately.

"I think an arrangement can be made, and I have a few ideas on how to make sure the guardian doesn't do anything inappropriate. But the day she turns sixteen, she'll be on her own. And if she were to run from a potential situation earlier? Well, arrangements can be made to make certain she is able to take care of the necessities. That can be extended later into life as well."

"What do you mean?"

"When guardians are flagged as problematic enough a divine interferes, there are steps the government takes to smooth things over. When she's sixteen, she'll have an easier time with obtaining a driver's license, especially in terms of permanent residency issues. She'd be able to get an exemption for her license, as well, in that she won't have the curfews newer drivers face, as we can't control her work hours. She'll also be legally able to work at a younger age. It's a permanent flag on her record, which employers, landlords, and the government sees if her name is run in the system."

"She doesn't have a last name."

"That's fine. We have a special form for that, so as long as her first name is unique, she has a birthdate in the system, and she has some other information, which the government will provide to her and only her, she'll be able to function."

"Will her lack of a last name be a problem?"

"No, not really. Not with the flag in place. Please come with me, and we'll take care of this somewhere a little more comfortable. Will you want to take the baby to her new guardian yourself?"

If I met the guardian in my current mood, there would be a murder, I wouldn't be able to storm the gates of hell to help my brother, and my life would be even more of a mess. "Can I decline? I'd rather this person understand the government is carefully watching her. However, if I could have a copy of her passport, birth certificate, and whatever other official documentation that is available for her, I'll hold them safe for her."

And, down the road, perhaps I could hunt for her and make sure she had a happy adulthood even though her childhood would be less than ideal. Something was better than nothing.

I could live with my guilt for that long—and once I had the Devil doing my bidding, I could make a real difference.

As far as plans went, I delved into the dark depths of insanity, but what was one more impossibility added to what I already intended to do?

"Yes, of course. I will make sure to send a pair with backup to impress upon the guardian that the CDC and FBI will be keeping a close eye on the situation."

I allowed myself a grim smile. "I don't suppose you can recruit an angel or devil or demon for that task, could you?"

"Normally, I would not mention something like this, but should you ever have children, ma'am, you'll be one hell of a mother. You've gone into momma bear mode, and you haven't even had custody of her for more than an hour or two at most."

I indulged in cuddling with the little girl, grateful she peacefully slept. "She deserves it."

"All children do. It takes a special person to be willing to take on such a burden for a child."

"She's my responsibility." It didn't matter

she'd only be my responsibility for a short while. I'd heard Michael. If I didn't show her love and compassion, who would?

"And that's special. I see a lot in my job, but it's rare for someone to take on such a burden for another's child. Most would flinch about the fee for once a year, and I bet the only reason you hesitated about once a month was you trying to figure out if you could afford the payments."

"Yeah. That's right. I'll figure out some way to pay it," I promised.

"If needed, I'm not above coercing an angel or find a charity to pay for it," Mr. Lemon confessed. "I can't do much, but I can do that much."

"I'll do my best to take care of the payment myself."

"I understand that, too." Mr. Lemon led me to an elevator and up several floors, taking me to a small office with a couch taking up the space his desk didn't. "This will take a few hours, so please make yourself comfortable."

I sat where he directed, settling the baby onto the cushion and retrieving my brother from my purse. Jacob gave me a dose of the cold shoulder.

"Is that a chipmunk?"

I held up his travel case. "This pain in my ass is my transformed brother, as he decided it was a good idea to make a deal with some stupid loan shark. They gave him a transformative. This is the result. If this adds complexity to my passport, I will understand."

"It sounds like you've had an interesting time of it lately, Miss Esmaranda."

"Yeah. You might say I'm having a devil of a time right now. It is what it is. Silver linings and all that. It could be worse."

"I'm afraid to ask," he confessed.

"I could be unable to do anything at all."

## FOUR

You're lucky I love you too much to
eat you, Jonas.

THE PAPERWORK WENT SMOOTHLY, but I delayed the proceedings because Kanika woke up and required care. Once fed and changed into a clean diaper, I fell prey to her charms, cooing and playing with her for almost two hours before I caved to the inevitable.

She needed to go to a different home, and I needed to storm the gates of the Devil's many hells to get my brother back. Revenge came second to that, although I would work hard on that front as well. No matter how much I wanted to keep her, I couldn't.

Handing her over hurt my heart, but I refused to say goodbye.

I'd see her again someday, so I wished her well and told her to kick ass in the process. Teaching a baby to curse wouldn't win me any points, but an archangel had already confirmed I'd be going to hell long before I saw any heavens, so what was one more infraction on my list?

Armed with an official copy of her pass-port, her birth certificate, her social security number, instructions on how to renew them all, more instructions on how to act as a su-per-secret guardian agent, and more instruc-tions on how to smooth the way for her into adulthood, I left the CDC's building and headed home with my brother in tow.

I dumped my brother on the front seat, buckled his cage in, and hissed at his wretched little car, one of the sources of my many problems. Jonas complained in a squeak and beat at the clear wall of his cage.

"You're lucky I love you too much to eat you, Jonas. I have a date with the Devil be-cause of you, so you better watch your pip-squeak mouth. Once you're back to human or the equivalent, I'm going to kick your ass so hard you can't see straight for a month. After you can see straight again, I'm going to kick your ass again. The number of times I kick your ass will be determined by how much you piss me off between now and returning you to your proper form."

That shut my idiot brother up.

"Good. There are some new rules I expect you to abide by. You will eat the damned chipmunk food and like it, you will not stage any escapes from your cage, and you'll behave for once in your fucking life. In exchange, I'll provide food, I'll let you out of your cage now and then so you can stretch, and I'll clean your cage every day. Because I'm having to deal with a fucking mafia because of you, I own your soul for the rest of eternity. You hear me?"

My brother squeaked but bobbed his head.

"You're a fucking moron, and you're lucky I love you." I drove him home, got the gun out of the glove box, and checked the street for unusual vehicles. Once satisfied, I got out, gathered my brother's cage, and kept the gun close and ready for trouble. I checked the mailbox, which had a letter addressed to me with no address, which I assumed came from the mafia. I returned to the car, grabbed my brother's gloves, and put them on before picking the envelope up. I shook it, watching for any telltale signs the envelope came with extras.

Nothing came out, and I heard papers rustling within. I turned it upside down and shook it again. Nothing came out.

Satisfied there were no basic powders inside waiting to make a mess of my day, I checked the front door of my home before unlocking the door. Everything was as I had left it, although I did a sweep of the place before sitting at my kitchen table and setting my brother's gun aside. I set Jonas down in the center of the table, went back to his car, and ferried all of his new supplies inside.

Setting his tank up in the living room counted as an asshole move, but I figured he could suffer with anyone coming into the house beholding him in all of his chipmunk glory. I considered tossing the television to the curb to add to my asshole move, but I left it alone, transforming the coffee table into his new home, turning the television on to his favorite channel, and dumping his ass into his new habitat.

"If you escape from your cage, I make no promises I won't eat you," I warned.

In reality, I would be eliminating chipmunk from my diet until he was returned to his proper shape, but I wouldn't tell him that. While the mafia hadn't scared sense into the idiot, maybe threats of being eaten by his sister would.

Jonas wisely settled in his new home, made himself comfortable, and watched the television.

With one problem solved, I returned to the kitchen and the letter, likely from the mafia who'd made a mess of my life. Using a fork and a letter opener, I tore into the envelope, and I snagged the grill tongs as my tool of choice to dump the contents out onto the table.

A business card and a letter waited for me, along with a few rose petals. I used the tongs to open the letter, which proved to be handwritten in neat cursive, first thanking me for not having added a new hole to one of the writer's sons and requesting to meet with me in a week. The letter contained an address in Manhattan, directions on how to get there by car and public transit, and a request to wear something that showed off my assets.

I twitched, well aware of Michael's warning of how the mafia would behave because of my status as a woman willing to shoot assholes who crossed me.

Great. Just great.

The business card informed me I dealt with the CEO of an investment firm, and I wondered why Lorenzo Gallo would be dumb enough to leave a trail of paper evidence I could take to the police. I thought about it, returned everything back to the envelope using my various tools, and dumped it into my kitchen drawer.

I'd think about how to deal with the letter in a few days. In the meantime, I had a bigger fish to fry.

Since the Devil was the only damned entity in the universe who could help my brother, storming the gates of hell came first and dealing with Lorenzo Gallo and his odd invitation came second. Taking over the Devil's hells long enough to secure a future home for baby Kanika came third, as I had sixteen years at a minimum to complete that plan.

It was important to set my priorities based on immediate need versus future desires, and I refused to fall prey to shortsightedness like my brother had. No, I'd play the short and long game, and the Devil would be the center of all my plans.

If I could tame the Devil, Lorenzo Gallo would be child's play in comparison.

I didn't even need to tame the Devil. I just needed to make him do what I wanted. I could trust an archangel to speak the truth and nothing but the truth, and he'd given me some very useful clues.

The Devil had an angelic streak in him, and I could use that to my advantage. But how? I went to the landline, picked up the receiver, and dialed the number Michael had given me.

The archangel answered on the second ring. "It did not take you long to seek my counsel."

"I have decided I'm hunting your brother, and I'd like to bargain for anything I might be able to use against him."

"You're hunting my brother?"

"I absolutely am hunting your brother."

"But why?"

"I need to rule his hells if I want to be in a good position to give that little baby girl a nice home later in her life, which means I have to conquer your brother. If I conquer your brother, then I have the full force of those hells at my disposal to make her happy. That's right, isn't it?"

For a long moment, the archangel remained silent. "You are very determined, I see."

"She deserves better. I'm going to have to rob your brother a little to pay for her monthly check-ins, too. They offered yearly, but that wasn't good enough. I requested monthly. I have to pay that bill, but your brother can afford it, right?"

"Yes, without difficulty. Bargaining is not typically the domain of angels, but we can come to an arrangement you will find acceptable."

"I'm listening."

"While my brother has fallen, he is still my brother, and I do love him dearly."

"Well, that could be a problem, as I'm fully intending on storming his gates and taking the place over. You said he had electricity and luxuries, and he might be a good enough protector for that little girl. I gave her instructions to kick ass before I gave her to the CDC to take to her blood relatives."

"She will," Michael promised. "There are, perhaps, some things you should know about my brother before you make any decisions."

"I'm listening."

"He cannot have children. That was a consequence of his fall."

I snorted. "He can dote on little Kanika when she grows up. Do I really look like the type that wants to deal with nine months of some brat kicking at my internal organs? Hell no. Apparently, I am the kind who might snatch unwanted babies and keep them. I really thought about keeping her, Michael. If my brother wasn't a chipmunk right now, I would have just taken that little girl home and made sure she had everything in her childhood she needs and won't be getting. But I can't guarantee anything for her right now. So, I'm going to whip your brother into shape and ruthlessly use him so I can guarantee things for her later."

The archangel laughed. "I know. You have no current interest in procreation, although you do have a general inclination towards mothering those in need of affection. My brother has already made a bargain regarding the child," Michael announced. "It was made upon her birth with her father. It will be some years before he will have to do his share of the bargain. He does not fully understand the consequences of the bargain he has made. He is somewhat blind in these matters."

"What are you talking about?" The Devil had already forged a bargain involving Kanika? I narrowed my eyes, turned my ears back, and growled.

"Please do not fret. There is nothing amiss with my brother's bargain. If anything, he is intrigued by what was offered to him. Kanika's father cannot tend to her for important and good reasons. As such, he bargained with my brother so that she might, after she turns twenty, have a divine eye guarding her. My brother does not yet understand he has stepped onto the path of becoming a father, although he has comprehended he will have some of the burdens and responsibilities of fatherhood. My brother is as dense as he is vain. *He* is quite amused over the situation, and *He* looks forward to watching his fallen son step onto a new path."

"Being a father is more than donating sperm."

"Precisely. My brother is limited in some regards, and he forgets this—or he simply does not understand what he has believed he can never experience."

"I saw her first."

"This is true. My brother has not seen her, nor will he for some years. The first time he is forced to move to protect her, my brother will discover emotions he had not believed himself capable of. I will enjoy spying on my brother and watching his latest fall."

"Finders keepers," I announced.

"Bargains do not work this way. He must fulfill his obligations."

"She's still mine. I saw her first."

Michael laughed. "Then you will have to move forward with your plans to conquer my brother. That would make what is his yours, correct?"

"Absolutely."

"Many have tried to conquer my brother since he fell, and all have failed. What makes you think you will succeed?"

"Well, if knocking on his door and asking nicely doesn't work, I'll figure something out."

"You plan on knocking on his door and asking nicely?" the archangel asked.

I giggled at the astonishment in his tone. "Well, that seems like the polite thing to do. It'd be rude to just completely go storming the place. I figure I'll ask first, listen when he inevitably starts doing what he does, and go from there. I'll refuse his generous offers to bargain, though. I'm not asking to bargain with him. I'm going to be telling him to do it because he's not completely awful."

"I am not certain of your chances of success, as I do not wish to ruin this surprise. I wish to behold his face myself when you do just this."

"Does that mean you'll take me there? Honestly, I called you for directions on how I might storm his gates. I don't even know where to start getting there."

"I can take you there, but my brother gets somewhat cranky when I step foot into his domain. He is not permitted to act unless I act against him. Bringing a soul to him is not acting against him."

"You're bringing my whole body with the soul, right? I don't know a lot about this, but I do know I need my soul."

"Yes, you do need your soul."

"Having an archangel for backup might be good. If I'm storming his gates with an archangel as backup, he might take me more seriously. Hey, do you happen to have any other brothers who would come along just for the joy of watching me storm the place?"

"As a matter of fact, yes. I could ask

Gabriel, and I am certain he would enjoy watching you storm the gates and do your best to conquer our brother."

"I'm accepting any free advice you might have for me to do this right. After paying for the monitoring bills for Kanika, I'm going to be beyond poor, and I still need to put together the cash for my idiot brother and secure revenge on those assholes. You hadn't been joking about them, had you? I found a letter with rose petals in my mailbox, and I was invited to meet with some dumbfuck, who wishes for me to showcase my best assets. I'm assuming he wants me to dress up like I'm easy. I'm really not."

"I recommend you inquire with my brother on your apparel for such a venture."

"Which one?"

"The one you wish to conquer."

"Do I want to know why?"

"He is as good at dressing women as he is at undressing them. It is one of his flaws. Should you conquer him, be aware he will wish to dress and undress you often. It is his nature, however flawed that nature may be. I am a benevolent being, and I feel I should warn you about what you face."

I considered my situation. "You said he has the powers of an incubus?"

"He has the powers of all demons and devils. That is part of who and what he is. So, yes. He has even more control over those abilities than incubi. Succubi are wary around him, because his powers surpass theirs. He does not indulge in women often despite his reputation. You might call him frustrated."

Hello. "Are you saying the Devil is sexually repressed?"

"Yes."

I twisted around and considered my plush and perfect tail. "Am I his type?"

"You are a woman. All women are his type. You will find him a determined hunter should you capture his attention, but he enjoys the game almost as much as the prize. He only chooses to use his incubi powers once he has won the game, as he loses if he has to cheat to interest a woman enough to join him in his bed. That is his angelic nature coming into play."

"You're very helpful for an archangel. I really thought you all were above such easy help. How do I thank you?"

"No thanks are needed but your consideration is appreciated. It is like this, Darlene. I do love my brother despite his fallen state. You have enough will to withstand me in the flesh. If you can withstand me in the flesh, you can withstand my brother. He does not want a woman he will inevitably break and mourn for all eternity. But I warn you, storming his gates will have consequences for you."

"All things have consequences," I replied, well aware of the consequences I would pay for my brother's crimes. "That's why I'm talking to you in the first place."

"When do you wish to act?"

While tired, I doubted I'd be able to sleep with the inevitability of paying the Devil a visit looming over me. "There's no time better than the present. I just need to grab my brother."

"I will impress upon him he should stay close to you, as his cage would inevitably melt. Do not expect your first meeting with my brother to go as you hope. He enjoys playing with his prey."

I smiled. "I'm not prey."

"This shall be fun. I will arrive soon with my brother, and we will escort you to our brother's door. Unless you are the luckiest—or perhaps unluckiest—of mortals, I expect we will be escorting you home shortly after."

"And that's fine. It wouldn't be fun if he gave in without putting up a fight for me. But then again, who knows? Perhaps he will enjoy having a woman run his hells for a while. By for a while, I mean however long is necessary for little Kanika to grow up and need a proper family in her life."

"I feel I should warn my brother of what I bring to his door."

I laughed. "You could warn him, but would he believe you?"

"I am an archangel, Darlene. I cannot lie."

"He can know you speak the truth without believing a word you say. That's how you lie without lying, isn't it? You tell him a truth so absurd he can't believe it, thus forgetting you're incapable of lying. Thus you deceive him with nothing but the truth. You can also choose to withhold important bits of information. For example, I will not tell your brother I'm planning on taking over his domain for personal reasons, leading him to believe I'm selfishly working only to restore my brother to a sentient form. I understand human might be a stretch. But sentient rather than rodent would be an improvement."

"You are a truly terrifying creature, and I find the more you speak, the more terrifying yet endearing you become."

"Does that mean you think I'm good enough for your brother?"

"I think you may be the most perfect punishment for him."

While I'd meant something entirely different, being the perfect punishment for the Devil would do if I got what I needed out of him. "That'll work. So, see you soon?"

"I will see you soon."

I hung up, and I smiled.

THE ARCHANGELS APPEARED on my doorstep, and only the color of their wings distinguished them. I sighed at their lack of nipples, clucking my tongue and shaking my head. If Michael had kept the nipples he'd put on earlier, he might have classified as male perfection. "What a waste of such beautiful chests."

"You have a severe chest fixation," Michael replied, and he gestured to his brother, who had red bands on his otherwise pristine feathers. "This is Gabriel. Arguably, we have the best relationship with our fallen brother, so that is why he has chosen to accompany us to our brother's door."

"What an interesting human you are," Gabriel said, his tone amused. "You will find my brother's chest quite attractive, I do believe."

"Does he have nipples?"

"He has all of the parts you, as a woman, find appealing."

Nice. "So he can make good use of his incubus powers?"

"Indeed," Gabriel replied.

"Seduction of your brother is not off the table if it gets me what I want, and I do not have a problem with his tragically monogamous ways. I'm a selfish bitch, and I do not have any intention of sharing should I select a man."

Michael chuckled. "You are hardly a bitch."

"Have you met me? I've been planning murder all day, and I'm going to take over hell so I can murder the bastards, send them straight to hell, and resume what I started. This is not a job I wish to leave unfinished."

The archangels, for headless beings, had quite the stare.

"What?"

"I have never met a human so capable of good yet also so capable of evil," Michael admitted. "It is quite startling, really. You have a strong capacity for kindness, but then I listen to you, and I realize your capacity for kindness is only equal to your capacity for..."

"Evil? Cruelty? Savagery?" I thought about it. "Cruelty might be the word you're looking for. And you're not going to hurt my feelings admitting that. I plan on making that mafia outfit pay for what they've done to my brother. I am assuming, for better or for worse, they have done the same or worse to others."

"Would it soothe you to find out they have?" Gabriel asked, his tone curious.

"Soothe isn't quite the word I'd use. Would I intensify my efforts? Absolutely. If they've done this to others, it's pretty obvious the justice system isn't going to do jack shit for the other victims or their families. I'm happy to cut checks on their behalf and dish out the suffering." I frowned, opened my front door, and gestured for the archangels to come inside. "This house isn't much, but it's what we have. I inherited it because my mother was worried Jonas would make a mess of things. I can't say she's wrong. I guess putting my brother on the coffee table counts as rude, but at least I'm keeping the television on for him so he won't get totally bored while he's a chipmunk."

The archangels walked to the coffee table and leaned over, which implied they had heads and peered at my brother in his glass prison.

Jonas squeaked and retreated into one of his tunnel toys.

"I guess he's not really all that fond of archangels. I'm sorry he's being rude."

"Your brother does not have your good tendencies," Gabriel informed me. "His nature recognizes us for what we are, and he avoids us as a result. You have sufficient good tendencies to not be offended by our presence."

"I'm offended by your lack of nipples."

Michael laughed. "Then you may find our brother appealing. His chest is much like ours, although he prefers darker skin, and he takes a great deal of pride in his physique. Darker skin hides the soot, and he's quite vain. He would spend many hours of every day preening if he had our pale countenance."

"So, you're saying he's a black man with a perfect chest? Are his nipples perfect?"

"He is any color he wishes to be. He adapts to where he goes. If you want him to be pale for you, he can do that. If you want him to be dark skinned, he can do that. If you prefer the complexion of a bronzed Greek god, he can do that. He prefers pitch black skin because it makes it easy to hide the soot and reveals the sins of humankind with ease. He takes advantage of that. He will play to your prejudices."

"I see." I frowned, as I certainly categorized people by their appearances, although I tended to keep an eye out for would-be rapists and the type of men who became loan sharks. "Let's say I wanted to storm his gates and take over the place in an efficient fashion. What would win me the war? Because really, I need him dancing to my tune sooner than later so I can take on this mafia outfit."

Gabriel chuckled. "You could, I suppose, try asking him nicely. I do not believe that has been tried before."

"Really?"

"He is who he is, and most who approach him do so expecting to bargain. They will tell him what they desire, he will counter, and the bargaining begins. No one asks him to do anything for nothing. A price is always expected."

"Interesting." I opened the lid to my brother's cage, plucked him out, and set him on my shoulder. "We have to go to pay the Devil a visit, Jonas, so stay there, behave, and try not to get kidnapped by some lesser devil or demon. I do not want even more work. You've given me too much work as it is. So, how does this work? How does a mortal make a trip to the Devil's door?"

Michael pointed at my brother's sporty car. "You can take that to a gate, or we can teleport. It would be safer for the vehicle should we teleport. It will be less comfortable for you. However, we will give you the address to the gate so you may storm his residence at your leisure."

"Obviously, I am in your debt for this."

Gabriel waved his hand and a black leather briefcase appeared and hovered in the air. He took hold of the handle and offered it to me. "You will find the contents of this useful. Consider us as paid in entertainment at our brother's expense. *He* has granted *His* blessing for our involvement, and *He* has granted us the freedom to deal with this situation however we see fit."

"But why? I'm just…" I waved my hand to take in our plain home. Having a home put us ahead of the game, but not by much. "Frankly spoken, we're poor as dirt."

"The beauty of mortals is their ability to change this world, for better and worse. This is not linked to how little or much you make. You seek to sway the Devil. Should you accomplish your goals, you will change this world."

I considered that. "I could run his many hells like a real dictator and make people want to clean up their act so they don't get an invitation to deal with me in a dungeon. I could inflict a lot of suffering given a dungeon and a good reason."

The first time I'd thought about killing a man, a friend of mine had been raped, and I'd spent many a night fantasizing how I could extend his misery as much as possible. I'd never been satisfied with my daydreaming.

My friend had never recovered from the attack, and a year after her rape, she'd taken her own life.

I'd learned a lot that bitter day.

"While my brother has fallen, he becomes justice, often unseen and unknown. He is the judge and jury. And, however much he resents his role, he works as much for himself as he does for *Him*," Gabriel said, and he gestured to my brother. "This may change your plans, but your brother does not have a place in the heavens as of this moment."

My brother squeaked at the archangel.

I thought about my childhood and the various things my brother had done, and I could believe my brother had done far more evil than good in his life. "Yeah. We're not particularly good people."

Gabriel reached out and stroked a finger over my brother's furry head. "Humans can change. Your nature is often unpredictable. That is as much of a blessing as it is a curse. Only he can decide what he will do with the rest of his mortal life."

"He'll cause me more trouble, that's what he'll do," I muttered.

Both archangels laughed.

My brother squeaked a complaint and waved his tiny rodent fist.

"What's in the briefcase, and should I take it when I stage my invasion?"

"It has paperwork, a laptop, and some funds to help you with your conquests."

I blinked, sat down on the couch, put the briefcase on my lap, and opened it up. Several stacks of hundred dollar bills, the promised laptop, and some paperwork filled the briefcase along with several pens. "I don't understand."

"The money will aid you in your cause and will close doors for my brother to manipulate you with. With the money, you have no need to bargain with him for it. No is a powerful word. Use it on him often," Gabriel advised. "The laptop is a new mortal tool, and you can use it for many things, including monitoring baby Kanika's progress. You will have a login with the CDC, and they will update it monthly so you can track her progress. If you become concerned, you can then act as needed. The cash is sufficient to grease the wheels of your revenge."

"Shouldn't you be discouraging me from seeking revenge?"

Michael strolled around my living room, examining the pictures of my mother and father near the television. "You call it revenge. We call it justice. Your motivation is revenge, yes, but you will be doing great good for others in the process. We are merely removing some of the problems that would bar your path. *He* uses you for the sake of justice. You would be wise to remember that. Your brother is likewise being used. *He* works in mysterious ways. Do bring our brother down low. He deserves such torment."

"Do you love or hate your brother?"

"We love him, of course. He deserves everything you will do to him. Do not hold back." Michael picked up the picture of my father. "These pictures are filled with your love. We could tell you of their fate if you would like."

"You can? They didn't just go wherever they were supposed to go after death?"

"Death is merely an ending and a beginning. Not all souls are suited for the heavens or the many hells. Your parents loved each other dearly. Heaven is only one of the many rewards *He* can grant worthy souls. *He* felt they were deserving of a second chance of a happy life together, so that is their fate. They grow, already smitten with each other, for their souls find comfort in each other."

"You can guarantee happiness in a future life?"

"To a certain degree."

"Why can't you do that for Kanika?"

"We could give her a kind childhood but rob her of true joy. It would be cruel of us to do such a thing. She will grow in adversity, yes, but her challenges will one day become her greatest triumphs. Allow her to endure life's discomforts. Only then will you be able to accomplish your long-term goals. This will displease you. Take your temper out on our brother in the meantime. If he cannot handle you at your worst, he does not deserve you at your best."

I closed the briefcase and rose to my feet, petting my brother with my free hand. Jonas wisely kept his teeth to himself. "Take me to your brother, please. And could you do me a favor?"

"What favor?" Gabriel asked.

"Tell me everything these bastards have done. I want to make sure their punishment fits their crimes."

"You will be challenged to make them suffer sufficiently. If you wish to learn their crimes, speak to our brother of such matters. You will learn all you need to know." Gabriel held out his hand. "We will take you straight to his gates, but I recommend you knock before you storm. It will be more entertaining for you should he have time to shore up his defenses. That will make your victory over him all the more satisfying."

# FIVE

## Would anyone believe you?

I HELD GABRIEL'S HAND, and a blinding light enveloped me. Spots filled my vision, and when they faded, a dark, barren landscape stretched out to the horizon, and gouts of flame shot towards a brimstone sky. Smoke filled my lungs, but rather than cough and splutter, the burn faded within a few breaths.

"*His* gift," Gabriel informed me, giving my hand a squeeze. "Your brother benefits as well. My brother's residence is behind you, but look closely at this landscape and think long on its existence. What do you see?"

In the brilliant blooms of flame, crystals jutted from the scorched ground, capturing the fire in their clear hearts.

"It's beautiful," I whispered, marveling at how something so desolate could hide so much. "What are those stones?"

"My brother's many hells are the birth-place of all jewels, for beauty so often requires adversity. You can find every stone throughout the universe here. Some are ugly, some are beautiful. Unlike the heavens, my brother's many hells touch all places within the universe. That is a secret most do not know."

"Yet you're telling me where my brother can hear?"

"Would anyone believe you?" Gabriel replied in an amused tone.

Huh. "Now that you mention it, probably not. Is it all like this?"

"No, not at all. There are many layers to my brother's many hells. Hell is unique to every soul. Should you earn a punishment from my brother, he will take you to the various options, I am sure."

"You sound way too happy about the idea of me facing a punishment from your brother there, Gabriel."

Michael laughed. "It is not much of a punishment if she likes it."

Oh. *Oh.* My eyes widened. "Nobody told me archangels were perverts. I feel like I have been deceived."

While headless, I got the feeling the archangels both smiled.

Freeing my hand from Gabriel's, I turned to face the Devil's home. In some ways, the sprawling stone structure reminded me of a gothic cathedral blended with a fairytale castle, with tall spires, looming crenellations, and a startling lack of gargoyles. A stone wall topped with wrought iron surrounded the place, short enough I could see over it but tall enough I'd have to put a little effort to get inside if I didn't opt to walk through the open gate.

The urge to close the gate so I could storm the place properly settled in, and I eyed the entry, debating if I wanted to make things more difficult for myself. "Think he's expecting company?" I spied an intercom mounted into a post, positioned where a driver of a car might be able to press the button and gain access. "This is rather civilized."

There would be plenty of time to be rude soon enough, so I strode to the intercom and pressed the button, amused at the chime that came from the speaker.

"If I didn't want you to come in, I wouldn't have left the gate open," a gruff, deep voice announced, and the intercom fell quiet.

"Is that your brother?" I asked.

Michael patted my shoulder and gave me a gentle push in the direction of the looming structure. "Indeed. He is annoyed. His voice gets growly and deep when he is annoyed. His guests have likely annoyed him."

"But I haven't even done anything to annoy him yet. I mean, I'm going to annoy him. I annoy just about everybody."

"The damned souls," the archangel clarified.

Oh. Right. Them. "You call them guests?"

"It is polite."

"Would you say they deserve to be here?"

"Absolutely," Gabriel confirmed.

"Call them fucking assholes," I suggested. "Guests sound like they don't deserve to be here."

"You are a ruthless being."

I marched down the cobbled driveway, which ended in a huge circle outside of the Devil's front doors, which were fashioned of wrought iron and decorated in a rose and thorn motif. "I'm just getting started. I hope your brother is hot. He better be hot."

The archangels followed me, and after a moment of hesitation, Michael asked, "Why must my brother be hot? Which sort of hot are we discussing here?"

"The kind of hot that tempts me into taking my clothes off. If I have to run this joint for a minimum of sixteen years, probably a lot longer than that, I'm going to need a lot of attention to put up with a bunch of fucking assholes. It's probably hard work educating a bunch of fucking assholes about why they should clean up their act in their next life, assuming they get one."

"He has all of the powers of an incubus," Gabriel reminded me.

"That doesn't mean he's hot. It means he has extra tools at his disposal to make me not care if he's as ugly as sin, but give me a break. I want him to be hot. I need some sort of perk outside of doing a lot of justice while also securing revenge."

"You worry me," the archangel muttered.

"I figure I became psychotic around the same time those assholes turned my brother into a chipmunk. Then to see that some assholes put a baby on a fucking cargo boat and abandoned her? Yeah. I'm a little psychotic right now. I want the fuckers responsible for that." I marched up the steps to the door, grabbed hold of the knocker, which was shaped like a rose, and banged on the door. I smacked it three times before searching for a peep hole. I scowled at the lack of a peep hole. "How the hell does he check who is at his door?"

Michael pointed at the top of the door. "That rose is actually a camera. As I said, my brother enjoys his luxuries, and he always gets the latest and greatest. Technology amuses him. You will enjoy stable electricity, good television, air conditioning, and all the creature comforts you can think of. He has a fascination with bathrooms."

"Aren't you supposed to talk people out of wanting to conquer the Devil and his hells? That's not talking me out of it. That's encouraging me. Does his fascination with bathrooms include really big tubs?"

"Indeed."

The door creaked open, and I stepped out of the way so I wouldn't get smacked with it.

"Isn't it easier to defend if the doors swing into the place rather than outwards?"

Gabriel pointed to the door, which was several inches thick. "Do you think it could be opened without the Devil's consent? He rules over every element of his many hells. Every gout of flame happens at his will."

"I hope he's able to program it like I can the VCR. That sounds like a pain in the ass, having to worry about all the fire and when it shoots up. There was a lot of fire out there. I'll make sure I delegate that to someone else unless I'm in a mood to landscape."

"I see you have decided you will be a ruthless ruler."

"Absolutely. I have more important things to do unless the spouting fire is scalding the shit out of some fucking asshole in need of punishment." I stepped into the entry, which reminded me of a grand cathedral on Earth. A painting on the vaulted ceiling drew my attention. "Oh *damn*, that's nice." I pointed at one of the scenes, which depicted unicorns during the Great Flood. "There are unicorns."

"Yes. My brother does enjoy his luxuries. You will have to ask him about the nature of the paintings."

"It's beautiful." I could lose hours staring up at the ceiling. I recognized some of the scenes, although one caught my attention, depicting a flaming, bronze-skinned incubus reaching out to touch the hand of the Christian god. "That's like that chapel in Europe."

"Do you mean the Sistine Chapel?"

"Yeah, that place. It's a chapel in Europe. But in the original painting, it's some random dude rather than a smoking hot incubus." I checked the incubus's chest, nodding my satisfaction at the presence of rather nice nipples to go with his striking face with a chiseled jaw and defined cheekbones. "I like that he's not white. He's a rather nice golden brown. He's also hot."

"Well, he is wearing fire."

"Wrong kind of hot. I mean, check out his chest. That is male perfection. Women must line up for a chance to play with that chest."

"You disturb me," Gabriel announced.

"If that's all it takes to disturb you, I'll make sure to go shirtless and wear flames in your presence," the gruff, deep voice announced, and a moment later, the incubus from the painting strode out from behind a column deep within the vaulted chamber. Rather than flames, he wore a black suit with black shirt and tie. "It's unlike you to bring a guest to my home, Gabriel."

"I only handled the teleportation. Michael issued the invitations."

"Really, Michael? You brought a human woman to *my* domain?" The incubus strode closer, looking me over, and his gaze settled on my brother, who hid in my hair the instant the Devil's gaze fell upon him. "Not quite human. A snow leopard? You brought a snow leopard to my hells? It is bad enough you would bring a woman, but to bring a feline?"

If the Devil was trying to paint a target on his pretty chest, he did an admirable job of it. I would have to put some thought into if I wanted to take over the place to get at the Devil or take it over for my other goals.

Why settle for one or the other? I'd enjoy the scenery while running the place.

"Indeed," Michael confirmed. "You are unwittingly in her debt."

I liked the sound of that. "I'll accept complete rulership of your hells until I grow tired of it or have no use of it as repayment. You could also do as I wish out of the generosity and kindness of your heart." Somehow, I kept my expression calm and neutral. "You'll do all the work I don't want to, of course, but Michael and Gabriel implied you have a dungeon, and I would like to make extended use of it."

The Devil's attention snapped from my brother to me. "You have got to be kidding me."

"Absolutely not. Originally, I was just planning on conquering the place so I could make use of the dungeons until I'm done with my dirty work, but after getting a look at you, I definitely need to add you to my conquering. Michael, why wouldn't the succubi want him? He's *hot*. I mean, he's the Devil, so it's not like I have to keep him long term unless he's that good, right?"

"I already told you succubi dislike monogamy, and for all his faults, my brother typically prefers his women one at a time. To pay them proper attention, or so he claims. He does not like admitting his angelic nature makes him wish to indulge in monogamy. The succubi do not wish to be monogamous for all eternity, nor do they wish to have the responsibilities of being the Queen of Hell."

"I don't care about titles, I just need to run the place for a while," I replied.

The Devil's mouth dropped open, but he remained silent.

I took another look around the entry, snapping my fingers at the doors. "Stop air conditioning the outdoors."

"Are you serious?"

"Absolutely."

The doors closed. "How am I in this woman's debt, Michael?"

"She secured the safety of an infant you hold responsibility for, and she has done so for a period of sixteen years."

I raised a brow, narrowing my eyes while considering the archangel. "You're playing both of us, aren't you?"

Maybe I couldn't see Michael's head, I suspected the asshole archangel smiled. "Perhaps."

"You know what? I don't care. Look, Mr. Devil, I need to use your hells for a while." I pointed at my chipmunk brother. "Some assholes did this to my brother, and I've the word of an archangel these assholes are in some serious need of justice, and you're my best chance of securing that. Killing the fuckers isn't good enough. After I kill them, I want to come here and continue my dirty work until they've paid for their sins. All of them. And the one? He sent me rose petals and implied I should showcase my assets for him."

The Devil didn't bother to hide his head-to-toe visual examination of my body. "Any man with functioning eyeballs would want your assets showcased for his enjoyment."

"Thank you, but I really can't afford to have some man—or fallen angel—distracting me right now. I'd really like to make use of your hells for a while. What do you say?"

"Perhaps, for a price."

"You already owe me. I'm also worried. You look pretty, but you don't look pretty re-liable." I circled the Devil, admiring the cut of his suit. "Michael, is this an incubus thing? Are they all like this?"

"An incubus does need to appeal to their target to work their magic. It is much harder to entice a human who has no interest. My brother has had many ages to hone his skills."

"That's nice, but I'm not here for a good time. Well, not that good of a time. He's defi-nitely worth admiring."

"It disturbs me how honest you are being about this. What an interesting human. You acknowledge your attraction for his current form, but you will not indulge in your human nature." Michael laughed, fluttered his wings, and shrugged. "It seems you have met your match this time, Lucifer."

"I think not."

Well, that wouldn't help me accomplish my goals. "Let's try that again. Would you please loan me your hells for a while? The duration will be determined by the completion of my plans. These include revenge on the assholes who did this to my brother, restoring my brother to an at least humanoid shape, and taking care of some other business involving a little girl who'll be a woman by the time I make my moves. I'll decide precisely what I'll do later for that."

"That's rather open ended," the Devil stated in a rather unamused voice.

"Yes, and? It's not like you have to kiss my feet and call me baby. You just have to do what you're told. Mostly, you'll run the parts of this place I don't feel like handling, inflict the appropriate amounts of punishment on the fucking assholes in residence, and help me accomplish my plans should I require your assistance. I'll try to inconvenience you as little as possible," I promised.

The Devil narrowed his eyes. "But what if I'd like to kiss your feet and call you baby?"

I shook my head. "Sorry, but I think not. This is business, and I'm not mixing business and pleasure. I'm sure you're a pleasure. You definitely look like you'd be a pleasure, but

I'm here for business, so you'll just have to convince a succubus to play with you for a while. You would probably have better luck with them if you set a time limit of maybe four or five hours. Have your fun, tire her out, tuck her in to bed, leave a chocolate on her pillow, and invite her to pay you another visit if she liked it. Maybe start a bachelorette contest to see if any of them happen to like your brand of sexy."

The Devil stared at his brothers. "Did you really bring a human woman to my house so she could give me advice on my sex life?"

"I did not expect her to give you advice on your sex life, my dear brother, but I am honored to have witnessed it," Michael replied. "I would like to mention she rejected you."

"That hasn't happened for a while," the Devil admitted. "I suppose there might be some succubi who could put up with me for an extended period of time. This idea of leaving chocolates on her pillow seems rather absurd to me. Most of them run away if I even think I might like to keep her around for a while."

"Most women like chocolate," I informed him. "Well, some. Personally, I prefer iced coffee after exercise, but chocolate is nice enough."

"Iced coffee?" the Devil blurted.

"Yes. It's coffee that is served on ice, usually with extra cream and sugar."

"Why did you bring her here, Michael?"

the Devil asked. "She commits terrible sins against coffee."

"She asked me nicely, I know the sins of the group she wishes to take on without any help at all if she can manage, and it would bring justice for many. You would also harvest many souls as a result."

"That's no reason to bring this sinner against coffee here. It's like you want her to take the place over, and she might take my proper coffee away from me. Sugar and cream, over ice?"

The more the Devil talked, the more I enjoyed offending him. Ruling over his many hells might prove even better than expected, especially if I could annoy and offend him daily.

Then again, perhaps not, especially if he convinced his succubi to visit his residence. I couldn't compare to a succubus. I wouldn't even come close.

"Now that you mention it, yes. That would be interesting."

I giggled at the archangel's tone, which came across as bored more than anything. "I'm happy to only mostly take the place over, as long as you do what I say. I'm sure it'll be no more than a few blinks of your eyes. Also, if your incubi get ideas, I'll cut their dicks off and feed it to them. I've made it through life this far successfully telling asshole men no, and I have no intention of changing that game plan now."

The archangels spread their wings and fanned their feathers.

The Devil raised a perfect brow. "And should I get ideas?"

"I have claws, and I'm not afraid to use them. I'm not nice enough to spice or grill your sausage before shoving it down your throat."

Both archangels vanished in a flash of silvery light.

"Damn. Think they'll come back to help me get back to Earth? Because I have a lot to do to bring down those fucking loan sharks." I thought about it and shrugged. "Whatever. I don't know what they're getting upset over. It's not like they even have nipples. Have you seen those two? Ruining those otherwise perfect chests through a lack of nipples. Offensive, that's what it is." I pointed at the Devil. "You better be packing nipples like the painting, or I'm going to have to go siege the heavens to have a talk with *Him* about this travesty."

The Devil stared at me, his mouth hanging open.

I planted my hands on my hips. "What part are you having trouble with?"

"The entire damned thing, really."

"It's simple. Loan sharks shoved transformatives down my brother's throat and forced me to watch while holding a gun to my head, now one of the bastards sent me some rose petals and invited me to show off my assets for his enjoyment. I'm going to bring their entire outfit down, I'm going to use you to do it, and the only payment you're getting is watching me torture their souls for however long I fucking see fit using your dungeon. It has to be stocked with everything I need to make sure their stay in your hells is particularly heinous. If they ever get out of this joint, they'll put angels to shame in their purity and good nature."

The Devil canted his head to the side. "You're going to kill them, send their souls to me, take over my many hells, and torture them in my dungeons while I watch? Not only will you torture them in my dungeons, you will do so until you give their souls a major alignment adjustment. Did I hear you correctly?"

"That sounds about right."

"First, you have no guarantees of the souls' final destination."

"The archangel said they've done far worse to others. If *He* allows that sort of filth in *His* heavens, well, I guess it's a damned good thing I don't give a shit if this ends up my permanent residence. I'll work hard to earn it, since when an archangel says I'm going to hell, I believe him. On the bright side, I get to secure some justice for others in the process. That means I've got about a week to dig up as much on these fuckers as I can. I'll show up and show off my assets, and I'll wipe the fuckers out at the same time. I mean,

I'll have to hit some of them sooner, so I'm really pinched on time. What's your next complaint?"

"Do you have any experience working a dungeon?"

"No, but I spent a lot of time fantasizing how I'd peel the skin off the fucker who raped a friend, leading to her suicide."

"Hmm." The Devil prowled around me, trailing a finger along my shoulders before flicking my hair. "You could practice on him if you wanted."

I froze, sucking in a breath. "You know who did it?"

I'd searched, but I'd never found the bastard. I supposed it was for the better. Had I found him, I would have carved justice out of his flesh and made my brother look like an angel in the process.

"I am the Devil. That's child's play for me. The rules of the heavens are simple enough. *He* never welcomes a rapist into his heavens. It is a supreme violation. Those souls all come here one day, no matter how remorseful those souls might be. *He* is not as forgiving as humans like to believe. The remorseful do not stay as my guests—"

"Fucking assholes," I corrected. "They are not guests. Guests enjoy privileges."

The Devil sighed. "Very well. The fucking assholes who show true remorse do not stay in my hells for long before they are evicted back to the mortal coil to see if they've learned their lesson."

"You rehabilitate souls, and you use torture methods to do it," I stated, regarding the Devil with a frown. "That so doesn't match your reputation."

"I'm the Lord of Lies, not the Lord of Sunny Afternoon Strolls. Why would I use other methods to do it? It takes true punishment to leave a mark on a seed of life or a soul. During the End of Days, my count of souls matter, but in the meantime? Why keep the fucking assholes longer than necessary?"

Huh. I understood the Devil a lot better than I did his brothers. "So, will you help me? It's a good deal for you."

"I fail to see how this is a good deal for me."

"You get to do your thing, but you're doing it at my say so, so whenever your underlings annoy you, you can just blame me for the edicts they don't like. I'm assuming you have underlings."

"I have devils and demons, yes. We'd be here for half an eternity if we discussed their types. I have generals who control facets of my army, and I have the army, but until the End of Days, they'll bicker amongst themselves and annoy me. They rarely like any of my edicts."

"Well, I'll carve chunks out of them if they get mouthy about your edicts, and I'll use your dungeons to do it."

"It doesn't work that way."

"It does when I'm running the place."

The Devil frowned. "I suppose if it is your hells, it is your rules, but I will tell you this much: neither my demons nor my devils will at all appreciate that."

"They aren't supposed to appreciate it. They're supposed to stand the fuck in line and do as they're told to avoid it. If they walk the straight and narrow, then they won't have chunks carved out of them, now will they?"

"So, you want to take over, have me work as normal, and take the dissenters to my dungeon, carve punishments into their hides, and teach them to never cross you?"

"Correct. And if they're just an annoyance, you can do the carving on my behalf. I might just observe while looking bored. Do you think it's more effective if you're doing the carving while I watch? I could work with that. It's only a few years. I'm sure it won't tax you too much. It's not like mortal years are long for you, right? You're eternal. You'll blink, and I'll be gone." I shrugged. "Or become one of the fucking assholes in residence."

"Let me take this from the top, simply so I can be certain I understand this situation correctly."

"All right. Shoot. I'll correct you if you get it wrong. I expect I'll have to correct you often."

He laughed. "You're such a bold woman."

"Well, I am a cat, I'm pissed, and I have a brother to save. You're the only divine in the entire fucking universe who can help my brother, so here I am. I've bargained with one pantheon to get this far, and I'm not dumb enough to bargain with you."

"You'll have to bargain with me if you want my help."

"No. You'll help me because you find this whole thing amusing, it's hardly more than a blink of your eye, and you're bored."

"We'll discuss that part of this arrangement later. You want to rule over my many hells, have me installed as your second-in-command, and maintain ruthless discipline over my demons and devils."

"Yes, that's correct."

"You want to do this so you can accomplish several goals. First, you want me to use my powers to restore your brother."

"That's almost correct. I want the other goals to happen first, as I lose my motivation if my asshole brother has been restored. Frankly, he deserves to spend a few weeks as a chipmunk. Once I'm done securing my revenge, I will be expecting my asshole brother to shower me with gratitude."

The Devil chuckled at that. "You're not incorrect. You might be interested to know that he is considering biting you."

"If he bites me, I'm throwing his furry ass into a lava pool and leaving him there."

"He is no longer considering biting you."

"That's because he is not a complete idiot."

"Your second goal is to murder all members of the mafia outfit responsible for transforming your brother into a chipmunk."

"That depends if all members of the mafia outfit are guilty of crimes worthy of death and a long, painful stay here with you. Tell me, Lucifer. Are they all fucking assholes?"

"So, you do care about their guilt."

"Yes, that's correct."

"Then your second goal is to secure justice for the guilty, send the guilty for their earned stay in my dungeons, where you will supervise and possibly participate in their rehabilitation."

"Yes, that's correct."

"Your third goal is to do a personal investigation of my chest to discover if my nipples are nearly as appealing as in the painting."

I raised a brow, eyeing the Devil. "You're supposed to be evaluating bachelorette succubi for one who is willing to put up with you."

"I will consider such a foolish endeavor should you be counted as one of the bachelorettes."

"I will consider it only after my brother is dealt with, I've brought that outfit to its knees before sending every last one of those fucking assholes to the nastiest dungeon here, and I've paid my bills off in full. I told you, I don't mix business and pleasure. You really are a vain creature, aren't you?"

"I am," the Devil admitted. "Business with me will be a pleasure, I promise you. That would be a suitable exchange. Not a bargain, but a business arrangement."

"Unless you're one of the mafia assholes who stuffed a transformative down my brother's throat, I have no business with you beyond taking your place over until I've done my dirty work. You'll probably survive."

"You are very bold."

"An archangel told me you were the only divine who might be able to help me, and I'm not stupid enough to bargain with you. I like my soul and wish to keep it where it belongs, in my custody, safe from your dungeons. I mean, I expect I'll be earning my long-term residency as one of the many fucking assholes populating the place, but I have shit to get done first."

"Would you at least hear me out before rejecting my proposition?"

"Show me this place while you pitch me. The amount of effort and my willingness to cooperate with you are directly tied to how comfortable your home is."

"This is a part of my hells, Miss Darlene. It's not supposed to be posh accommodations."

"Bullshit, Sir Lord of Lies. An archangel told me you're spoiled and require your luxuries. That means you have posh accommodations you don't share with anyone because you have to maintain your appearances as the world's most notorious bad guy. As such, you're selfish, require training on how to share nicely with others, and otherwise need to undergo some serious reforms before a woman would even consider you to be husband material. You're also a man who indulges in sin at every opportunity, so you probably wait maybe five seconds between women. That plays into most women not considering you to be decent husband material."

"Do you have a death wish?"

"For me? No. For people who cross me right now? Yes. I've had a really bad day, and I don't need any idiot man getting in my way right now. You can make this easy, or you can make this difficult. If you make this easy, I might actually consider your pitch, assuming it isn't bullshit wrapped in even more bullshit."

"Being seduced by me is never bullshit." The Devil reached out and touched my cheek. "Your spots are lovely. How many of them are you hiding?"

The Devil could growl, and the cat in me appreciated the sound. "I said you could pitch me. If you want to negotiate for permission to count my spots, it better be a damned good pitch. There will be rules, Lucifer. You will follow them, or we're finished with negotiations, and I will resume my hostile takeover of your hells until I'm done with them."

"What are your rules?"

"At no time will you bargain for my soul. You can do nice things for my soul, but you can't do mean things like steal it. It's mine, and you cannot have it. I'm already scheduled to come here after death anyway, so you may as well just learn to be patient."

The Devil chuckled. "And once your soul comes into my many hells?"

"Well, I assume you'll enjoy punishing me however you see fit. I guess I'll find out once I get here as one of the fucking assholes in residence. Hey, that's an interesting question. Do you know if I've done time here before? Souls are recycled, right?"

"Your soul does not have the weight of a prior lifetime. It's new, so you're corrupting it nicely without any help from me. Good work. Keep it up."

I pointed at my brother, who still hid in my hair. "How about him?"

"I've had a few rounds with him already. Really, he's a pain in my ass. He refuses to learn, or he just enjoys a round in the dungeon. Maybe he just likes me and can't get enough of my attention."

"Damn, Jonas. You need to improve your general learning capacity. Me? I'd learn the first time. You're a fucking moron."

My brother squeaked a complaint.

"If you bite me, I really will toss your furry ass into a lava pool. I've put up with enough shit for one day solely on the grounds of being your sister. You have used up all my benevolence towards you, possibly for a year. Be happy I spent a ridiculous amount of money on your new home."

"It concerns me how honest of a being you are," the Devil admitted.

"Second rule. I do not mix business with pleasure, so if you want your business to include pleasure, you're going to have to help me finish my business first. I may consider adjusting this policy if you make a good enough offer, but really, my momma taught me boys are nothing but distractions, and she was right."

"My chest is a good offer."

I wondered if tossing the Devil into a lava pool would do anything beyond tickle. Considering he depicted himself as wearing flames, he likely enjoyed any pain lobbed his way. "You have plenty of succubi you can seduce. Just make sure you're clean and free of diseases between seducing a succubi. That's polite. I expect you need a lot of tutoring on being polite company." I needed to have a chat with the archangels, who hadn't warned me the Devil might be seriously desperate for some positive female attention.

"You're really rejecting me."

"Business *before* pleasure, Lucifer. This isn't a hard concept. And the pleasure part of this equation only happens if you have a damned good sales pitch and you haven't gotten tired of me running the joint. I suspect you'll be more than ready for me to head on home once I'm finished around here." I regarded the ceiling with interest. "The interior decoration of your entry is sparse but gorgeous, I'll give you that. You could use a few sofas or lounge chairs scattered around here to make viewing a little easier. Did you go cathedral theme throughout the whole place?"

"I have modern rooms."

"Because you're spoiled and need your luxuries?"

"You're really calling me spoiled. In my own house."

"If it makes you feel better, I'd call you spoiled outside of your house, too."

My brother sighed.

"Your brother wishes to communicate that he is convinced you will die a terrible death at my hands."

"He's probably not wrong. I'm viewing myself as having low odds of general survival anyway, but if I'm going to go out and earn my way here, I'll do it in a spectacular fashion. You can't kill me until I've paid the CDC's bill, though. That's the third rule. Murdering me so you can torture my soul for however long you see fit is definitely not on the table for discussion."

"Any other conditions?"

"Yeah. Show me your bathroom." If I had to move into the Devil's house for a while, his bathroom would give me a pretty good idea of if he was actually spoiled or just a talker.

"I assure you, I make no boast without being able to back it. Do you want to see the guest bathrooms or the master bathrooms?"

"I wish to see my entire domain, if you please. And honestly, even if you don't please. If I'm going to be making my permanent residency here after I'm done fucking over the rest of my life, I'd like to see what I'm taking over and if it's worth it. And if you bite me, Jonas, I will make you suffer for all eternity."

"She really will," the Devil warned. "But very well. If you wish to go on a tour of my home, then let us go on a tour of my home. We'll begin here, which was the first room I built of this residence, as I had the fucking asshole of a painter in residence. Painting the ceiling at my whim rather than his seemed like punishment enough, and once he finished painting, I had him work as a maid for a few years before sending him off. Really, his job as a maid was the real punishment. However much it disgusted me, he loved the painting of my ceiling almost as much as I do. So, that's mine, and you may not have it."

If I owned the Devil, I owned the Devil's prized ceiling, so I shrugged. "Whatever you say, Lucifer."

"Remind me to torment my brothers for the rest of eternity for bringing you here."

"How do you torment a pair of archangels? Truth be told, I'm a little annoyed they abandoned me here before telling me how to get back to Earth. Then again, maybe they expect me to successfully storm your gates and conquer the place, which means you could probably return me to my home in the proper time and in good health." I shrugged. "And if not, well, I'll come up with a new plan."

"For some reason, I find this worrisome."

"What's this? It's possible for a man to be smart and pretty?"

"I'm not a man."

I pointed at the painting of his perfect chest and flame-shrouded body. "Close enough. You're male, and you're pretty. Therefore, the probability of you being smart is greatly decreased."

"Yet you've rejected me."

"Smart and pretty doesn't make for a good husband there, sweetheart. And if I was in the market for a man, I wouldn't be living with my brother. You'll just have to get over it."

"You don't have to marry me to come to bed with me," the Devil complained.

"I already told you how this works. Business and pleasure do not mix, and if you want to get to the pleasure portion of any arrangements we might make, then you better have a damned good proposal for the business portion of my ventures. You might make a good advisor on how best to approach this. If I had my way, I'd just poison them all with the nastiest transformatives I can find coupled with a poison to make sure they slowly died in their new form. But I could settle with just stabbing them repeatedly, but I figure an eye for an eye is appropriate, except I don't just get mad, I get even and charge interest."

"I can't believe you're really rejecting me."

I rolled my eyes. "Show me your bath-rooms, Your Sulfurous Majesty. At least try to pretend you're worth conquering."

## SIX

The Devil had more bathrooms than
sense.

___

THE DEVIL HAD MORE bathrooms than sense,
and he had a tendency to create them with a
theme in mind. His Chinese-themed one,
which he saved for last in his tour of his
home, displayed priceless treasures. I bet I
could steal one of his vases and make enough
off it to live the rest of my life in comfort.

I spent a shameful amount of time debating if I could fit one under my shirt so I
could steal it.

"I would definitely notice if you tried to
steal one of my vases, although I would find it
amusing enough to allow you to try to get
away with it until it was time to go, which
would be when I would enjoy doing a very
thorough searching of your body to make
certain you weren't trying to steal anything
else. I have decided my current goal is to
count all of your spots. They're lovely, and I
want to investigate each and every one of

them." He paused. "Preferably with my tongue, but I'll settle with my hands first if needed."

I spent a few minutes considering his offer. How would he manage? While soft, fur was fur. When I wasn't rocking a fur coat, I did have a collection of freckles scattered over my body, enough to keep him amused if he needed something to count. It didn't take me long to come to a conclusion there would be no counting of my spots in his near future. "Obviously, I'm going to need to either leash you or keep a supply of willing succubi ladies around to keep you amused while I work."

"You could keep me amused."

"I'm sure the succubi will be far more talented at keeping you amused and satisfied than I." I snorted at my general lack of experience with men, as every time I thought about landing a man, he chickened out believing he'd catch some disease or another from me —or he proved to be an asshole. Add in my asshole brother, my mother's warnings, and decent observation skills, and I'd gone through life more frustrated than anything else.

"Virgins are an extra special treat, and half the fun with them is teaching them how to be the perfect lover. I don't have to go through the hassle of undoing any bad habits."

"What makes you think you're good enough for my first time, anyway?"

The Devil spluttered. "Have you forgotten who I am?"

"No. You're the Lord of Hell. The Lord of Lies. You have a great chest, I'll give you that. But I'm not here to take you to bed. I'm here to take over. I don't need you in bed to accomplish my goals. Also, if we could not talk about my lack of a love life in front of my brother, that would be great. He'll start bringing his unsavory friends home with him, assuming I might actually want one of them. And don't get me started on the idiots who assume my ears and tail mean I'm infected with some disease."

"I could resolve those problems for you while counting your spots. You have many spots, and I wish to count them. I do not like when there are pretty things in my home I cannot have. Let me count your spots."

"Business," I reminded him.

"But I don't want to handle business. I want to handle you and your spots."

"Then I suggest you come up with an effective and satisfying revenge plan, acknowledge you'll be running this place at my whim rather than yours, and make yourself useful. Only then will I consider such a reward for your good behavior."

"Good behavior? I'm the Lord of Lies, not an obedient puppy."

"That's such a shame, then. The Lord of Lies doesn't get any spots. The obedient puppy might get spots. Your bathrooms are really nice, I'll give you that. You are obviously very spoiled. Do I want to know how you bargained for these antiquities?"

The Devil pointed at one of the larger vases. "That one was a bribe to be somewhat merciful on a particularly nasty soul. I agreed, opting to be more brutal over a shorter period of time as part of his rehabilitation program. It worked rather well."

Huh. "You can bargain on things like that?"

"Anything can be bargained away, Miss Darlene. Even your spots."

"Take my spots away, and I will cut off your nipples."

"That does not sound particularly pleasant. I was meaning we could bargain for my ability to count your spots."

"I've been here less than two hours, and you're already obsessed with counting my spots? What's wrong with you?"

"Well, I am the Devil, and you told me no. Being who I am means I really enjoy the pleasures of the flesh and indulge at every opportunity. Being told no is absolutely infuriating, and that means I just want what I was denied even more. I will get my satisfaction out of you, mark my words. In good news, I'll make certain you like it."

My brother squeaked at the Devil.

"You don't get a say in this," the Devil stated.

"He's right, Jonas. He who gets poisoned with transformatives doesn't get a say in what I do. Maybe if you hadn't made a deal with loan sharks in the first place, I wouldn't be storming the gates of hell right now."

"I do feel you could use some work on the storming the place front," Lucifer muttered.

"I brought two archangels with me and walked in. I stormed your gates just fine."

"I opened the gates because I found you amusing, although I will concede your choice of archangels for this venture to be wise. You could have put up a good fight had they waged war on your behalf. I might have had to work at it brawling with both of them. Then I would have been delighted to accept your spots as payment."

"The answer is still no. I have too much to do right now to worry about you and your desire to count my spots. Anyway, you'd choke on my fur."

"I'm the Devil, Miss Darlene. I can take any form I want, including that of a male snow leopard with a tongue suitable for counting your spots."

Hmm. "Demonstrate, please. You're the Lord of Lies, so I need to see evidence you can do as you say. I will permit you to count a single spot of my choice should you show me this form of yours."

"Which spot?"

Smiling, I held out my arm and pointed at

one of my favorite spots, a perfect ring on my wrist. "That one."

"How would you like me dressed?" the Devil asked in a purr.

"I do quite like that suit, but perhaps you could add a splash of color with the tie. Red might work. A good crimson. Black, white, and crimson always work well together."

"Dressing appropriately is key to a proper seduction," he replied, and a dark fog enveloped his body, and when it cleared, he took on a more human appearance with a snow leopard's ears and tail, and he opted to keep his face clear of fur, with his coat starting just below his chin and covering the rest of his body. As requested, he wore a red tie. "I've opted to give just a little of a rough tongue for your enjoyment should you wisely opt for a more thorough exploration of your person."

I held out my wrist for him. "You get one and only one spot. Consider it a preview of what you're going to be missing until I'm finished with all my dirty work. If you put up a fight over being conquered, you'll just have to wait even longer for even a chance to access more of these spots."

"You are quite cruel," the Devil complained, but he took hold of my hand and traced a finger along the perfect ring, flicking at my fur. "Your coat is quite plush. Much softer than I expected. I must factor in the softness of your fur into my willingness to make sacrifices to gain spot counting privileges. This is one glorious spot, but I find myself wishing to possess two glorious spots."

"Well, you only get one spot, so enjoy it while it lasts."

"Cruel."

"You haven't seen anything yet, Lucifer."

I GAVE THE DEVIL CREDIT; he didn't joke around examining his one allowed spot. He stroked my fur with a gentle touch, and after he satisfied himself with his first touch-based exploration, he lifted my hand to his mouth and gave the spot a single kiss. "You are far more patient than my succubi."

I raised a brow at that, as his ten minutes of dedicated attention to a single spot promised good things later if he successfully navigated the dark waters of business before pleasure. "Once, I kept a boy company in a stairwell for three hours, and we spent most of it fencing with our tongues. Perhaps if I didn't like that sort of thing so much, I wouldn't be a virgin right now. If your succubi don't enjoy the slow approach, perhaps you should train them better. You only have yourself to blame. Patience is a virtue for a reason."

"Had patience been presented as a virtue

suitable for pleasant pursuits, perhaps I would have cultivated more patience. You are a feline, and felines are curious creatures. I'll have to account for your nature should I win a second spot. Or, perhaps, entice you with an offering?"

"Business before pleasure," I reminded him.

"You are excessively cruel."

"View it as a good qualification to run this place for a while. I'll even be a fairly benevolent dictator and mostly allow you to do what you want."

"Mostly does not mean I get to do everything I want."

"That's correct. For example, you do not get to count my spots." I freed my hand from the Devil's hold. "Once I bring my targets here, you don't get to send them out of this joint until I've had my turn with them. I will allow you to critique my torture techniques, however. I figure you have to be a little decent at it."

"A little decent? I'm the Devil. I'm the supreme master of torture techniques."

"As I said, you're a little decent at torture techniques."

"You are an infuriating woman."

"I am an infuriating woman who has what you want, so let's get down to business. I need your place for a while. You also need to settle down and find a succubus who is willing to put up with you. You can amuse yourself with that business while I'm running the place. Your current level of sexual repression can't be good for your health. Perhaps you're tiring your succubi because you're repressed and wait until you're frustrated before joining one in bed. I feel those archangels dumped me here to knock some sense back into you. Do the bachelor seeking a bachelorette thing, try to contain yourself at least a little, and maybe you'll find a suitable woman to become the queen of your domain."

"Her being a queen implies she'll have run of the place."

"Well, yes. Having a queen around to knock sense into your minions would probably be helpful."

"My minions are the generals of my many hells, and cut their teeth on sin and violence," the Devil replied.

"Well, she better be one hell of a woman, then. Moving on. As I expect to be visiting here often, I'll need to take over a room."

"You may stay in my bedroom."

"You really have trouble with rules, don't you? No more spots if you can't follow the rules, Lucifer. My rules state you don't get any pleasure before my business is completed, so I will not be residing in your bedroom. Anyway, I don't play games with men, and I don't engage with men who have side chicks, so you'll have to maintain your bedroom for your bachelorette succubi. Surely you have at least one good guest bedroom in this place?"

"Why would I have a guest bedroom?"

"For guests. Not fucking assholes, for actual guests."

"Why would I bring guests into my home for longer than a few hours?"

"This is why your succubi do not want to engage in a long-term relationship with you. You need a guest bedroom. You need multiple guest bedrooms. For example, I'll have my pipsqueak of a brother here with me, and he needs his own guest bedroom. I get my own guest bedroom, and you should have at least two or three other guest bedrooms for visitors."

"This sounds like a great deal of work. Why can't I just throw the guests into the dungeon? I already have dungeons."

"The dungeons are for the fucking assholes unless you have a guest who wants to experience the dungeon."

"I don't like your rules."

"Deal with them. Guest bedrooms, Lucifer, not excuses. Moving on. I'll need an office, as I'm sure you have more paperwork than sense."

"I feel personally attacked by that statement."

"That is because I personally attacked you with that statement. I swear, you must have gotten kicked out of the heavens for your tendency to whine, complain, and talk back."

"You're not wrong," he admitted. "It's a little more complicated than that."

"I really don't care. You're a stepping stone, buddy. I have goals, and I'll use you to accomplish them."

"For every day you control my many hells, I get to count a spot," the Devil announced. "This is a fair arrangement. If you control my many hells for more days than you have spots, I get to count spots a second, third, or fourth time until I have counted a spot for every day you've taken the place over."

At a minimum of ten minutes per spot with a mix of hands and mouth paying attention to each and every one of them, he would need at least an entire day to get through the spots on my chest alone. I narrowed my eyes, considering his offer. "You're supposed to be checking out the eligible bachelorette succubi. You're really not clear on how this works, are you?"

"Oh, I'm very clear about how this works. Most succubi will run away, although some will play the game to see if they can gain more power here. I'll spend a great deal of time chasing my succubus around; they do like to stray. Often. Daily, really. I can't blame them. I made them that way. Then I keep getting these defective incubi and succubi. Those are the ones who think it's a good idea to shack up with an angel and a human."

"Maybe you should shack up with a succubus who is generally inclined to shack up with an angel. They are loyal to their triad. I mean, I'm a human, and even I know that."

"Shapeshifters are hardly human." The Devil stared at my wrist and the spot he'd been granted permission to admire. "Humans do not have such lovely spots."

"I have some freckles when human."

"You have my attention."

"I feel your brothers should have warned me you have a spot fetish."

"I feel I should thank them for their failure to warn you how much I intend on enjoying your spots."

"There is zero chance of you having anything to do with my spots until I've fully secured revenge on my brother's behalf. Can't you see I'm traumatized over what I was forced to witness here?"

"Your sarcasm is almost as appealing as your spots," the Devil purred.

"Put your perverted little brain on a different track for a while there, tiger. Revenge first, family securements second, then and only then can you beg and plead for the right to count another spot."

"You keep telling me no, and I am utterly baffled over why I have not wiped you from existence yet. I find this to be disconcerting."

"You want to count my spots. If you wipe me from existence, you can't count my spots. I really thought you were smarter than this." I heaved a sigh. "Taking over the place might be doing your underlings a favor. Do you have a responsible adult in this place I can talk to about appropriate management practices?"

"I am the responsible adult."

"Goodness. No wonder this place is a mess. I'm done with my cordial visit, and I am moving into the hostile takeover phase of my day. Show me your office, assuming you actually do any work in this place. I need to see what I have to work with."

"But do I get to count spots when you've completed your hostile takeover? Will you use the whips and cuffs?" The Devil gestured out of the bathroom in the direction of the hallway. "Will you chain me to my desk?"

"You sound a little hopeful there."

"It's been a while since a female of any species was willing to chain me to my desk," he admitted.

"I will chain you to your desk should you give me a nice present I will enjoy with no strings attached."

"My office is this way. Would you like to use silver, gold, platinum, or iron chains?"

"That's a dumb question. I'll use them all."

I CHAINED the Devil to his desk as requested, used the chains to make a gag, and left him there while I examined the rest of his office. Michael hadn't been joking about the Devil's luxuries. His computer was nothing like I expected, with a large enough screen it re-minded me of a television. Rather than ask him where he'd gotten it, I ignored my jealousy, moved the keyboard within the Devil's reach, and ordered him to tap in his password.

He obeyed, grunting at me. As I didn't understand grunting, I ignored him, sat in his large, comfortable chair, and explored. As promised, he had a good internet connection. With minimal poking and prodding, I discovered the Devil kept meticulous notes, and he even had a system of files and folders dedicated to his various minions. Names and descriptions of roles simplified my work, and I brought up the files of Belial, Asmodeus, and Abaddon, all three who might be useful for what I needed done. I considered their roles, eliminating Abaddon as my first choice. While he'd likely do a wonderful job of destroying my enemies, he'd likely do his best to make sure my plans were also destroyed. Wholesale destruction worked in some cases, but I needed more refinement than what he likely offered. As Asmodeus embodied wrath, I'd have a decent time convincing him to work with me.

I had plenty of wrath to share.

Belial, however, would accomplish my goals in such a way I could render long-term satisfaction from the assholes who'd acted against my brother for a measly five thousand dollars. According to Belial's file, unlike the other two devils, he had a phone number. I grabbed the phone, dialed as the file directed, and listened to it ring.

"You are not Lucifer," a male voice growled in my ear after the second ring.

"Oh, good. You're not stupid. Excellent. I've chained your lord and master to his desk because he annoyed me. I have a job for you. I'm running the place for a little while, but if you piss me off, you get to deal with the Devil. Cooperate, and I'll be out of your hair sooner than later. Come to his office, and wear something nice. A good suit, make sure you wear a colored tie. I've decided we're going business wear until further notice, because if I have to deal with this damned joint, at least I'll surround myself with pretty devils. Make yourself pretty, then come here. I require your advice." I hung up, propped my feet onto the Devil's desk, and took the time to pet my brother. "I could get used to this," I confessed.

The Devil, tied up to my satisfaction on his desk, sighed.

"It's your fault. You gave me the chains and let me do it. And since you want to count spots, you're going to stay there and do as you're told. Once Belial gets here, I'll see about something to smack you with. But don't worry. I'll make it hurt real good for you."

He seemed like the type, and I needed to work out some of my frustrations.

Belial didn't leave me waiting long, tele-porting into the office with a flash of orange light and the stench of brimstone polluting the air. Much like the Devil, the devil associated with ruin wore a pretty face to cover his nature. Heat wafted from the devil, and as directed, he wore a suit much like the Devil's, although he'd opted for an orange tie. "How unusual. You truly chained him to his desk, and it seems you've made him like it."

To my amusement, the Devil shrugged.

"I have what he wants, and he doesn't get what he wants until I'm satisfied. As for the chains, I just promised him I'd ask you about something I can hit him with when he gets annoying. As he can't get what he wants until I've secured revenge for this travesty, well, here I am." I grabbed hold of my brother and held him up. "This is Jonas, and I'm very offended he has been turned into a chipmunk."

"He can only be changed from that form by conversion into a demon, a devil, or an angel," Belial replied. "You do not need to take over the hells to accomplish that. A simple bargain would suffice."

Ha! That explained why the Devil was the only divine who might be able to help me. "You're useful. I like that. You're the bringer of ruin, are you not?"

"I am."

"I have all the motivation in the world to do the job, but I'm uneducated in the methodology of how to best bring ruin to a mortal mafia outfit. Inconsequential to you, I'm sure, but I want to give them all a miserable invitation to here, after which I will take extensive lessons from the Devil on making certain the fucking assholes have the absolute worst stay here possible. I'm not here for easy. I'm here for satisfying, truth be told. My brother's debt? About five thousand dollars. An utter waste for so little, really."

"That is a very small sum to bring so much ruin. You have my attention, little mortal."

"Darlene. So, what do you think?"

Belial tilted his head to the side, and he regarded me with glowing orange eyes. "You have made many plans and fantasized long about how to assign justice to sinners."

I could only assume Belial dug around in my head to get the information he wanted.

"Yes. It is a power of most devils. Nothing is secret in this domain."

"Well, if I cared about that, I'd be worried, but that simplifies things. Good. Were any of those ideas good?"

"They are sufficient, and they could make for excellent ruin of your targets with the correct implementation."

"Good. I need something I can use to smack the Devil with. If you'd like to help plan some ruin, you can acquire excellent transformative substances that the CDC won't be able to readily identify, as I do not have a wish to spend the rest of my life in prison. You can bring proposals on how best to end their miserable lives on Earth before they enjoy their stay here. I'm accepting lessons on torture techniques when the idiot I've chained up is tired of playing tutor."

"Did you just call Lucifer an idiot?"

"Yes, I did."

"Why have you not struck this creature out of existence yet?" Belial asked his master.

The Devil shrugged.

"He likes it, I have what he wants, and I keep refusing to give it to him. Right now, I'm the holder of the Devil's chain, but it's going to be business as mostly usual. I do recommend you don't cross me."

Belial's eyes glowed hotter. "Why not?"

"The Devil's mine, and I'm not afraid to use him."

"Understood."

"Oh, and Belial?"

"What is it now?"

"The Devil needs to meet some eligible bachelorettes. He probably takes all his frustrations out on you poor devils because he's sexually repressed. Spread around to the various succubi he's looking for a suitable bachelorette to be his queen. Just remind them that he brings a lot of power with him at the annoying price of sexual loyalty. Honestly, he's probably so repressed she'll have to put her life on halt for a few weeks while he gets it out of his system, but she'll survive. I'll do what I can to make him a little more considerate, but he's raw material right now."

"Are you not an eligible bachelorette?" Belial asked, his tone curious.

"Are you kidding? You do not want me permanently taking over this place."

"May heaven forbid," the Lord of Ruin muttered.

## SEVEN

Do you even know what the word
chastity means?

BELIAL BROUGHT me a riding crop with a
black leather handle, a silvery shaft, and a
rather wicked flaming leather swatter on the
end. I accepted it with a grim smile and eyed
the Devil, who remained on his desk, still
chained as I left him. "Thank you, Belial."

I didn't need to suggest the devil get out of
my hair. He teleported away, and he didn't
bother with the brimstone theatrics. I slapped
the riding crop against my leg to test it.

It stung nicely, and flames danced across
my leg before extinguishing. "Remind me to
thank your brothers for this later."

To make it clear I meant business, I
slapped the small of the Devil's back with the
crop, earning a delightful grunt out of him.
"Also, remind me to thank Belial for this, too."

That earned me a baleful glower.

Setting the crop in easy reach, I sat in the
Devil's chair and drummed my fingers on his
desk. On a whim, I typed Lorenzo Gallo in

the search box. According to the computer, there were thousands of matches, and I scowled. "Does this thing have every damned soul in it?"

The Devil nodded.

I stood, reached over, and pulled the chains out of his mouth. "You have earned some talky time with that. The specific Lorenzo Gallo I want to ruin. How do I find him in this thing?"

"Type his company name in, and you will find the one you're looking for."

I patted the Devil's head. "Good boy. For being so helpful, I will permit you to admire a second spot today."

The Devil's gaze locked onto one of the spots right above my cleavage.

"That is a special spot, and you don't get that one unless you've really earned it."

"I should get to choose the spot," the Devil complained.

"You should sit there, look pretty for my enjoyment, and be grateful I'm patient and will allow you to admire a second spot today." I added the fucking asshole's company name, and sure enough, the field narrowed to one result, and I clicked into the folder to find numerous files on Gallo, from childhood history to his adult operations. I started with his childhood, my brow raising as the file registered him as a reincarnated soul who'd done six hundred years of time in the seventh level of the Devil's hells. "Is there anything special about the seventh level?"

"There are numerous branches of my hells. That specific branch has nine levels. Eight and nine are devilish and demonic residencies, and they only bring special pets in with permission," the Devil replied. "Right now, there are six fucking assholes who are staying in those two levels. The seventh level is the current deepest pit for offenders, and they do not get many breaks from their torment. It's designed for particularly heinous souls who are unlikely to be successfully rehabilitated. Lorenzo Gallo has a history, and truth be told, that soul only leaves when there needs to be a balancing."

"A balancing?"

"When there is too much good in the world, seeds of darkness must be planted to maintain the balance. The End of Days is when everything has fallen out of balance, and I will wage the final war with my heavenly father. The End of Days is a great deal of work for me, so I actively work to prevent it from happening. *He* does as well. It's not precisely something either of us desires, but it will one day happen. The worlds cannot begin anew without it. The End of Days is as important as the Beginning."

"You mean like the story in Genesis?"

"Precisely. Humans mangled the history of humanity, but that is to be expected. History is always rewritten by the victors to best suit their needs and purposes."

I frowned, reading over Lorenzo Gallo's file, which gave me no information on what he'd done to deserve hundreds of years of torment at the Devil's hand. What I did read, however, lit a fire under my ass. At age twelve, Lorenzo Gallo had already raped three girls. By eighteen, the Devil simply made a star notation, not bothering to count the infractions. He'd murdered plenty of people, too, but he preferred to keep his victims alive, transforming them into other forms. Most disappeared.

Many of his victims remained alive, pets in his menagerie, which he kept in his primary residence in Maine.

"It looks like I'm doing the Earth a favor getting rid of this asshole and his operations."

"It disgusts me when people do evil acts and it is ultimately an act of good. *He* is more likely to overlook those evils if they are for the better of everyone. That means I get fewer souls to play with, and that's simply no good."

"Does that mean *He* might actually like me if I eliminate enough of these fucking assholes? Because if the others have files anything like this, I really am doing the entire world a favor."

"No. I can't count your spots if you're keeping my father company."

"Attention on work, Lucifer. You can

count one spot of my choice after work." I already knew which spot I'd pick, too. The best spot, right on the back of my neck, did an excellent job of inducing the best naps ever, and I would shamelessly use the Devil to secure an excellent nap.

I probably deserved my long-term residency in one of his hells.

"I hope it's a good spot," the Devil replied.

"It's one of my best spots, so behave until it's time for you to enjoy it."

"I should resent how easily you're controlling me, but you have so many spots I haven't met yet, and I want to possess them all."

"You need to teach your succubi how easily you can be manipulated through the careful rationing of spots."

"None of my succubi take the feline approach for some reason. It's like they fear I'll keep them permanently or something. Also? Recruiting Belial was ruthless, and I haven't been so turned on by an act of evil in centuries. Bringing him into this? An act of pure evil, Miss Darlene."

"I don't have enough time to look into all of your minions, and adding some ruin to go with my revenge seemed like a good idea. What is he going to do about you being chained to your desk?"

"He will tell everyone, of course."

"So, all of your various residents now know the place has new management?"

"That is a reasonable assumption."

"Excellent. Hey, Lucifer?"

"Yes?"

"Is it possible to have a dress that shows off my assets while giving me plenty of places to hide weapons? I'm going to need a weapon if I'm going to take out Lorenzo Gallo at this meeting. I might need a chastity belt that's magically sealed, too."

"I can offer you something better than a chastity belt."

"You can? Do you even know what the word chastity means?"

"Unfortunately. It is a very foul word, and I loathe how much it's been used today."

I laughed. "You'll survive."

"I'm not sure I will survive if you decide to wear a chastity belt for any period of time. After all, I have to sufficiently reward you for permitting me to count your beautiful spots. I cannot do that should you be wearing a chastity belt. Unless I'm allowed to destroy the belt during your reward. I would enjoy that greatly."

I needed to talk to the Devil's brothers about the situation, as I worried managing over so many fucking assholes had warped their fallen brother. "You're still only getting one more spot today."

"I feel we should negotiate for a third spot today. I could be useful to you. I will prove my usefulness to you in exchange for access to a third spot."

One spot, two spots, three spots... what

was an extra spot or two if he helped me accomplish my goals without putting up too
much of a fight? I had plenty more spots, and
exposing three of them to the Devil wouldn't
do any harm. "I will listen to your proposal."

"I will compile a list of all those who were
directly involved with your brother's current
state, a list of their crimes the police have
been unable to prove, provide the evidence
required for the police to take action, and I
will direct Belial to give you a rather potent
substance suitable for your revenge. I will do
this in the next twenty-four hours, after I
have had sufficient time to explore both
spots. There are many substances that would
work, and he might make some... unfortunate... choices. In exchange, you will allow
me to pay attention to a third spot of your
choice today. I will need at least an hour per
spot, but I will limit my attentions to two
hours per spot."

If the Devil paid that much attention to a
singular spot, I'd enjoy a very good nap. "I
like that you acknowledge I will be the one
selecting the spots you can investigate."

"I am a being of great wisdom."

"Don't you mean great naughtiness?" I
muttered.

"Well, yes. But for today, I am a being of
great wisdom, and I really want to explore
your spots."

"You will escort me back to my house
with my brother before you get to explore my

spots, and you will bring me the information and evidence I need within the twenty-four hour period. If you get something particularly juicy for me, I might allow you to make a secondary exploration of one of my spots as a reward for good behavior."

"As I cannot have my precious spots at risk, I will establish wards around your home. Until I have conquered every spot, I cannot have interlopers interfering."

If the Devil wanted to act as my home security, I wouldn't stop him. "I will be utterly distraught should my brother come to harm, and when I am distraught, it's obvious I would be in no state to want any man enjoying my spots."

"Obviously, I should put you in charge of negotiations. You are wicked."

"If I'm going to be making my residency here, at least I'll earn it."

"Oh, you will," the Devil promised.

SEVERAL HOURS into my research project using the Devil's computer and entertaining myself with random swats of my chained prisoner, Michael and Gabriel teleported into the office.

Both archangels laughed at their fallen brother.

"He talked me into sharing three of my spots with him, but he's saving me a great

deal of work, so I thought it was worth indulging him. He's like a child. If you give him
a taste of candy, he'll do what you want in
hopes of another piece. However, I'm concerned his time spent here dealing with
fucking assholes has slightly warped him."

"You chained him to his desk," Michael
observed. "I do not think anyone has done
that before."

"Well, if he didn't want to be chained to
his desk, he wouldn't have provided me with
the chains."

"While this is true, it is a little unnerving
to witness my brother chained in such a
fashion."

"Don't worry about him. He likes it. If he
gets sad, I hit him with the riding crop Belial
gave me. That perks him up for a while before he gets whiny again."

"That riding crop is rather hellish. In fact,
it is rather painful to be hit with."

"I tested it against my leg before I went to
town on your brother. He'll survive. It doesn't
sting for that long. If that little pain is too
much for him, he needs some time in the
dungeon for a refresher on what painful actually is."

Despite their lack of heads, I felt the
archangels staring at me.

"When I take her to her home, I get to
count two new spots. As she would set limits
if I didn't set them, I had to negotiate for only
two hours per spot. Under most circum-

stances, I would blind you for looking upon her, but are her spots not beautiful?"

Gabriel chuckled, and it amazed me the archangel's amusement could brighten even the Devil's many hells. "She is a stunning creature. It is as though *He* is aware of your every failing and triumph and put such a woman on the sweet Earth for you to enjoy. Assuming, of course, you can convince her to allow you to enjoy her company. I do not hold much hope for you."

I snickered. "I told Belial to start spreading word the eligible bachelorettes need to work their magic on him. That much repressed sexuality can't be good for his health. I mean, he's been brought low by three spots. If he realizes how many spots I have, he might swoon."

"I do not swoon."

"Men who do not swoon do not get the extra special spots."

The Devil stilled. "There are extra special spots? What makes a spot extra special?"

"Location, location, location." I picked up the riding crop and slapped the Devil's hand with it, and he yelped. "I am almost done with my preliminary research, so your twenty-four hours to gather the information I need will begin when you start exploring the second spot you've earned, so you better manage your time properly."

"Ruthless," the Devil complained. "You brought a truly ruthless creature to my domain. She's taken it over without remorse, too. She ordered Belial to come in here dressed in a suit and looking pretty for her, and he obeyed. I've never been so turned on in my life."

"We do not need to know anything about your current restless state," Gabriel replied with zero evidence of sympathy. "Belial is wise and recognizes when someone is in a position to ruin him, and he does not wish to test her willingness to bring ruin into his domain. She is a predator, and she has made no effort to hide her predatory ways. She is a very determined predator at this moment."

"How much help did you give her for this scheme? She did not even flinch with both of us in here giving her our full regard."

"We did not handle that matter. *He* did. You will have to put thought into your situation. *His* blessing will not last forever."

The Devil grunted. "Meddlesome."

"I'm sure *He* will have a favor to ask of you soon enough, probably in the form of expanding our numbers."

"Wait. I thought the hosts were fixed. That the armies of the heavens and the hells always had the same number."

"Not precisely. They are *balanced*," Michael replied. "As such, the heavens and the many hells have a balanced number. My brother has only so many devils and demons, and the heavenly host have only so many angels and archangels. When an angel falls, for example, the balance of power shifts in my brother's favor, and the angelic seed must be reclaimed and replanted before the End of Days comes prematurely. When demons or devils perish, my brother must claim those seeds, although he sometimes opts to leave them as seeds for a while, permitting the scales to shift in the favor of the heavens for a while. It is a delicate balance. When there is great evil in the world, my brother tends to leave his claimed seeds unplanted, because that maintains the balance. It is part of what he is. While *He* keeps a close eye on the balance of things, it is actually our brother who does the most work. In many ways, view my brother as a great gift from the heavens for all he earned his fall."

"It is truly disgusting," the Devil muttered. "I am the consequence of free will. I am the symptom of free will. Without free will, I would not exist. I am also the price of free will. Before my fall, there was only a set fate and destiny. There was no sin, for there wasn't the freedom to sin. I was given the freedom to sin, which is perhaps the greatest of gifts humanity could ever receive. But that freedom comes with consequences." The Devil shrugged. "I'd wave my hand, but it seems I'm facing certain restraints right now."

I ignored the Devil's antics and said, "People like me exist. Like my brother. Like Lorenzo Gallo. But on the other hand, people like my father exist, and so do people like my mother."

"That is correct," Gabriel confirmed. "Humans are free willed creatures, and they can choose to make themselves into anything they wish."

I pointed at the Devil. "He claims *He* tends to be more forgiving towards those who do great evil for the greater good. Is that true?"

"You could do the greatest of evils doing an even greater good, and you would still find your way into our brother's many hells. Only some sins *He* does not forgive, like rape," Michael replied, coming around the Devil's desk and patting my shoulder. "It would be hard for you to run the place if you did not come here often."

I laughed at that despite my awareness I'd be on the naughty list. "That is true."

"My brother would chase you to the heavens and get himself into even more trouble should *He* allow you to step foot there. Do you truly believe merely three of your spots would satisfy our brother?"

"Hey, I'm considering allowing him to recount a spot or two. I'm not totally cruel."

"That definitely would not satisfy him, knowing there are many more spots for him to explore." Michael laughed, and he caught my hand in his, pulling my arm up to show off my spots. He touched my elbow. "You have seventeen spots on this elbow alone for him to admire, and he will resent I have touched a spot he has not yet enjoyed, for he is a selfish and jealous creature."

That he was. I twisted my arm for a view of my elbow, straining to count the spots, amused over how many tiny spots were on such a small surface. "I've never really noticed there were so many tiny spots there before."

"Have you had a need to count how many spots were on your elbow before now?"

"Well, no. I guess not. I see I will have to do a complete spot count to be aware of how much bribe material I have in my hands. I've gotten him busting his ass to earn the three he's getting as it is. To be fair, one of those spots is my favorite. It's perfect."

"It really is perfect," the Devil agreed. "I don't want to fight you over her spots, Michael."

"I have no interest in forming a triad with her, no offense intended to you, Darlene."

"Michael, you ruin that perfect chest with no nipples. We would fight for my entire lifespan over your lack of nipples. It would not work out. Meeting you taught me a very important lesson: my men need nipples. My men also need other important parts."

"Indeed. You are free to be told no by her for however long you wish, my brother. We will enjoy witnessing your rejection."

"She's already trying to sell me off to a succubus. She's also made some suggestions about how I might keep one around, and why I have terrible luck keeping them around. My lack of guest bedrooms is only the start of my problems, if she is to be believed."

"She is to be believed. You have plenty of empty rooms. Convert some into guest bedrooms. I recommend you give her the garden as her personal domain. A comfortable bed, a private bathroom for her use, and some moderate renovations would appeal to her. She is, after all, a feline. You will want to make a room suitable for a snow leopard as well. She becomes quite saddened when she cannot go play in the snow."

"Snow," the Devil blurted. "You want me to put *snow* in my house?"

"It would make her very pleased with you and might earn you some spot counting."

I considered the archangel's words. "He's not wrong. I love winter, because winter is when the snow comes to visit me. I'm too poor to go up to the mountains to visit the snow. Last year didn't have more than a few inches of snow. It was terrible."

"But *snow*?"

I couldn't help myself. I grinned and replied, "I guess that means there's a snowball's chance in hell of you getting to count any more spots."

The Devil growled. "I should punish you for that."

I slapped his wrist with the riding crop, and he yelped. "You will not."

"Wicked feline!"

"Yes." I returned to my work, printing out

the file I'd constructed on Lorenzo Gallo and his assortment of bullying mafia members. Unlike the printers I was familiar with, his printed on both sides and wasted no time spitting out the sheets. "Okay. I'm ready for you to take me home, where you can enjoy counting two spots of my choice before you have to do your share of the work. And anyway, don't feel too badly, Lucifer. I already told you business came before pleasure, and until my work here is done, you really do have a snowball's chance in hell of getting to count any more spots. You'll get over it, I'm sure."

"I absolutely will not get over your cruel mistreatment."

Laughing, I released the Devil from his chains. "You'll survive. And I'll survive, too, because if you kill me, you can't count my spots, and I'd just be yet another fucking asshole in residence here."

"She has you figured out, Lucifer," Gabriel announced.

"You came here to witness my defeat at the hands of a mortal woman, didn't you?" the Devil accused.

"That plus to pass a message," Michael said.

"A message? What message? When *He* wants something, he usually bothers me personally, because *He* knows it annoys me."

"Do not panic," Michael replied, and a moment later, both archangels disappeared.

The Devil frowned. "Should I be worried?"

"That depends. What would make *you* panic?"

"That's the problem. I don't know. How odd." The Devil hopped off his desk and held out his hand. "Shall I take you back to your home? I must count my two owed spots, handle my promised share of the work, and pay my heavenly father a visit, as I now have some questions for him."

The Devil would be busy, and I smiled, taking hold of his hand. "Just don't lose my brother on the way. Despite appearances, I do love him."

"Don't worry. I intend on taking good care of your brother. It would not do to lose hope of counting your spots due to his demise."

I suspected Jonas would make me pay for the Devil's attention later, but I'd cross that bridge when I came to it. "Keep dreaming, Lucifer."

## EIGHT

Fine lines separated revenge,
vengeance, and justice.

WITHIN FIVE MINUTES of the Devil taking me home and placing my brother in his new cage, I staggered to my bed, showed him the two spots he could fiddle with to his heart's content, and passed out. Waking to a persistent knock at my door annoyed a growl out of me, and still dressed in my rumpled clothes, I stomped across my home, checking the peephole to discover two of the mafia goons standing at my doorstep.

One held roses, both wore suits, and the absurdity of the situation gave me pause. I picked up my brother's gun, which had somehow gotten onto the stand in the entry, checked it over, and without disengaging the chain, I cracked open the door. "What do you want?"

"Our boss sends a gift and his regards, and he wishes to know if you will be accepting his invitation."

Well, as accepting his invitation would be

critical for my plans to send him straight to
the nastiest hell I could find for him, despite
my lack of coffee and foul mood, I forced myself to cooperate. I straightened, closed the
door, disengaged the chain, and let the assholes in. "There are a few rules in my house.
Even look at my brother wrong, and I shoot
you. I'll even go dance naked on your grave
and invoke the Devil's name trying to make
him show up and make sure you get to hell. If
you're pulling any tricks, I recommend you
don't even try it with me today. I'm not in the
mood."

"We have no ill intentions," the asshole
with the roses replied, offering the bouquet
to me. "Our boss wishes to apologize for his
lack of foresight in this matter, as he was unaware of how interesting a woman you are."

Having read Lorenzo Gallo's file, I recognized when that meant he wanted to take me
to his bed whether or not I wanted to join
him, but he'd use enticements before settling
for rape. I accepted the roses, opted against
sniffing them in case they'd been laced with
something, and transferred them to my
mother's vase on the end table. She'd always
kept an empty vase out just in case flowers
wandered her way and required containment.
"Apologies won't bring my brother back."

"He is aware of that, and wishes to discuss
an arrangement with you, which is why he is
so eager to learn if you'll be accepting his invitation."

"I have a condition." The last thing I needed was to go anywhere private with a known rapist and murderer, so I'd have to do my best to arrange the situation to protect myself while leading to his downfall. "I want to pick the location, and he has to pay for it. If he's going to be sending roses, then I may as well enjoy the wining and the dining while listening to whatever proposal he may have in mind. I get to pick where we go, but I'll keep his proposed date and time. If he wishes to change the proposed date and time, you know where to find me."

The two assholes exchanged glances, and after a moment, they shrugged. While bereft of roses, the asshole who'd brought them in nodded. I gave him credit; while he had more scars than sense, he had enough brain cells in his skull to recognize when to be wary.

I'd enjoy sending his ass to the Devil's many hells and refining the art of torture on him for his long collection of sins.

I'd seen parts of his file, too, and he'd crossed every last one of the Devil's lines.

Fine lines separated revenge, vengeance, and justice, and I meant to dance on them all with a ballerina's grace. When I finished, the triumphs would balance the tragedies, and I expected I'd earn my place in the Devil's many hells before I finished my work.

Another reason crept into the back of my head, one that wouldn't have mattered to me the day before yesterday.

When little Kanika grew up, there would be filth in the world still, but I would personally eliminate some of it so she might never experience the terrors they inflicted on others. That alone would make eternal damnation worth my while.

Somebody had to care what happened to her in the future, and there was nobody else.

"We'll let him know," the asshole replied. "And should he wish to meet with you sooner?"

"I'd rather not. Family is important to me, and he's broken mine. I doubt any offer he can make will do any good, unless he's willing to bargain with the Devil to undo what he's done." If he wanted to get screwed by the Devil instead of me, the final destination mattered more than the method, as long as the asshole found his way into a dungeon where I could sink my claws into him.

I'd have to ask Belial to loan me the riding crop again, as I bet it'd be an excellent tool in my arsenal.

"The Devil?" the asshole blurted.

"I've been told by an angel the Devil is the only one who might be able to help my brother now, and I've nothing to offer him."

Well, except the right to count my spots to his content, and I intended to withhold my spots as much as necessary to get what I wanted. Trusting the devil to have only counted two spots while I'd slept classified as a moronic move on my part, but the Devil came across as the kind who enjoyed his victories and found no satisfaction in taking the easier road.

I understood and respected that. Hell, if I'd been in the Devil's shoes, I wouldn't have counted any spots at all because the game couldn't be half played. I'd have to find out if the Devil had endured even more frustration because of my exhaustion.

Poor Lucifer. He'd survive. Maybe.

"If you'd had the money, you wouldn't be in this position in the first place," the asshole conceded. "It is unfortunate he, until now, had been unaware of you and your exotic beauty." The fucking asshole stared at my chest, as did his buddy. "He would have accepted other forms of payment on your brother's behalf. Perhaps an arrangement can be made."

I read between the lines, but as I needed to play the game, I ignored the implication I could sell sex to cover my brother's debts. "I'll think about it, but I have to get ready to go to work."

Someone knocked at my door, and tempted to scream at the invasion of people I wanted nothing to do with, I checked the peephole to discover the Devil had come calling, and if I hadn't known better, I would've believed him to be an unusually hot human in a black suit. To my amusement, he'd gone with a bright blue tie for a splash of color. I opened the door. "What can I do for you?"

The Devil smirked and held out an extra-large iced coffee. "It's not chocolate, and it's not on your pillow, but I figured you'd prefer this in its mostly frozen state rather than melted and messy."

If spot counting while passed out got me my favorite treat, I'd put some serious thought into driving the Devil mad with my criteria for being able to count a single spot. I accepted the drink, took a sip, and sighed. "Enjoy your math lessons yesterday?"

"My tutor became sadly unavailable. May I come in? I noticed you have company."

*Fucking assholes, both of them,* I mouthed to the Devil.

He smiled, and the rather unfriendly nature of his expression intrigued me.

Who knew something as simple as a smile could be full of promise and lies?

"Sure. They were about to leave." I took another sip of my coffee, wondering how much of a fight the succubi would put up once they realized the Devil could be trained to be the ultimate morning provider of necessary treats, such as iced coffee. If he brought me treats after skipping his owed spot counting, there was hope for him. Poor succubi, unable to train the Devil to be a provider of excellent treats. Maybe I needed to go take over the place to teach them how to train the Devil properly. "Is there anything else I can do for you gentleman?"

They glared at the Devil, as though they

expected their scarred faces to deter my divine guest. When that didn't work, they left, muttering curses the entire way to their black car parked at the end of my driveway.

I waited until they were out of sight before closing the door and returning my brother's gun to its rightful place on the entry stand. "Thank you for the coffee."

"I forget how tiring my presence can be for mortals."

"It was more I'd been up way past my bedtime than anything else. Yesterday had been long and hard. What time is it?"

The Devil checked his cell phone, which was far smaller than the portable bricks most carried with them, oddly flat and compact, with more glass than plastic. "It is a little after two."

Shit. To be on time for work, I needed to teleport three hours into the past. "I'm blaming you when I get fired for not showing up at my job."

"I will offer you a competitive salary for access to a single spot per day."

As he hadn't specified it needed to be a new spot, I considered his offer. "Monetary incentives only, with a five minute minimum and a thirty minute maximum of how much affection you can display to the spot of my choice."

"Yes, those terms are acceptable. I will include a clause where I can attempt to negotiate for up to two hours with the spot your choice. Otherwise, it will be a standard employment opportunity. As I want continual access to your spots, I will even give you fair terms, excellent health insurance, and daily opportunities to tell me no."

Damn. When the Devil wanted something, he made damned good offers. "I'm going to have one of your brothers review any and all paperwork involved with my employment. Let me call my boss and notify him I'll be quitting before he calls and fires me for not showing. I'll just tell him I was sick today. I'm obviously delirious and running a high fever. Then you can pitch me a figure. Think about if there's any other real work I can do for you, because I work hard for the money despite my inability to show up at my job today."

The Devil pulled out his odd cell phone, dialed a number, and held it to his ear. "Michael, could you smooth things over at Darlene's place of employment? She is acquiring employment elsewhere. What? No. I am not hiring her to be a sexual deviant."

Did spot counting classify as sexual deviance? Considering there'd been no sex on the table, his desk, or anywhere else, either the Devil had some strange kinks or he just liked plush fur.

"I'll be paying her for her operations involving my many hells, and I have been issued a hiring incentive of one spot per weekday. She even set time limits on how much attention I can pay to the spot of her choice. It's cruel, really. I'm even letting her tell me no. She would like you or Gabriel to confirm the paperwork so I don't try to pull any tricks on her. I really would, too. I am who I am, and I want what I want, and I really want access to those spots. Do not make me pluck your feathers for admiring her spots too intently. You can admire them a little, at a distance."

"Lucifer, neither Michael nor Gabriel have nipples. That's a dealbreaker for me."

"Hold on a sec, Michael." The Devil pointed his phone at me. "You were looking at their chests?"

"If they had nipples, they'd have perfect chests. Michael put on some nipples for a few minutes, but he made them go away again. You better believe I was looking at their chests! If you want to keep your nipples, you better change your tune, Lucifer. I can look all I fucking want. You got it?"

"Can I respectfully ask that you do not touch unless you're touching mine?"

I thought about it. "You can ask, but considering you have a gauntlet of single succubi to worry about, you have more problems than whether or not I want to touch some man's nipples."

The Devil put his phone back to his ear. "Can you believe this, Michael? What did you do to her? She has no fear of me, she really just does not give a flying fuck if I become upset with her, and I'm rather dismayed how interested she is in your chest."

"No nipples," I reminded him. "Deal-breaker means I'm not interested without the nipples. If I am forced to cut your nipples off, you become vastly less interesting than you currently are, so I recommend you take good care of them. They're mandatory."

"The rest of my body is equally appealing, thank you," he muttered.

"Is it?" I shrugged and sipped my iced coffee. According to the painting, he was a prime specimen any sane woman would want to enjoy repeatedly. However, as he boasted the title of the Lord of Lies, I would withhold judgment. "Maybe it is, maybe it isn't."

"Do you hear this, Michael? She's utterly unrepentant!"

"There is a reason I'm going to hell. Being unrepentant is one of those reasons."

"You're going to hell because you walked in and decided to take it over yesterday," he countered.

"Well, yes. But after I kick the bucket, there's a good reason I'm going to hell. Scratch that. There are a lot of good reasons I'm going to hell. Try to keep my torture reasonable, please. I've been bad, but I haven't been *that* bad."

The Devil grunted, and he held the phone out towards me. "Michael wants to talk to you."

I eyed the device. "How does it work?"

"Just put the glass part against your ear. It's a phone, it's just oddly shaped. I cheat."

"How did you cheat this time?"

"Advanced production, and I fully intend on bargaining with some idiot human to develop these sooner in the mortal world so I don't have to keep cheating to have half-decent technology." The Devil put the phone into my hand. "This is the top, and it goes near your ear."

"But it won't reach my mouth."

"It doesn't need to. Just hold that part to your ear and talk like normal. He'll be able to hear you."

Considering my landline had enough trouble, I had my doubts, but I held the device as directed and said, "Hey, Michael."

"Darlene," the archangel replied. "Is my brother bothering you?"

"He brought me an iced coffee, so no. I owe him two spot counts because I decided it was nap time when I got home, and he seems to want to indulge in spot counting while I'm conscious."

"It does tend to be more entertaining for him if his partner is conscious."

"That's something. What can I do for you?"

"Did you handle the flowers given to you?"

"Only long enough to put them into a vase. I opted against sniffing them."

"They are poisoned," the archangel announced. "The delivery service has been given the antidote, but you will begin experiencing symptoms within the next day. Your target plans to use your worsening condition to gain your compliance."

"Well, that's rude."

"It is a rather lethal toxin with a slow onset. By the time of your meeting date, you will be quite ill. The envelope you received was likewise contaminated, but you had minimal exposure due to the care you took. I have been monitoring the situation."

"Well, that's *really* rude. Not you, but him."

The archangel chuckled. "It is quite rude of him, indeed. In good news, there is an antidote, but he intends to deceive you by giving you a less potent antidote to make you reliant on him."

"That sounds like a damned good reason to send him to fucking hell in a handbasket."

"What is it with mortals and going to pay me visits in baskets? What is with your obsession with baskets? I do not understand why mortals insist on coming to me in a basket. Where would you find one large enough? Why a basket? If you're going to visit me, you should at least travel in comfort."

I stared at the Devil. "Really?"

"What? What is it with you mortals and baskets? Really. I want to know."

"Handbaskets are pretty and usually used to send gifts, I guess. I don't know. It's just a saying. Go sniff the poisoned flowers if you want to have a reason to whine."

"Did you just suggest my brother should go poison himself?" Michael blurted.

"Why not? It's not like it's going to kill him or anything. I'm sure he'll just want to whine." I went to the roses, wrinkling my nose. To all appearances, they seemed normal enough. "There's nothing obvious on them."

"That is because he took care to disguise it. He spritzed them with water with the colorless substance, so it dried onto the flowers and wrapper. Should you touch the roses and rub your fingers, you will feel the toxin."

Well, since I'd already gotten poisoned somehow, I obeyed, and I rubbed my fingers together after rubbing one of the big blossoms. Sure enough, something a little sticky but otherwise invisible clung to my fingers. "And it's absorbed through the skin?"

"Yes, and it has a minor aerial radius, so if it came too close to your face, you could breathe it in. It is a rather illegal substance... or will be soon enough. Your sickness will be what makes it illegal, should you opt to turn evil into good."

"Sure. What's a little suffering?"

"You are such a curious being."

The Devil eyed the roses. "These were poisoned?"

"Yes, Lucifer. They're poisoned. It's not the end of the world. There's an antidote. I'm sure I'll be fine." Eventually. "It just gives me the justifiable part of the homicide verdict. Hey, how much does ruling over your hells earn me, anyway? I seem to be out of a job and have been poisoned."

"You're taking this in stride."

I pointed at my brother. "I'm just a little poisoned. He's a chipmunk. Apparently, I'm a prize, and he wants me badly enough to try to manipulate me into having sex with him through the use of lethal poisons."

The Devil twitched, and he held out his hand. "May I please have my phone?"

"Your brother wants to talk to you." I handed over the device, as even I had some shred of self-preservation left. When the Devil's eyes burned brighter than any flame, screwing around with him probably wouldn't work out in my favor. I sipped my iced coffee and watched him with interest.

Fury was a good look on the Devil, especially when he wore a nice suit. He turned and graced me with his back, and I tilted my head while admiring the scenery.

Nice. I'd have to make the Devil fetch things for me often when I was ruling over his hells.

"You're saying I can't destroy the roses," the Devil stated, his tone colder than my coffee.

Poor Michael. "I'm sure your spot supplier will be fine. There's an antidote, and you could always bargain with the archangel for a cure. I hear they'll do medical miracles for a fee."

The Devil twisted around and shot a glare at me. "You shouldn't sound so chipper after being told you've been lethally poisoned."

"I'm not dead yet."

"Yet."

"He already said there's an antidote. Why are you whining so much? This is perfect. We know where the poison came from, and we've the word of an archangel. We know who sent the flowers, we know why he sent the flowers. He wants me to show up to manipulate me, and he's willing to poison me to get his way. This totally removes any feelings of guilt I may have suffered for contemplating doing terrible things to him in your dungeon. I'm also going to make plans for the two who delivered those roses knowing they'd be poisoning me and getting an antidote. There will be a special place in your hells for them. Am I understood?"

The Devil raised a brow. "Are you seriously ordering me around?"

"Yes. They need a special place in your hells so I can come play with them whenever I want. It will be brutal. I might even accept your assistance in adding additional brutality to my planned brutalities."

"That's the hottest thing a woman has said to me in a long time."

I rolled my eyes at that. "Ask a succubus to

flirt with you. I'm sure she can come up with something hotter."

"They don't like coming with me into the dungeons for some reason, unless they're asking for a punishment, and is that really a punishment?"

"It's not a punishment if she likes it," I confirmed. "Consenting punishment definitely isn't punishment. The consent part is key."

"For some reason, I like the begging."

"Well, yes. You're the Devil. It would be strange if you didn't. Also, should you be conversing with me when you have your brother on the phone?"

"He's talking to Gabriel, as he is offended you have been poisoned. Archangels get rather pissy at times, so I figure I'll be a good brother for a change and wait while he works his temper out. I'm sure *He* will be brought into it, because *He* gets cranky when his archangels are pitching fits. Basically, *He* is cranky all of the time. I come from a very dysfunctional family."

"A dysfunctional family that will ultimately end the world."

"Yeah. We're a little more dysfunctional than most. Truth be told, it's not like any of us actually *want* the End of Days to happen. But humans are humans, and because they're humans, it must. If we had a choice in the matter, we'd dodge it for all eternity. But all beginnings have ends. In good news, all ends have beginnings, so the End of Days is merely the end of an old beginning and the beginning of a new end. It's complicated."

"Hey. Can you ask what kind of poison the fucker got me with?"

"The kind that will kill you within two weeks if you aren't given an antidote or other treatments."

"I was hoping for some specifics."

"Do you need to know more than it will kill you within two weeks if you aren't given an antidote or other treatments?"

"Well, yes. Can you ask Michael if the envelope with his name and the rose petals in it has more of the poison available in a detectible fashion? I'm happy to give it to the police. It has his name on it. It's his invitation. I didn't touch anything on the inside. I used tongs. I should throw the tongs and crap out I used to open that envelope, shouldn't I?"

"Are you fond of this house?"

"Yes."

"You won't let me solve this problem with the appropriate usage of fire, will you?"

"That is how you destroy evidence, Lucifer."

"I don't care about the evidence."

"I do."

"That's unfair."

"I don't care if it's unfair." I pointed at my vase of toxic roses. "They're mine, they were given to me, and I will resent if you destroy them. That's my evidence, damn it! I need the evidence to bring ruin and destruction to them."

The Devil sighed. "Michael, why must she always argue with me?"

I wondered if the archangel would tell the Devil the obvious, or if I would need to remind the Devil I held the true power in our ridiculous relationship.

I controlled the spots, and she who controlled the spots controlled the man wanting access to the spots.

My spots held great power, and as I meant to earn my stay in hell, I would use my every spot to my advantage.

I waited, allowing myself a smile and taking a sip of my iced coffee, which had become the first of my trophies claimed from the Devil.

"She's smiling at me, and I find this somewhat concerning. You, an archangel, notified her she was lethally poisoned, and she's *smiling about it.*"

"Oh, stop being a baby. It's not lethal yet." I eyed the roses. "However, that said, my brother is teeny tiny right now, and I'm concerned the dose would be lethal for him far faster than it'll kill me, so if you could ask Michael to escort some lovely police officers over and verify the toxins, claim the envelope, which is likewise poisoned, and otherwise start the wheels moving on that, I'll probably be forced to owe him a favor. Pretty please."

The Devil relayed my request with minimal adjustments, and it amused me he refused to say 'pretty please' to his brother. "I said pretty please."

"I refuse to use those words. There are limits."

I sipped my iced coffee. "Access to a fourth spot will be barred until you use those words in the appropriate order in a meaningful way."

The Devil took his time thinking about it. "Michael, she's making me say dirty words to gain access to a new spot."

I laughed. "I'm such a cruel dictator." I tilted my head to the side and pointed at a rather nice spot along my throat, one that made me purr whenever someone stroked it. "This is a particularly nice spot, and I may consider introducing you to it should you learn to use those words in the appropriate order."

"I will help escort all of your enemies straight to hell for that spot. I will do so in a fashion so brutal mortals will quake in fear for a hundred years."

"Pretty please are the words you need to say if you want this spot."

"You're really going to make me say dirty words to gain access to that spot?"

"And you can hire me, but you won't be getting to meet any new spots until you use those terrible, awful, tragically dirty words." I pointed at the spot on my wrist. "You will get this spot for all eternity should you fail to use those dirty words."

"Ruthless," the Devil complained. "Michael wants to talk to you again."

I took the phone and placed it to my ear. "How can I help you, Michael?"

"He has not used the equivalent of please in a thousand years. It is not a part of his current vocabulary."

"Excellent. He can demonstrate how badly he wants access to a new spot, then. What are the symptoms of this poison, if I may ask?"

"It is primarily neurological, so you will experience tremors in your hands, a weakness in your grip, potentially blurred vision, and a difficulty remembering things. You will forget people and names fairly early, although you will be aware of having a relationship with them. This will, frankly spoken, create some issues with my brother, as he will find your adjusted behavior intolerable. It will be like you are walking through a thick, dense fog. You will experience severe head pain, and by the time the meeting happens, you will be quite pained. Lorenzo Gallo meticulously planned the onset to make certain you fall into his hands when you are most pained and pliable, but before you reach the point of no return."

"Well, that's rude of him."

"You are aware of his nature. This is nothing compared to the things he has done to others."

"And should I pass on his generous offer for the antidote?"

"In the later stages, you will remember nothing of who you are. You will eventually fall into a comatose state. Death comes shortly after. The comatose state is unpleasant for those witnessing it, although you won't really feel the seizures and other symptoms as your brain goes into the final stages of death. It is a nasty toxin. He intends on giving you a compound that will slow the progress. Every now and then, he would give you something that would mostly reverse it, essentially enslaving you. He does not care for your happiness. He only cares for his end goals, and you are exotic. You could live for a very long time like that."

"Is this something you can help me with?"

"It is within my power to purge the poison from your body. My brother forgets, but it is within his powers to purge the poison from your body as well. He has not lost his heavenly flames. This is but one of his many flaws. He can heal many things should he choose. To be fair to my brother, he has not healed anyone in many years, for he spends little time on the mortal coil. His work in his many hells keeps him occupied, and until now, he has had no reason to handle mortal affairs directly. He visits but always with a purpose. That is what makes my brother who he is. He changes."

"And you do not," I guessed.

"You are mostly correct. I do not change often. We can learn, and we change when we learn, but we rarely experience new things. My brother is far more curious than the rest of us, although we do find humans to be sufficiently entertaining from time to time."

"You change within allowed parameters?"

"Precisely."

"When will the symptoms start?"

"By tomorrow morning, you will no longer recognize anyone without intervention, although you will have most of your memories intact. Events you will remember, but the names of people, places, and things will be significantly hampered."

"That does not sound like a good time for me."

"I expect you will be approached again tomorrow, likely with another poisoned gift to help speed the poison's progression, especially when you did not opt to smell the roses you were given. They will be monitoring you."

"This doesn't bode well for me securing revenge, Michael. I cannot plan revenge when my brains are dribbling out of my ears."

"You speak the truth, but it would be wise to allow the toxin to do the work for some time."

"Are you looking into the future?"

"Perhaps a little."

Okay. That was cool. "Can your brother do that?"

"He can, and he does at his whim. He does not wish to look into this future for his own reasons. He enjoys surprises. I am more methodical on this matter than him. He is a creature of passion, and the methodical approach does not appeal to him at this point in time. That may change."

I pulled the phone from my ear. "Hey, Lucifer?"

"What is it?"

"You can count spots on my arm tomorrow, one spot for every time I can't remember your name, but you can only ask me once every twenty minutes as a part of monitoring this poison's progression. However, you must trust Michael to tell you when it's the appropriate time to pull the plug on this little experience."

Michael laughed, and I returned the phone to my ear in time to hear him say, "Should you make that bargain, he will do nothing but count spots all day tomorrow, and you have yourself to blame for this. Is it wise for me to control your fate?"

"I expect you'll take me right to the point of no return should we proceed."

"Yes. There is a reason for this."

"And will this win me more than it will lose me?"

Michael took his time considering my question. "Much of the answer depends on you."

"Illuminate me, Michael."

"You will lose things. You will win things. I cannot judge the value of what you will win and lose. Some things I hesitate to look for in the future, for those futures are often uncertain and unclear, and I do not wish to lead you astray."

"Hey, Lucifer. Do you think I'll win more than I lose scheming with your brother?"

"Win," he replied without hesitation.

"Justify that statement, please."

"If my brother waits until a more dire point, I will be very eager to rid this Earth of these people, and you will get to enjoy tormenting them in a very special place in my hells, for I will be highly motivated to give them their fair share of attention."

"Okay. Lucifer is all right with this. I can handle some suffering for a good cause, and if it does good down the road, then it's worth it to me."

"Your capacity for good is only equal to your capacity for..." The archangel sighed.

"Evil?" I suggested.

"Viciousness might be a better word. You do not precisely do evil. You work for a greater cause."

"I can get vengeance on behalf of those who cannot get it for themselves."

"Yes, and while your method is rather vindictive, you do so with good intentions, so I cannot precisely call it evil. You are the swiftest hand of justice available, but you are as brutal as you will be swift. You have chosen your weapon well."

"Well, unleashing the powers of hell on Earth to get rid of a few bastards is a bit overkill on the weaponry front."

"The powers of the heavens, too. You are in league with both the heavens and the hells for this."

"Does that mean I can storm the heavens, too?"

"Would you like to?"

I laughed at the curiosity in Michael's voice. "Perhaps. Do you think I could get away with it?"

"I am sure *He* might grant you an audience at some point."

Huh. "For someone like me?"

"You stormed the gates of hell for the sake of another. *He* finds things like that admirable. Not many can say they have spoken with *Him*. It might be worth your while."

"You know what? I'd like that. I think I have a question for him." I glanced at the Devil, who engaged in a one-sided glaring match with my poisoned roses. "I'm a curious mortal."

"That you are. There is one thing you will need to know."

"Tell me, please."

"You may permanently lose some memories because of this venture, but they will be painful ones you are better off without. Do you consent to that?"

I thought about it. "Do those memories define me?"

"No, but they would redefine you in ways you would not appreciate," the archangel replied. "Without them, you can define yourself."

There were worse things I could do than place a little trust in an archangel. "Then I do, although if I need to know one day in some future, I am trusting you to make things right in its proper time and place."

"I shall," he promised.

A shiver passed through me, as though some gentle hand touched somewhere deep in my chest. The feeling faded, but unnerved, I asked, "What's next?"

"Amuse my brother with one of your spots while I handle the matter of bringing the police and someone in the appropriate safety gear so they are not also sickened. I will see you soon." Michael hung up.

I handed the phone to the Devil. "Michael has suggested I amuse you with one of my spots." I pointed to the one on the back of my neck. "I recommend this one."

The Devil's amusement would be my enjoyment, and if my memories would fail me soon enough, I wanted to remember his gentle affection.

## NINE

Just keep your hands from wandering
inappropriately.

A WISER WOMAN would have kicked the Devil out of her home, but I invited him to straddle my lower back and play with a rather lovely spot. As expected, he possessed a gentle touch, and he took fiendish delight in stroking my fur. The instant he figured out the spot made me purr, he chuckled and indulged me. "I see I am being cruelly used for your pleasure."

Yep. "I like back rubs, too."

"Women usually do. It's not counting spots if I'm massaging you, is it?"

"Just keep your hands from wandering inappropriately."

"Most cruel," the Devil murmured.

"My brother will disapprove of anyone giving me a back rub, so you can indulge in your evil ways through quiet feuding with a chipmunk. While you're rewarding me with a back rub, I'm going to plot revenge."

"You don't have a chip on your shoulder.

It's a mountain," the Devil muttered. "It has been centuries since the last time I was actually concerned over how far a mortal would go."

"Are you going to bitch and moan about the lethal poisoning thing again?"

"It is disturbing I feel I must, as you will not."

"Well, yeah. I've the word of an archangel he can deal with the whole poison thing. Pain and suffering aren't really my thing, but I'll deal with it for the sake of some justice mixed in with a healthy dose of revenge. Maybe you're the one who needs a back rub. Do you even know how to relax?"

"If I say I know how to relax, does that mean I won't get a back rub?"

The Devil amused me. Had anyone told me I would like him a few days ago, I would have laughed long and hard. "I'll think about it."

"We are making your brother rather uncomfortable for some reason."

"That's because he's almost as much of a pervert as he is an asshole."

"I'm a pervert," the Devil announced with pride.

"You're a lecherous spot counter, it's true. More rubbing, less talking," I ordered.

"Bossy."

I stretched, cradled my head in my arms, and waited for my owed massage.

If anyone learned that the Devil had magical hands meant for offering massages, he would be mobbed, I would be robbed of future back rubs, and I bet he could gather the souls of many in exchange for his work. It took him all of five minutes to reduce me to a purring mess.

"This is how you work a woman, Jonas. First, you buy her nice things. Your sister seems to have a strange appreciation for hot beverages perverted into becoming cold beverages. Find out what they like and make small offerings to test the waters. Should the tentative offering be accepted, you begin the next phase." The Devil's fingers dug at my right shoulder, and I melted under his touch. "Most women will turn into women-shaped puddles when properly massaged. This makes them rather pliable, although some have hidden swords rather than bone for spines, so they are only pliable for however long you're massaging them. You need to be clever about the timing. Seduction attempts are far more likely to succeed should you pounce during a massage when she is happy, relaxed, and potentially more receptive to your pouncing. Weak men, much like that Lorenzo Gallo fellow, are unclear on the concept of how to make a more satisfying conquest. Really, it's a much more intense power trip when you get a woman to beg through a drawn-out seduction. Of course, there is a time and a place for tortured screams, but it's ideal if your woman wants to help you make

the screaming happen with a mutually disliked target."

My brother's indignant squeak from his
cage on the coffee table made me giggle.

"He is absolutely horrified I am educating
him on the art of seduction while I have my
hands all over you, his sister. It's delightful. I
am accomplishing so much through a single
act. I haven't had this much fun since my last
visit to my dungeon to give some fucking assholes some personal attention."

"You're going to ruin your reputation if
you keep this up," I warned him. "You have
ventured into gentleman territory, and your
reputation very clearly states there is nothing
gentlemanly about you. Yet here we are, with
you trying to teach my brother to be a slightly
perverted gentleman."

"But will gentlemanly behavior result in
me being able to count extra spots today?" the
Devil asked. "Some sacrifices are worth making, especially if there might be some pleasant
screams in my future."

I could think of three types of screams,
one of which belonged in the positive cate-
gory and two which belonged in the fear and
suffering categories. Upon close consideration, depending on how the Devil's dates with
his succubi went, I would consider being
game for all three, although the Devil would
have to earn his keep if he wanted me in any
position where I might be screaming for any
reason. "Do you count Gallo's screaming as

pleasant? Because I am not a good person right now, and I would be very pleased by his screams."

"After today, his screams will be the sweetest of music in my dungeons. Does an extra good massage earn me an extra spot? I'd really like an extra spot."

I pointed at a random spot on my upper arm. "Is there a spot there?"

"There is," the Devil confirmed.

"You can count that one, but you have to massage until I nap, and then you can count that spot however long you like, just do your work between spot counting sessions. Try to leave some of my fur intact. Rubbing all my fur off would be rude and likely bar you from future spot counting sessions."

"See, Jonas? I brought the goods to the table and received a prize for my excellent behavior. However, I have lost this war, because I absolutely do not want to indulge in spot counting without the subject of my attention being fully present. I have won, yet I have bitterly lost."

My brother squeaked, and the soft tap of tiny paws on the glass cracked me up.

"You're just lucky you're good with your hands. I'm expecting you to work for that spot, and you have to pay it at least ten minutes of attention while I doze."

"You can't just change the rules at your whim."

"I absolutely can change the rules at my

whim. They're my spots. If you want free range spots, grow your own."

"I could be talked into growing spots of my own if you would like to engage in a spot count exchange," the Devil countered.

"You're tricky." I yawned and waved my hand in the direction of the poisoned roses. "When your brother and the cops get here, make sure they take a blood sample or whatever it is they need to do, and then ask your brother for details about this poisoning, and conspire with him about the best way to bring this entire outfit down. Also, get that stuff I asked Belial for. I'm going to get mad and get even. I'd rather not be forced to force you to discipline some big bad devil for failure to do his share of the work."

"He'd like it."

"But will you like it if I'm making him like it?" I could only assume the Devil possessed some of humanity's faults, including jealousy, pride, and greed.

"I absolutely would not like it if you made him like it." He snorted. "And you call me tricky."

"More massaging, Lucifer. Do I look like I have all day here?"

MICHAEL BROUGHT GABRIEL, four cops, and a pair of CDC representatives in white containment suits that covered them from head to toe with enclosed helmets into my home and introduced them, but their names went in one ear and out the other.

The Devil's magic hands had something to do with that. Every time he went for one of his allowed spots, he'd massage my neck, I'd melt, and he'd earn more time to indulge in his spot counting habit.

Until I developed a headache, I'd blame Lucifer for my inability to care who invaded my home as long as he kept up his sinful work.

I observed from my prone position beneath the Devil, evaluating if I wanted to return to my nap. As I'd already been disturbed, I pointed at the vase of roses. "Apparently, I was poisoned just from touching them, and there's an envelope in my kitchen drawer that's likewise contaminated. I had the envelope on my table." While my house counted as small, I pointed in the direction of the kitchen. "Kitchen is that way."

One of the CDC agents went for the roses while the other headed for the envelope, and they carried several thick, plastic bags with them and a jar of pink powder, which I could only presume was neutralizer.

I'd never seen the stuff in action before, as the CDC struggled to find a way to produce the substance, which required dust from pixies and similar species. As plucking a pixie from a tree and giving them a good shake counted as cruel and unusual punishment, the government needed to negotiate with the hyperactive menaces, who were paid more by legalized shops to offer highs.

Maybe my idiot brother should have gone into the pixie dust business. I bet he could've afforded a nicer car without having gotten himself turned into a damned chipmunk.

"Yes, that is neutralizer," Michael informed me. "The CDC wishes to test you to see if it will purge the toxin from your blood. They will take the samples from the roses and the envelope, and your cooperation with their experimentations would result in you being paid rather than you paying for your care. This is beneficial to you."

The Devil growled, and he stroked the spot on the back of my neck I'd offered for his enjoyment. I relaxed and struggled to keep from purring, as purring would lead to potentially hissing to evict everyone who wasn't the Devil from my home.

I bet I could talk the archangels into caring for my brother for a while. Training their brother would take a great deal of time, effort, and uninterrupted concentration.

"You are an annoyance," Michael informed his brother. "Humans need to establish if things like this will work without us holding their hands every hour of their existence. It will not bring harm to her."

"But will it help her?"

I suspected the archangel smiled. "Try it and find out if you are unwilling to peek into the future. I already gave my word I would halt the toxin's progression should the humans prove incapable of handling the situation. They wish to question you, Darlene."

I eyed the cops, one of which I recognized from the station, but to my dismay, I couldn't remember his name. I lacked the headache, but I shot Michael a glance.

He shrugged, and if he had a head, I wondered at his expression. Then, after a pause, he said, "It begins."

Damn. I wondered what would go next— or if I'd even realize something was going wrong by the time the toxin got done slaughtering my poor brain. As I couldn't do anything about it, I pointed in my brother's direction. "The same fuckers who did that to my brother brought the flowers along with an invitation to meet somebody in their operations. Lorenzo Gallo. He probably wants to take advantage of my poisoning, and he probably believes he's the only one with an antidote. Apparently, I'm attractive and exotic."

"You are attractive," the Devil replied. "Isn't she exotic, Michael?"

"Only to annoying devils and idiot humans," the archangel muttered.

"Gabriel? Don't tell me you're going to side with him."

"I am siding with him." Gabriel stretched his wings out and rolled his shoulders. "A foolish question, truly."

"Don't side with him. He's obnoxious enough."

The complaint in the Devil's tone amused me. "Is he always so whiny?" I asked.

"Yes," The archangels chorused.

The Devil sighed. "I require you to be in good health so I can selfishly count your spots. I am not whining. I am making these idiot archangels understand you are attractive and exotic, thus you should be treated better than some experiment. The only experimentation I enjoy takes place in my dungeon."

Having seen the Devil's bedroom, which resembled a dungeon for perverts out for a good time with cuffs and whips and other implements I wasn't quite ready to even imagine, I recognized his statement could be taken one of several ways. I chuckled. "He thinks I'm attractive and exotic, Michael. He might need some help. Maybe his lack of support for his various issues is why he is like he is now."

"He is like he is now because he is spoiled, vain, greedy, and rather selfish." Michael chuckled and strode towards my kitchen. "I will observe the human so there are no mishaps. This toxin's potency is what makes it so dangerous. It only takes a little to kill."

"What questions do you have for me?" I asked, propping my chin on my hands. If they wanted me to get up, they'd have to move the Devil, and I got the feeling he wouldn't be cooperating without a fight the mortals would lose without question.

"When did you first come into contact with this Lorenzo Gallo?" the cop from the station asked.

I really wished I remembered his name. "Never that I know of. My brother is the idiot who made a deal with his thugs, not me. I just caught his attention when I told the bastards to get the hell off my property, and I enforced it with a firearm. I have a conceal carry license, and no shots were fired."

"Yes, we are aware of your concealed carry license." The cop approached my brother and leaned over, and I tensed. "Has Mr. Esmaranda changed since his transformation?"

The Devil stroked the spot on the back of my neck. "There will be no changes."

"I didn't ask you, sir."

I raised a brow, wondering if I'd have to explain to the other cops why their colleague had come to a brutal end at the hands of the Devil. Intervening would keep things mostly cordial, and I could use a small spot to keep things calm. Lifting my head, I held up my right hand and pointed at the spot on the tip of my index finger. "You can play with this spot if you behave and give me a back rub at a later time of my choosing."

The Devil stilled, and I grinned at having made him stop and think about whether he wanted my spot or to take his temper out on a cop. "There still won't be any changes to your brother."

"You still have to behave and give me a back rub at a later time of my choosing if you want access to this spot."

Heaving a sigh, the Devil muttered, "Very well."

With a low chuckle I'd count as wicked had it come from anyone other than an archangel, Gabriel stepped between the cop and the Devil. "With the due respect owed to an officer of the law, be aware of whom you speak. Lucifer really does not care for mortal laws, and *He* does not typically intervene should *His* fallen son create trouble for you. Right now, my brother works at the young lady's whim, and it would not be wise for you to test those waters."

Everyone stopped and stared at the Devil.

"You're Satan?" the cop blurted.

"In the flesh," the Devil replied, and he resumed massaging my shoulders. "She prefers this guise, although I am willing to give you a taste of what it means to stand in my presence if you'd like."

"If you stop rubbing my back, I'll put you in your own damned dungeon for at least a year, and I'll make sure you don't like it." I would, too. I'd already gotten Belial to stand in line. I could find another one of his devils to do my dirty work. If I ganged them up, I could get my way, then I'd kick everyone else out of the dungeon and have some fun at the Devil's expense.

I'd like it. A lot.

In my kitchen, Michael laughed. "She really will, brother mine."

The cop spluttered, but after a moment, he asked, "What is so important that two archangels and *Satan* have interest in this matter?"

The cop's indignant tone annoyed me, and I flattened my ears. Not even the Devil paying extra attention to my favorite spot soothed me. I wanted to bite the officer, but I settled with a hiss. Did he dare imply my brother was not worth the attention of two archangels and the Devil himself? Sure, my brother had done some stupid shit, but I didn't give a shit about that.

However much Jonas annoyed me, I would still consider storming the heavens should my takeover of the hells fail to go to plan.

He was my brother.

After taking a moment to consider my situation, perhaps I needed to storm the heavens to fully earn my trip to the Devil's many hells while also recruiting more help for my cause.

I'd have to put some thought into it later.

"Forgive her," the Devil requested. "She's a passionate, jealous creature."

Was I? I took a few moments to consider that, too. "No, I just need you for the stuff I want to do. I saw you first, so they have to wait their turn, assuming I decide their turn will come. You agreed, so you're stuck with it. You should be happy I'm a generous and kind woman. I let you have spots when you display a capacity for good behavior and general obedience. You're happy I'm generous and kind, aren't you?"

"I recognize when I can't win this one. My answer is yes, I am happy you're generous and kind to me and only me in regards to your spots. I'm a jealous being. I refuse to share the spots I've earned."

"This is a bargain you have lost, brother." Gabriel laughed at the Devil. "Keep a close eye on him, Darlene. He was never good at being obedient. I do not expect that to change now."

"He'll be obedient if he wants to continue enjoying access to any of my spots. I have retained rights to revoke access to my spots at any time."

"She is a most cruel creature." To my amusement, he continued his massage. "I do enjoy being bribed and coerced into obedience. It's one of my many sins."

Gabriel went to my brother's cage, took off the lid, and captured Jonas, stroking his furry back. Wisely, my brother kept his teeth to himself. "This one will vex you greatly over the years. I thought you should know."

"They always do. I am debating how best to handle the situation."

"He will need to be quite durable to survive his sister's temper. Do keep that in mind. She would become most distressed should something happen to her brother, no matter what unsavory forms of address she assigns to him." Gabriel tucked his wings close to his back. "Darlene, I will take care to detoxify your home once the humans leave, although I will leave it to the humans to determine if any of their number came into contact with the toxin. They would do well to take every care."

"Thank you, Gabriel. That's kind of you. I appreciate it."

"Of course. It is but a small matter, and acts of kindness such as this please *Him*. You are also keeping my brother amused, which means things are a little more peaceful than usual. For the moment. Things may become less than peaceful in the near future, but only a fool would expect any other result from this situation."

Any other day, I believed the cops would have been thrilled to question me for hours, but I figured the presence of three divines unnerved them. The CDC representatives packed up the flowers and my envelope, hauling them outside in layered plastic bags. After Gabriel's comment, I wondered how many would be poisoned before it was studied and contained.

No, I already knew the answer: too many.

For the sake of my revenge, I didn't give a shit I'd been poisoned.

Anyone other than me was too many people, and the archangel's warning implied someone else would be sickened from the toxin. For all I knew, the Devil could be poisoned, although I doubted anything as mundane as mere poison would do anything other than annoy him.

No, I wouldn't worry much for the Devil. He could take care of himself. Unlike me, I doubted anything could actually hurt him.

"You would be surprised," Gabriel said, and it unnerved me I could feel the archangel staring at me despite his lack of a head.

"Has anyone ever told you that reading someone's mind is creepy at absolute best?" I complained.

"Yes. It is amusing how unsettled humans become when they realize their thoughts are no longer private."

I pointed at the Devil. "Why isn't he listening in, then? Well, at least it doesn't seem like he's listening in."

"He is not, unless he deems it to be important. Who knows what he deems to be important? My brother enjoys playing games, and your thoughts would bereave him of his enjoyment of the games he plays. He particularly finds satisfaction in the mystery you are, and he does not wish to ruin that. He is monitoring you for evidence of the toxin, but he is only listening whenever you attempt to remember someone's name."

"You're an asshole," the Devil announced.

Gabriel laughed. "You are annoyed because I speak the truth, and you do not wish her to know the truth for you think you are sly when you are, in actuality, rather pathetic."

"Gabriel." While Lucifer's growl promised violent retribution, he continued to rub my back.

The cops, rather than try to ask me any more questions, fled from my home and closed the door behind them.

"Mortals," the archangel muttered. "One little complaint out of you, and they flee."

Michael sighed. "Limit the bickering for later, if you please—and even if you do not please."

"Is it bad I know I can't remember that one cop's name?"

As one, the archangels shrugged.

"Let me rephrase that. Is the toxin progressing faster than you anticipated?"

"It progresses as anticipated," Michael replied. "Within a few hours, you will remember only those who have had close ties to you. Your brother's name will be the one you cling to the longest, but within the next eight hours, even his name shall be gone from your memories. Once that occurs, you will begin experiencing significant discomfort,

and your general awareness of your sur-
roundings will diminish."

"Which is when I'd be most pliable so this
Gallo asshole can take advantage of me."

"Correct."

The Devil growled.

"Lucifer, please try to contain yourself at
least a little."

I couldn't help but laugh at the absurdity
of my life. "That's rich. An archangel is asking
the Devil for a miracle."

"It happens from time to time." According
to Michael's tone, the Devil performing miracles annoyed the hell out of him. I couldn't
blame him for that, although I found the di-
chotomy of their relationship intriguing.

The Devil liked his brothers, and they
seemed to like him, too.

Someone had lied to me as a child. What
had happened to the eternal struggle between
good and evil? Why were representatives of
both sides of their conflict in my living room
acting like long-lost friends? I couldn't ask
how the hell I'd gotten dragged into it; I'd
thought it'd been a good idea to participate in
a hostile takeover of the Devil and everything
he owned. The fault went to me on that one.

I appreciated the perks of having lost my
mind, though.

"Essentially, what you're saying is that I
have no longer than eight hours to complete
my revenge before I'll forget the details on

why I'm seeking revenge in the first place. Is that correct, Michael?"

"Not precisely. You will still have your memories, but your ability to access them will be severely hampered. You will be aware of some elements of your situation, including your determination to indulge in revenge. Your brother's name will be no longer accessible, but you will remember you have a brother and you care for him deeply enough you would storm the gates of my brother's many hells for his sake."

"Yeah, about that. It was a lot easier than I thought it would be. What's the deal with that?"

"My brother is a glutton for punishment, he has an enjoyment of soft things, and he loves beautiful things. That you are beautiful and soft pleases him greatly, especially as you make him work to get his hands on your soft beauty. Doling out rewards in spot-sized pieces was quite wise of you. I recommend you use this as a primary weapon in your arsenal against him."

"Don't give her such a terrible idea," the Devil complained.

"I am not giving her a terrible idea. I am giving her a wise idea, one she should use ruthlessly, for you are a ruthless menace upon this Earth."

I giggled. "No apocalypses in my living room. Gabriel, tell them they're not allowed to start any apocalypses in my living room, please."

Gabriel sighed. "If you wish to start any apocalypses, please do so outside. We are guests."

"Could you wait to start any apocalypses until after I've died and gone to hell, please?"

Both archangels snorted.

Damn. I'd met my fair share of assholes over the year, but the archangels took the cake. "If I swipe my hand over your shoulders, will I hit your neck?"

Once again, both archangels snorted. The Devil halted his massaging duties, rose, and waved his hand where his brothers' heads should have been. "Pretty cool parlor trick, isn't it?"

"It is disconcerting and strange," I replied.

"To look upon the face of an angel is to look upon the face of God, and no mortal may see *His* face and live to tell the tale. It is not a sight for mortal eyes, although divine blood can make such a vision survivable." The Devil strode into my kitchen and returned a few minutes later with one of my mother's clear glass vases. "You'll find this useful, along with the other six or so of these things you have in your cabinet."

I resented the loss of my massage, but rather than voice my opinion over its conclusion, I got up, stretched, took the vase out of the Devil's hands and set it next to my brother's cage. "Those things are vases. Mom liked fresh flowers. Why will my mother's vases be useful?"

"You're going fishing."

Great. The Devil had lost his mind. "I don't fish."

According to the Devil's expression, I had struck him with a cruel, low blow. "You don't fish?"

I pointed at my rodent brother, who beat on the glass of his cage, probably trying to prevent me from doing something he wouldn't like. "When I want fish, I make him get it for me. He's lazy and goes to the grocery store. Most times, he gets a can of tuna and tells me to cope." When I ran as a snow leopard, I hunted for fish as often as possible, but I never called it fishing. "Do I look like I fish to you?"

"You're a cat. Cats like fish."

"Yes, I do like fish. I like fish when someone provides fish for me. Why would I fish when I can have someone else fish for me? I prefer my hunts to be where the water is frozen and unsuitable for fishing."

"Ice fishing is a thing."

Was the Devil serious? "You live in a fiery hell hole. Where, precisely, would you go ice fishing?"

"I could make it work."

Men. Why was I plagued with men? I resented the Devil's general manliness and his ability to annoy me with a single sentence. "You'd probably have an easier time creating fish capable of surviving in lava than making a place suitable for ice fishing in your home." Shaking my head, I picked up the vase, turning it over in my hands and examining it for damage. "Why would I need a vase to go fishing? You use fishing rods and bait to go fishing." I thought about that for a moment. "You can use a net, too, I guess."

"You wouldn't use the vase to go fishing with. You'd use it to keep your new pet fish. The vases are clear, the fish will be small, and you can amuse yourself with admiring your new prizes this way. One of the perks of running my oh-so-many hells is to tour the various dungeons and admire my prisoners. It's satisfying. Using the vases prevents you from having to do additional investments."

I considered the vase in a new light. "Don't fish need special water?"

The Devil shrugged. "It doesn't matter to me. It would just speed up the process of getting them into my hands if they do need special water and you fail to provide it to them."

"Fish need to live in treated water," Gabriel announced.

"And what happens if I don't treat the water?"

"Death is probable. The treatments remove chemicals unhealthy for them from their water."

"So, you're saying if I put a fish into tap water, I'll be slowly poisoning them?"

"It might not be slowly, but yes. You

would be poisoning them. Some fish are more sensitive to the water than others."

"I guess I need to get whatever it is fish need to make the water safe. I guess it'll be another trip to the pet store, then." At least I had enough money to handle it. "Can you do me a small favor, Gabriel?"

"What do you need?"

"I need someone to pay the CDC to handle a certain issue, and I've already imposed on your brother enough."

Michael chuckled. "She will not be satisfied until that matter is properly addressed. But you are not imposing upon me to ask for such a small thing. I will handle it on your behalf, as that issue is more of my responsibility than his."

"Thank you. Do either one of you know what I would need to best care for these fish?" I spent a moment wondering, then it occurred to me the only fish I would care for would be the ones responsible for my brother's current shape. "While they may deserve to be slowly poisoned, I should care for them properly."

"Stop being good. Being good involves extra work," the Devil complained.

"Why would I want to kill one of my prizes?" I asked, and however much I disliked the loan sharks who'd hurt my little family so much, it seemed like a waste of effort to kill something I went through effort to transform and catch.

"Because they would end up in my hands faster, of course. I want them, Darlene."

Right. I dealt with a sadist, one with a reputation of greed with a significant dose of sin splashed in. "Why would I want my pet fish to end up in your hands?"

"I'll do an excellent job of torturing them."

"While I don't doubt your general torture skills, that does not answer why I would go through the hassle of fishing only to give you my prizes."

"Do I get to count extra spots if I demonstrate I have a base understanding of what it means to be patient?"

"No."

"You're a most cruel creature. Why would you deny me your spots?"

I considered my entire situation, and I wondered if forgetting about the Devil and his wicked ways would be a blessing or a curse.

"It would be both," Gabriel informed me.

"But would it be more of a blessing or a curse? This may become important, especially if he's angling for more spots. He is greedy, so I will assume he wants more of my spots. I'm not sure he's appreciated the spots he's already received."

"I appreciate the spots I've already received very much, and I will not be satisfied until I've explored every single one of your spots."

"Don't you have a herd of succubi to review for marriage purposes?" I countered. "Go count their spots."

"They don't have spots."

"I'm sure they could apply spots to their persons for you to enjoy."

"It's not the same as enjoying naturally occurring spots."

"You got kicked out of heaven because you're a pain in the ass."

"I got kicked out of heaven because I'm disobedient, but me being a pain in the ass was a factor."

"I'm not sure I have enough spots to teach you even limited obedience," I muttered.

"You're probably right," he agreed with a smirk.

"Should you revoke spot access, you have an infinite number of spots to work with," Gabriel stated. "It would be prudent of you to revoke spots when he indulges in disobedience and other unwanted behaviors."

"You're not helping, Gabriel."

"I am not supposed to be helping you in this matter."

"That's just cruel of you. I'm surrounded by cruel beings. What did I do to deserve such cruelties?"

I couldn't tell if I loved or hated him for being such an annoyance. "You're the Devil. Perhaps your very existence is the reason you are deserving of such cruelties. You might also be a masochist in addition to being a sadist."

"I'm definitely a masochist, especially if it results in access to more of your spots. If no one has told you this, your spots are lovely."

"Were you dropped on your head as a baby?"

The Devil huffed. "*He* would never accidentally drop a baby, although *He* does not tend to keep *His* angels young long. I was undoubtedly the cutest of the babies in the heavens."

"Which tells me *He* dropped you on your head when you were a baby quite on purpose," I countered.

"Your cruelty knows no bounds, I see." The Devil sighed. "Michael, why did you encourage her to storm my gates?"

"She needed no encouragement. She decided to without any intervention on my part, and she did not have any interest in being deterred, so I aided her cause for *His* reasons."

"That's one of the sexiest things I've ever heard."

Great. The Devil viewed my invasion of his home for my nefarious purposes as sexy. Then again, I could use that to my advantage, as I'd never had much interest in learning how to flirt with anyone, mostly due to the general belief I was diseased thanks to my prized tail and my ears. "I think you're confused and possibly desperate for positive female attention."

"I wouldn't say I'm confused, but I will not deny my desperation for positive female attention, but only if the positive female attention includes your spots. I can be very focused when I wish to be."

"Most people call that obsessive."

"I would be pleased to be appropriately obsessive over your spots."

Why hadn't anyone warned me the Devil was in serious need of therapy? "When is it ever appropriate to obsess over my spots?"

"Always. It's always appropriate for me to obsess over your spots. I want them."

"You're like a child but worse."

The Devil shrugged. "I know what I want, and I want your spots."

"But they're my spots. You can't steal my spots."

"If I steal you, then your spots become my spots."

I narrowed my eyes. "I'm already the owner and operator of what used to be your many hells. You can't steal me. I already stole you and everything you own."

The Devil took his time thinking about that. "But does that mean I can have your spots?"

I considered throwing my mother's vase at his head, sighed, and thought better of it. Rather than commit an act of assault against the Devil, I regarded the clear fish prison with interest. "Is there a way to make sure those assholes become fish?"

"Yes," the archangels and the Devil replied.

"Should I be concerned that the pair of

archangels seem somewhat enthusiastic about this?"

Michael came to me and patted my shoulder. "You do an act of great good with evil intentions. While we dislike the sin, you do a greater good, and we see what will change because of what you will do. As such, it would not be prudent for us to interfere with your evil ways. We assist for the sake of the greater good, for all your heart quite enjoys its evil ways."

I shrugged. "What can I say? If I'm going to end up one of the fucking assholes inhabiting that asshole's hells, I may as well earn it. What kind of fish am I getting?"

"You shall find out soon enough," the Devil promised.

## TEN

You devils are all insane, aren't you?

BELIAL SHOWED up at my house with a beautiful box decorated with fish with long, flowing tails. Upon his arrival, the Devil sulked, pretended to ignore the other devil, and spent his time in my kitchen muttering curses. The archangels lingered, and I didn't need to see their heads to get the feeling they did not possess a cordial relationship with the devil associated with ruin.

Whatever. I didn't care. I was grateful I still remembered the devil's name. I took the box out of his hands. "Thank you, Belial."

"I've been asked to continue assisting you, as my true visage will not bring harm to your mortal soul."

Ah ha. The Devil resented Belial could do something he could not. "Given an hour or so, I'm not going to remember your name, so please accept my thanks for your help now."

Belial inclined his head. "You are a bold

mortal, and it would be a pity to bring forth your ruination prematurely."

"You devils are all insane, aren't you?"

That earned me a grin, a rather vicious one revealing pointed canines. "To a certain degree."

"He's jealous because you can show yourself and won't wipe me out, whereas he can't. Is this correct?"

"Yes."

I turned towards my kitchen and stomped my foot. "Stop being a baby. The archangels aren't whining they have to put their heads into storage to keep me from kicking the bucket, so get your ass in here and act like a gentleman."

"I'm hardly a gentleman," the Devil retorted, although he did come into my living room, and he scowled at me.

"If you want to ever see a spot again, you'll be a gentleman. I deserve a gentleman, especially in my house. If I don't want a gentleman, I'll tell you, and then you can earn a spot through encouraged ungentlemanly behavior."

The Devil blinked, and he furrowed his brows. "Do you want gentlemanly or ungentlemanly behavior?"

"Gentlemen might, through displays of gentlemanly behavior, earn spots. The only time ungentlemanly behavior is rewarded with spots is when I specifically request the ungentlemanly behavior. I would like to mention I can shift so the only spots you see are the ones on my ears and tail. You should be grateful there might be some succubi willing to put up with you. I have standards."

"Your standards are cruel, and they are too high," he complained.

"A spot earned is far more satisfying when claimed."

"Can we discuss the claiming process?"

"No."

The Devil growled. "You're ruthless in addition to cruel."

"And you're a whiner."

"Does whining earn me a spot?"

"No."

He grunted, scowled, and said nothing.

I turned to Belial. "Now that he's taken care of for the moment, I have a few hours before you're some nameless entity floating around in a world of pain. What's your general proposal for this box?"

"I will kidnap you, lure the humans to a quiet, remote location, and begin your fish collection." The devil associated with ruin and general suffering gestured to my new box. "Some devilish influences and the careful cultivation of substances have resulted in a compound capable of guiding their transformation to a certain extent. In short, upon exposure, they will become finned aquatic creatures. An additional compound, chosen specifically to garner favor with you, will reverse their age to a rather young state. They'll be babies barely capable of survival. My sources indicate you enjoy the presence of young creatures."

I turned my glare to Michael. "You tattled, didn't you?"

"I prefer to think of it as encouraging you to care for your new pets rather than flush them down the nearest toilet, however satisfying dumping them into your septic tank may be. View it as extending your revenge in a somewhat merciful fashion."

"The one that abuses his family deserves to be flushed into my septic tank."

"That one will be aware of his past transgressions as he lives out a very extended life waiting for his time in my brother's many hells, assuming he survives long enough to be turned into your pet. Should he survive, you will have a beautiful pet, and he will be brought low until it is time for him to face his punishments."

"Just how beautiful of a pet are we talking about here?"

"He will become a Mandarin dragonet."

"He'll be a what?"

"A Mandarin dragonet, sometimes called a Mandarinfish. He'll be a very beautiful and colorful fish, the prize of any aquarium," Michael explained. "As a gift to you for putting up with my brother, I will help you set up his habitat, and I will teach my brother how to care for your new prize. He is beautiful but toxic, fitting his nature. You will enjoy many hours watching him. I will help you establish homes for all the new species of pets you acquire. You will need an entire room in your new home dedicated to your living trophies."

I regarded the Devil with interest. "I'm going to need a room for my pet fish, and I am willing to offer you a payment of one hour with a spot of my choice for this space."

"Monthly, like rent. I get an hour with the spot every month as rent for these fish I cannot eat or torture until their natural deaths."

"Deal. I'll pick the spot after I have these fish in my possession and have approved of their new habitats. They're treasures, so they get excellent habitats so I can show them off to those I don't like. Belial, it is possible to get more of this substance should I need it, yes?"

"Of course."

"Okay. What's this about kidnapping me?"

"You will be impaired, and being kidnapped will be well within your capabilities while you're suffering from your poisoning. Lucifer can satisfy himself rescuing you once the main work is done and I have secured your new pets. I will safeguard your pets while Lucifer indulges in one of his fits of temper."

"I do have quite the temper," the Devil admitted. "Indulging is my specialty."

I bet it was. "And how are you going to kidnap me?"

"You will go to one of the addresses your brother has, and I will snatch you with witnesses, and I will have some of my lesser devils lure them to the appropriate locations. They will be disguised as humans, of course."

"Okay." I eyed the Devil. "Get your protesting out of the way now."

"If Belial wishes to forge an alliance with you, I'm not going to stop him. Try not to abuse my devil too much, as while he is annoying, he's very good at his work."

I found it amusing he thought Belial would need to be protected from me. "I'll think about it. The only rescue I'll particularly require is from this poisoning, so that's your problem."

"Yes, it is a problem. I dislike maintaining this ruse."

"Deal with it. Belial, try not to damage any of my spots. He gets unreasonable about my spots."

"I have noticed this," Belial replied. "Your spots are safe, although I fear for my sanity."

I pointed at the Devil. "You live in one of his hells. Were you ever really sane to begin with?"

"You make a good point."

Pointing at the Devil led to trouble, as the Devil leaned over and gently seized my finger between his teeth.

Right. I dealt with the Devil, and he was not a sane or sensible being.

"I'm sorry, Belial. You have to deal with this all the time, don't you?"

"He does not usually handle females in this fashion."

"Well, aren't the other females basically succubi seeking sex or demonesses of some sort?"

"Yes. He does not indulge in mortal women often."

"Oh, joy. I'm an exception."

"You are. If he's busy playing with your finger, he will stay quiet, so let us attend to business while he's amused. I have, as you have requested, gathered interested succubi, taking the time to make certain they are aware His Most Sulfurous Majesty is seeking a permanent partnership. I took the liberty of notifying them that you have taken over, and that you will be observing the festivities."

Something about Belial's tone warned me of trouble. "Did you tell them I'm competition?"

The devil shrugged. "He is suckling on your finger as you won't give him anything else. It seemed only fair to warn them that they compete against a mortal woman capable of bringing His Sulfurous Majesty to the point of desperation."

"It's more of a nip than a suckle," I replied. As I could be an asshole, I reached over with my other hand and smoothed the Devil's hair, which was in dire need of a good shampooing and some conditioner. "Your home environment isn't doing you any favors." I concentrated, shifting my hands enough to remove the fur up to my wrists before rubbing strands of the Devil's hair between my fingers. "Belial, as I have zero doubt I'll forget by the end of the day, I need to take him somewhere to do something about this disaster. If he's expecting me to keep my fur soft and pristine for his enjoyment, this mess needs to be addressed."

"Are you planning on grooming his hair for your enjoyment?"

The Devil definitely counted as handsome, and if he softened his hair a little, I could see myself losing hours toying with him at my leisure. I shrugged. "Sure. Maybe if I make him pretty enough, I'll make the succubi work to get a chance at him."

"I suspect His Most Sulfurous Majesty is more interested in you giving him a chance at this point in time."

I stared at the Devil, aware I'd reduced him to the equivalent of a prized toy in my head. "Are you an idiot?"

Both archangels choked, excused themselves, went outside, and laughed hard enough I could easily hear their chiming amusement through the door. Whatever. If the Devil's brothers wanted to laugh, I saw no reason to begrudge them their fun.

The way I figured it, they lived in the heavens, which seemed like a rather stiff and stuffy place.

"It really is," Belial replied.

"Is there any way to stop you devils from reading my mind?"

"There are ways, but there is no time to teach those ways to you right now."

The Devil released me and straightened. "I will teach her."

Belial smirked.

I wiped my finger off on the Devil's sleeve. "I have some rules for my kidnapping. First, no violations. I know you devils like your violations, but you're just going to have to bide your time and violate someone else, preferably one of the fucking assholes or some willing person seeking violation. Second, you can tie me up, but the Devil is going to have to massage out all the kinks later. Third—"

"I accept your terms," the Devil interrupted. "Will I be rewarded with a spot for the proper massaging of all your kinks?"

When phrased that way, I realized I'd stepped in a filthy trap, one occupied by one hell of a man. Did the Devil count as a man? I frowned and stared at Belial.

"Yes," he replied. "For your purposes, he does."

Okay. I could work with that. It was just a little filth and perversion, and if I was going to delve into the dark depths of perversion, why not aim for the Devil himself?

"That would be the toxin talking, as it already begins to impair you."

Well, shit. "Okay, so I'm out of my right

mind. That's fine. Back to my rules before I forget what they are. Third, I can't remember the last time I had something to eat at this point, so one of you has to make sure I'm fed dinner while I'm a captive. Don't let me eat my new pet fish."

The Devil chuckled, pulled out his wallet, and handed Belial a card. "You know what to do."

Belial took the card and disappeared, leaving behind a faint hint of brimstone.

"This whole mind reading thing is weird."

"It has its uses, including my ability to have an entire conversation to Belial without you being aware of it."

"Except now I'm aware of it."

"You're unaware of what we were discussing."

"I'm not going to remember his name by the time he gets back from that errand, will I?"

"Very probably not. Belial is particularly talented at judging a human's state. He enjoys knowing how much ruin he can bring when he toys with mortals. He's able to tell even the minor changes, the ones you're unaware of." The Devil reached out and touched my forehead. "The toxin is attacking here. It will spread soon enough. Michael?"

The archangels strode in through the door with no sign they'd left so they could laugh at me. "Yes, my brother?"

"How long until her memory is impaired?"

"It will happen soon. She is resilient due to her determination, but she already loses focus. Belial does truly intend to garner favor with her as much as he can. He is masterful in his manipulations."

The Devil grumbled curses. "I will destroy them all if they hurt her."

"Yes, you will," Michael replied, and without another word, both archangels disappeared.

"I don't know about you, Lucifer, but that sounded rather ominous."

"Yes, it did," the Devil agreed.

THE HEADACHE STRUCK with blinding force, and my world narrowed to the misery of my existence. Much like the relentless waves in a storm-tossed sea, the pain crested, crashed, and surged, eroding away at me. Closing my eyes kept me from drowning, and every sound stabbed at me.

Little remained, save for the knowledge I'd paved my way to some dark hell.

A soft and gentle laugh broke through the agony and calmed the storm, reducing the thundering waves to gentle, soothing ripples.

*"Hello, Darlene,"* a still and quiet voice whispered to me. *"Do not open your eyes quite yet. It is not time."*

Even if I wanted to, I doubted I could disobey *Him*.

The entire situation flustered me. It was one thing to deal with the Devil, but it was another to deal with *Him.*

My father would have given anything to be in my shoes, and I would have rather fled back to the general safety of the Devil and his sinful, spot massaging hands.

*"Treat me as you would my fallen son, and you will find my presence is not as terrifying for you as you believe."*

Somehow, I had missed the memo *He* liked playing jokes on wayward mortals. "Are you sure about that? I mean, you're here to tell me I'm about to go to hell, aren't you?"

*"While you are going to my son's many hells, it is not for the reason you think. You have not fallen out of my favor."*

"I haven't?" I blurted. "But why not?"

*"Is it so hard for you to believe?"*

I considered everything that had led up to the moment I'd been poisoned. "Well, yes."

*"You have not fallen out of my favor because your purpose was never to be a child of my heavens. You are a beloved creation, one born in adversity so you might thrive in adversity, just as my fallen son is beloved for all he is fallen. My fallen son's domain is full of adversaries you will need to face."*

"Well, that's one way to put it. He has lava for landscaping. Also, in case you weren't aware, you have one dysfunctional family."

While I could not see *His* face, I felt *His* smile, and it warmed me from deep within.

*"Yes, this is the truth. I do not usually interfere this directly, but this is something only I can do, so I will do it. My fallen son will make a mistake in a moment of passion, one thousands of years in the making—and a necessary one, for he grows beyond my original purpose. It is part of his journey, and it will become part of yours."*

"You are a master at being vague," I complained. "Just tell me what I need to do, as I figure if you're telling me something is going to happen, I may as well get to it. Have I died from being poisoned yet?"

*"Not precisely, although your death soon comes. I am here to prevent that death from having permanence, but it will leave you changed. All I will do is bar you from crossing through the boundary between life and death, but you must face your death in this moment. I cannot break the universal laws, but I can bend the rules—and I will, for the sake of my fallen son, who has learned something precious."*

"What has he learned?"

*"That he, like the rest of his brothers and sisters, is capable of what he has denied himself since the day of his fall."*

"What, the realization that you love him despite the fact he's a bastard who hates doing what he's told?"

*He* chuckled, and I became aware of *His* presence surrounding me, and *He* chased away the lingering discomfort with a wave of *His* perfect hand, which shimmered and came into focus while the rest of *His* body remained hidden. Something about his thumb bothered me.

"Your thumb has a third joint, like a finger."

*"Would a hand more like yours comfort you?"*

I shook my head. After a moment of hesitation, I reached towards *Him*.

*He* turned *His* hand so I could better view *His* thumb, and like a moth drawn to a flame, I touched *Him*.

*He* radiated a gentle warmth, and *His* skin felt a lot like mine. My curiosity took a firmer hold, and I stroked my fingertips over the extra joint, marveling over how one little detail divided us, yet I couldn't help but think *His* hands were somehow gloriously human despite being different.

*"You were made in my image, but humans are as humans are. Humans bring change. Humans are change. Humans are a great many things, including defiant. Because my son fell, humans could be. My son's fall is one of my greatest gifts to mankind, for I gave my son the freedom to fall —and thus the freedom for mankind to choose its own path. Sometimes, I believe I made a rather severe mistake."*

With the suffering I often witnessed in the world, I could understand why *He* believed our freedom was a mistake, and a rather severe one at that. "I guess I should thank him for that, shouldn't I?"

*"You should. You fluster him. You will continue to fluster him, and I find this amusing. He*

*has his regrets. You will help him overcome those things with time, I am sure. That is part of your purpose."*

"I feel like my birth certificate should have come with a disclaimer that I'm a pawn in a game between your heavens and his hells. It would have been polite."

*"A disclaimer would have changed who you became, and that would have been a poor thing for all parties. You are as you need to be."*

"Is it true you can't help my brother?"

*"Do I possess the power to? Yes, but the method in which I could do so would destroy him in your eyes, and it is not the solution you desire at all. You were told the truth. The only one who can give you the outcome you seek is my fallen son. Of course, it will not be the outcome you expect, and it will undoubtedly vex you, but he will remain your brother, although perhaps a little more troublesome of a being than he was before. But your brother's life will ultimately come at a price."*

I shrugged. "All things have a price. I expect to pay some fairly high prices for storming the hells and taking the place over. I'm sure Lucifer will get tired of being amused soon enough. At that point, I expect he'll be carving out chunks of my flesh to feed to his various devils for daring to boss him around."

*"If by that you mean he will stalk you to gain access to your spots, yes."*

"He needs therapy."

*"Intensive spot therapy. You were created to be*

*my fallen son's ultimate temptation, after all. Your spots and forms are all my masterpieces. I am quite proud of the work I put into your making. I even went so far as to skirt one of the universal laws for my fallen son."*

"Will it hurt you to just call him your son?"

*"He prefers the distinction."*

"Well, he's not here to whine about it. I have noticed he whines a lot. After dealing with him for a few hours, I've come to the conclusion you kicked him out because of the whining, and you have been hoping he would grow up and come home. Except he's a rebellious child and seems to have skipped that phase of reconciliation."

*"You are a most irreverent being."*

"Is this where I'm supposed to say you made me this way?"

*"It is."*

"Why did you make me this way, anyway?"

*"I am sometimes inflicted with unfortunate amounts of sentiment."*

"You know, if my old man found out you're quite the sass, the entire world would shift on its axis."

*"Your father was among the best of men, although it saddened me how much he struggled with the rise of magic. Your mother was quite the interesting human as well. There are few couples capable of tempering a child like yourself. I have rewarded them well for their care with you."*

"Can I ask a question?"

*"Of course."*

"Why me? Why not some, well, better person?"

*"A gentle soul would break beneath my son's hand. You are a strong sword, forged for a purpose. But for you to be as you are, you needed to be born a human with a human's mortality. That is why I am here, as it is that mortality I must address."*

"Dying sucks, and I think I'm rather done with the dying thing, if you please. I'd say even if you don't please, but you could wave that hand of yours and just wipe me right out of existence if you wanted."

*"But why would I want to? You are a flower I have cultivated from a seed, but it is the nature of your seed that is flawed for your future purpose. So, while this is typically my son's domain, you and I must bargain."*

Uh oh. "Bargains are trouble. Am I going to lose my soul over this?"

*"For a time."*

Double uh oh. "That doesn't sound promising."

*"For all my son does take care to prevent mortals from seeing his true form, he slips from time to time in moments of rage or passion. This time will be both, for one of his devils seeks to sow chaos through your destruction, specifically so a succubi this devil has allied himself with might become the Queen of Hell."*

"I'm going to die from sheer stupidity, aren't I?"

"I recommend that you punish him through the restriction of your spots, for it took him a very short time to grow fond of them, and he is disturbed over how fond he has become of you. That is not, in his opinion, his nature."

"He's an idiot, isn't he?"

He chuckled. "Perhaps."

"You do realize I basically browbeat your archangels into taking me to his house so I could take it over, right? And he likes that?"

"It is a first for him, and you did not need to browbeat them into it. They are very fond of their brother, and it is their nature to want to see to his happiness. Do not bother trying to tell my son that. He is more stubborn than any goat and will not believe you."

"Let me see if I have this straight. I'm going to not-quite kick the bucket because he's going to have a temper tantrum, possibly because one of his devils wants to get rid of me because the Devil likes my spots, and because he likes my spots, he won't pick some succubus to be the queen of his many hells?"

"That is mostly correct."

"What part is wrong?"

"Like is too weak of a word for how he feels about you and your spots. He just fawns over your spots because it is simpler for him to express himself through his greed. My son is not a sensible being. But yes, at the heart of the matter, you are correct. As such, we will bargain. Your soul will endure some hardship for a time, but because of a kindness you have shown, that hardship will not *last long. You will find yourself with some diffi-culties facing my son's true self, but that will ease over time. In exchange for giving you what you require to survive, you must do a simple thing."*

"What thing?"

*"You must hold a seed for me, and you must plant it in a moment of darkness. This seed will balance the new seed of your life, which will grow while you walk through the valley of the shadow of death. That is the first part of our bargain."*

"How am I supposed to plant this seed? What is this seed?"

*"It is the beginning of a soul."*

"This seed is some person's soul?"

*"Not precisely, but you are not far from the truth. The seed will eventually grow to become a soul. It is not a soul quite yet. There are several ways you can plant that seed. I recommend you lure my son to your bed with the intent of taking the seed and making it your own, and thus al-lowing nature to run its course. As a consequence of his fall, he cannot create a seed of life on his own. There is nothing in the rules that state I cannot provide the spark that allows a seed of life to take root and become a child. However, that seed's nature will be particularly vexing for my son, who gets delightfully upset over beings with insufferably good natures."*

My eyes widened. "You want me to have a child with the *Devil*?"

*"Yes. That is the price of this bargain. You love children, and you already find yourself intrigued by my son. In time, you will understand. All of*

*this has been arranged to be a natural choice you would make for yourself. In exchange for your soul's survival, you must nurture the seed I have made for you and my son, which you will use to turn the impossible possible. But there is a catch."*

"What catch?"

*"You will forget this bargain in its entirety until an opportunity comes for the seed to be properly planted. I do not wish for my son or all of the angels of my heavens to be aware of what I do. They believe, in truth, my son cannot produce fruit, and there is some importance that their belief remains as such. The child you safeguarded will be my son's first venture into fatherhood, yet another deed of your hand, and your first experience of what it is like to be a mother. You will remember the important details as necessary, so you might act when the time is right. She will be of great importance one day. She will also make an excellent babysitter."*

Kanika. "This is an elaborate prank, basically. But the prank is a *baby*?" I frowned. "Multiple babies, if you count Kanika and the seed."

*He* remained silent for a long moment, and *His* soft chuckle skirted giggle territory. *"Kanika is not of my making, but she is special and deserving of your safekeeping. Your future child? I will merely state you are deserving of it. My son will be most pleasantly surprised after he rages, as he will make ridiculous assumptions despite knowing, without even the shadow of a doubt, you are incapable of being disloyal, just as he is incapable of disloyalty. He will annoy you, and you will make him sleep in your den until he chills his temper. You will enjoy yourself, for I made you as you are to best handle his fits of temper. When he has chilled his temper, he will realize what has occurred. Then I will get scolded most severely, and the heavens and hells will both wait with bated breath to see if the End of Days begins. It won't of course, as my son will be too busy fretting over how to be a father, a problem he doesn't believe possible, nor will he until that moment. This is truly a gift to myself, and I will enjoy it immensely."*

"Jesus Christ on a cracker. This is one fucked up and dysfunctional family." I froze, realizing what I'd blurted. Heaving a sigh, I bowed my head. "I'm sorry. My mouth is going to get me blasted out of existence, isn't it?"

*"Why would I go through so much trouble to provide you and my son with a seed only to blast you out of existence? The whole point of this is to prevent you from being blasted out of existence."*

Right. "Can we go back to the part about me and your son having a child together in the first place?"

*"You charmed him from the moment you invaded his home. As he is a greedy, selfish being, he wants to keep you all to himself, and he plans to work hard to secure you as his. As you enjoy his attention, you will not mind him following you around, thus encouraging his advances. This will result in the formation of mutual affections. Of*

*course, you have stirred the ire of his succubi, and they will become an annoyance to you when they flirt with my son. You are a jealous being. I made you that way quite on purpose, for my jealous son requires a jealous woman. Of course, my son will also pretend to stray to enjoy your jealousy, for he understands its source. You will recognize that he does not actually stray, but his posturing will annoy you enough your fur will stand on end. That will draw his attention back to you, and he will take a great deal of time toying with your spots. I have created the ultimate infinite loop of affection. I am quite proud of this working, if you must know. You are a jewel among all of my creations."*

"I was right. This is seriously one fucked up and dysfunctional family. And I'm not even going to remember most of this conversation?"

*"You will not, not for some time. One day, you will remember the entirety of this conversation, but that day will be many years in the making. But when the seed is ready to be planted, you will know what to do and how to go about it. You'll enjoy yourself, I'm sure. My other sons will also enjoy themselves when you come knocking at their doors to handle various favors for you, and they will be eager to do their various duties as uncles. They are all alike in that regard. They love being fathers and uncles. Or mothers and aunts, should the right human man cross their paths. I encourage them perhaps too often."*

Wow. While the Devil earned parts of his

reputation, *He* was something else. "You're an asshole, aren't you?"

*He* laughed. *"Through your eyes, I suppose I am. It is not unreasonable for you to think such thoughts about me. I do not mind. You are justified, for I have manipulated every element of your existence, all so my son might find some peace through you."*

"Peace? Don't you mean eternal frustration? It sounds like you're setting him up for a severe case of eternal frustration. I know me. I'm pretty damned frustrating."

*"Peace, eternal frustration... whatever makes him happy. You and your spots will accomplish that. Then you will encourage him to bring Kanika into his life as a cherished daughter and his heir as a method of completing a bargain he has made, although some of your choices will annoy him for a while. He will not like when anything brings harm to his little cupcake."*

Laughter bubbled out of me. "His little cupcake?"

*"My son is a sentimental creature with a fondness for sweets. This name will annoy her, which will goad him into using it often. There is reason I gifted you with patience. You will need it. Most importantly, having Kanika as my son's heir will allow for the seed you bear to be a child born of love rather than duty."*

"I missed the memo about me going along with this."

*"You will. The first time you witness a succubus trying to lay a claim on my son, you will*

*understand I speak the truth. And do not try to convince me you were not wanting to remove my son's clothes."*

Crap. "You do not play fair."

*"I do not, not on matters of importance."*

"I expect Christmas presents yearly, and birthday presents would be nice. If I have to put up with your son, I should be pampered the two days of the year presents are commonly given."

*"If you wish to bargain, perhaps you should bargain for something that falls beyond traditional familial customs. Even Lucifer receives gifts for most holidays. You are my favorite of my gifts."*

"I'm now a present for him?"

*"You were born on the same day I breathed life into his seed and welcomed him into my heavens, although thousands of years separate you. The day you stormed his gates is the same as his fall. This was no accident. I moved the seas so the ship would arrive precisely when it did, and I made other arrangements so that your brother would face his fate when he did, although I did not need to do much on that score. I have listened to your every breath so I would not miss the moment you would witness my son in his glory, for only I can ensure you stay on the right side of death's cold boundary. I have put many plans into motion, all so this moment could come. Your soul will suffer for a time, but you will one day truly thrive in my son's glory."*

I raised a brow at that. "And here I

thought my desire to rampage and kill a bunch of assholes was mean. That's downright evil."

"Not precisely. Evil would have been nudging events so your brother faced his death rather than transformation. Rather than anger, you would have faced grief had I not interfered. Your revenge will lead to much good and justice once you can go about your business properly. You will get to try that again. The seeds of a tolerable plan were planted, although my son's less obedient devil and that succubus interrupt it rather thoroughly."

"Well, since you're here and being pretty helpful, how do you think I should handle this?"

"Personally, I believe flushing them into your septic system would be a great deal more merciful, but as they deserve their fate as your trophies, I view it as an early start to their owed punishments. They have no place in my heavens. As for that pesky devil, should he be destroyed in a moment of my son's fury, a better seed can be created to take its place. To keep my son from whining, I shall handle that matter when he looks the other way. It is an important enough seed."

How had my life taken such an odd and dark turn? I cringed at the thought of my family, and if I had not learned their souls had moved on to new lives, I would've believed they rolled in their graves. "My father would be pretty disappointed in me for not being a good little girl, going to hell and all."

*"You are not just going to hell, Darlene. You will be ruling it."*

If my father found out *He* loved the Devil, wanted *His* son to find happiness, and meant to use me to do it, he'd die from a second heart attack. "That doesn't make this any better!"

*"You will get used to it in time."*

"What else are you going to tell me that I won't like?"

*"You will not precisely remember this, but it will exist within you as a gut feeling or instinct. Belial will prove to be one of your greatest allies. While his role is ruination, his loyalties are firmly entrenched with my son. Like you, he was made that way. The notes you read lead you a little astray. Belial is the ruination of all who oppose my son. I have taken steps to make certain he is aware of your importance. Cultivate Belial, and he will serve you and my son even beyond the End of Days."*

"Wait, *beyond* the End of Days? I thought that *was* the end. You know, the apocalypse, world goes kaboom?"

*"The End of Days is only the beginning of an end and the end of a beginning. It is ever present, but it may never be present. It is a paradox. The threat of the End of Days must exist because nothing is meant to live forever. There must be the opportunity for renewal. But the time of that coming is always in motion."*

I sucked in a breath. "Are you saying the End of Days might not even come?"

*"Precisely. There are conditions which must be met for it to happen, and even then, the time of the end is ever fluid. For as long as the balance remains, the balance I helped to create through allowing my son to fall and gifting humanity with free will, it may never come to pass. However, it will always linger on the horizon, waiting for its moment. And should it come, all things will become new. That is what it means for the End of Days to come. But you will have a place in the beyond, although I suspect you shall be the cause of my son's next fall, a change from the helpful push or two I gave him to make him choose his own path. However annoying it can be, change has its benefits."*

Great. I'd been plunked straight into the heart of an utter disaster, and *He* fully meant for me to hitch and whip the damned *Devil* of all people. In good news, *His* son packed heat in all the right ways, and I found myself challenged to find any disadvantages with going along with *His* plan. "How does this put my relationship with the potential in-laws?"

*"When you need some unconditional love, come knocking on my door. You will find my home a welcoming place to visit, but you cannot stay more than a night or two. You would try to take over if I gave you but a single chance. It is quite amusing when my son pays me a visit, and where you go, he will surely follow. He has some strange notions over our relationship. He can visit, but he cannot stay. If he stays, you will stay, and*

*you really would try to take over if given a single chance."*

I laughed at that. "I really would. Answer me one last question, then?"

*"Ask your question."*

"What will my death do to him?"

*"It will change him for better and for worse, but once he is able to look beyond his newfound fear of loss, he will discover that not even death can take you from him. He'll be cranky and clingy. That is why I am here. The price for your survival is one he will find easy enough to bear, as will you. Now, there is the matter of your brother we must deal with before it is your time to face death's shadow."*

"I should flush him into the septic tank," I muttered.

*"You would regret that before he even made it into the tank. You would find the tank opening and fish him out, and nobody would be happy."*

"Just because I would regret it doesn't mean I'm not going to think about it while grumbling."

*"It is your nature to think such things. The price is simple. My son must either destroy the traitor's seed so your brother may have a future, or he must ask me to create a new angel for my heavens. That is the price that must be paid to maintain the balance and keep from breaking any of the universal laws."*

"Why not just make a new angel, tell your son to deal with it, and if he doesn't like it, well, he should have made sure his devils hadn't gotten out of hand. Probably again, the way I figure it."

"Again. And they will again in the future, and you will find this element of being his queen rather annoying. If I gave you the choice, you'd make angels out of his devils, and you would throw everything out of balance. Your job is to help maintain the balance, not thoroughly crush it when certain devils and demons annoy you. And they will."

"Do new angels come fully formed, or are they little baby angels?"

"They are as I wish them to be."

"I guess I can't take a little baby angel to his house, can I?"

"And you wondered why I assumed you would have no problems becoming a mother in the future."

Busted. I shrugged. "Is that a no?"

"You would create much whining should you take an infant angel into my son's home, and we would have the problem of having to balance even more angels, devils, and demons. The numbers must stay balanced."

"It would be a little weird carrying around a headless baby, I guess."

"Only a little. How about a kitten instead? I can create a kitten suitable for your new home, and she will stay young, playful, and affectionate towards you for all her days. It would be trivial to create such a small seed, and I will create something similar in my heavens to maintain the balance, perhaps a playmate for your kitten when *you come to visit. No, that wouldn't work. My kitten would simply follow you home. I suppose you must have two kittens of opposite natures to keep you company. Such a tragedy. You are not a solitary creature, and she will keep you company during the days my son must attend to work he does not wish for you to witness. He will want to spare you from discomfort."*

"You would give me a kitten? Wait, two kittens?"

*"You can consider them a birthday present, and they'll make adjusting to your new home a little easier."*

"I've never had a kitten before."

*"I know."*

"Will the kittens bother Lucifer?"

*"Immensely."*

I grinned at the thought of yanking the Devil's tail. "Okay. That sounds reasonable. Is it strange that I'm not really afraid? Shouldn't I be afraid?"

*"It is not terror that kills a mortal soul upon seeing our faces, Darlene. It is the awareness of everything that humans are and are not, and the beauty of it is too much for a soul to tolerate. You will emerge on the other side changed, but not all change is bad. Change is change. You will understand soon enough. I have prepared you as much as I can. You have nothing to fear, for I am with you."*

## ELEVEN

How could someone so beautiful
exist?

THE DEVIL HAD MANY FORMS, and the dark-skinned beast he'd become intrigued me. With black leathery wings sheathed in flame to cloven hooves that burned wherever he stepped, a sane woman would've feared him. Add in his long, curved claws dripping a rusty, thick fluid, and fear would have been a sensible response.

A few scraps of stubborn fabric, charred on the edges, clung to his wrists. Had his beautiful suit survived the transformation before being incinerated from his heat? The loss of his clothes annoyed me.

How dare he show off his perfect chest to anyone who might come wandering by? Unlike his angelic brothers, he possessed nipples, and the flames crackling around him did a good job of hiding the rest of his physique.

Damn it. I turned my ears back and lashed my tail at that, and I opted to focus on his face before the mystery of the rest of his body either drove me mad or my temper snapped a lot like his. The lingering remnants of my headache had something to do with my irritation.

I forced my attention upwards with a slight detour to admire his chest for a few extra moments. Beyond darkening and the presence of fangs and horns, the Devil's face remained as I remembered. The unbridled fury in his expression promised death.

If I hadn't known better, if I hadn't seen the Devil masquerading as a human already, I might've believed the man dumb enough to face off against the Devil was nothing more than a mortal man, handsome enough to turn heads wherever he went. A red gleam in his brown eyes gave him away.

The urge to get up, unsheathe my claws, and leave some marks across his face as a reminder of why he shouldn't cross me *or* the Devil roused. I flexed my hands, and I concentrated on the wild part of me, the one that led to fur over my skin and the manifestation of my perfect, beautiful spots.

Growing claws hurt, but I accepted the pain and focused.

The unfamiliar living room irritated me, as did my place on an old, worn, and comfortable couch. Movement in the corner of the room drew my attention, and Belial regarded me through narrowed eyes. I flexed my hands, slid off the couch, and debated how to best tear strips out of my new opponent.

Belial raised a brow, and at a glare from me, he raised his hands in surrender.

"You dare to disobey me?" the Devil demanded, and the fires of his many hells crackled in his voice.

"You allowed a human female to undermine your authority," the lesser devil countered. "Be rid of her, or I will get rid of her myself."

Blue sparks danced over the Devil's skin, and the flames cloaking him flared white before brightening to an icy blue. His form shimmered, and much like a glass dropped to the floor, something around him shattered, sending a cascade of shards raining down, which sparkled before dissolving away to nothing.

The beastly visage fell away to a golden skinned man with sun-bright wings, each feather clouded with white and tipped with blue. Something about the Devil's face had changed. From the gentle curve of his jaw to his eyes, which had shifted in color to the sapphire of a winter sky, I found no evidence of human imperfection.

My breath caught in my throat and lodged there.

How could someone so beautiful exist?

Even if I could have breathed, I wouldn't have for fear he'd vanish like smoke whipped on a growing wind.

How could someone so perfect exist?

How could I compare?

I couldn't.

Mocking laughter rang out, but I couldn't tear my eyes away from the Devil's face. I could understand a moth's determination to fly close to the flames. I couldn't compare, but I yearned to touch and discover what perfection felt like.

Part of my very soul despaired for what I could never be, withering away while my lungs burned for the breath I refused to draw.

A cold darkness crept in, stealing away the Devil's golden beauty and leaving me with nothing but shadows reminiscent of his glory. While my eyes could no longer focus or pierce the black shrouding my vision, I could still move my arms.

The shadows drew closer, and I lifted my hands and smiled at the warmth suffusing my hands, tracing his perfect face with my fingertips in the hopes of etching his image into my memories. I closed my broken eyes, but his visage slipped from my grasp, lost in the relentless dark.

*"Breathe,"* a still and quiet voice ordered.

I obeyed, and the world fell away into nothing.

"YOU SHOULDN'T KILL HIM YET," Belial stated, and something about his tone annoyed me into growling.

I was warm and comfortable, and some damned devil was blabbing about not killing somebody? I considered doing my best to kill him, but after a moment of thought, I decided against it.

Killing useful devils wouldn't help me down the road, and for all Belial could be annoying, he had his uses.

"I absolutely should kill him," the Devil replied, and his growls were a great deal deeper and louder than mine.

How unfair. There needed to be a rule against that. His voice rumbled in his chest, which was in close proximity to my head, a situation I quite liked.

His chest and my head needed to maintain a close and personal relationship. I purred, snuggling closer to the source of warmth, which I determined was likely him.

"In order to kill him, you would have to move her, and I can hear her purring from here. He isn't going anywhere. I'll see to that. I will quite enjoy helping with his complete ruination. Your lady seems content where she is at, and you would become more upset should she be disturbed. Perhaps this worm can be the first of her toys. Cats require many toys, do they not? Gift him to her so she can practice her arts, for she has much to learn. You can occupy yourself with building her a dungeon all of her own, filled with toys to keep her from becoming bored."

"Who is he and why are we killing him?" I asked, and I cracked open an eye to discover the Devil had taken on a more human form, and to my disappointment, he hid his beautiful chest beneath a crimson shirt partnered with a black suit jacket.

Belial stood on the back of a struggling man, his suit torn and covered with soot. To all appearances, the devil should have been able to escape, although upon a second, closer look, I realized Belial's feet had transformed into hooves equipped with curved claws, which impaled his victim.

"Alloces," the Devil replied, and his chest rumbled with yet another one of his growls. "He thought he could defy me."

"He wanted to kill you, Darlene," Belial announced with a rather offensive amount of good cheer. "You are delightfully resilient. I am not sure who was more startled by the most unexpected intervention, although Alloces lives only because His Most Sulfurous Majesty turned his attention to you. What would you have me do with him?"

I eyed the squirming devil pinned beneath Belial's clawed feet. "Turn him into a cute and harmless fish that can live in one of my tanks, and then I can show him off."

"A toy for your amusement?" Belial asked.

"If I feed him to another fish, can he become a fish again so I can keep feeding him to other fish?"

The Devil remained tense, although he did chuckle. "Make the concoction particularly hellish, Belial. I'm sure you can make the appropriate arrangements to ensure his punishment is as thorough as possible before he is sent to Darlene's dungeon to be used as a training tool. Locate the succubus who conspired with him and make an example of her."

"Verify she actually played a role first, please," I requested. "He could just be an idiot who thinks he's being helpful when he is not. But if she was involved, I will not object to more pretty fish to play with."

"I will see it done." Belial reached down, grasped Alloces's throat, and vanished in a dark plume of foul-smelling smoke. Unlike before, the stench wasn't that of brimstone.

Sniffing, I frowned. "What is that smell?"

"That would be benzeneselenol. It is a rather toxic acid, and it's one of Belial's favorites. He is in a mood, and when he is in a mood, he enjoys warning those around him he is not to be trifled with. I requested he give proper warning to others of his state of mind to keep things somewhat peaceful among the various devils and demons inhabiting my hells." Without any sign I weighed well over a hundred pounds, the Devil got to his feet, cradling me in his arms while he regarded the bloodied spot on the carpeting with a disdainful expression. "I have changed your plans. I will be having a few of my more trusted devils participating in some games with Gallo, leading him around while you have some time to recover. I will also deal with your brother's situation at the same time. I intend to bargain with him, and unless he wishes to remain a squeaking rodent, he will become the equivalent of your personal secretary and gopher. That should keep him busy. You can boss him around however you see fit."

"Does this change of my plans mean I won't be walking?"

"You're not walking."

"Why not?"

"I said so. That's why not."

"I am disappointed you put your clothes back on." I thought being separated from his perfect chest justified my pout. "I feel a lot better now. My head doesn't hurt."

"That is only because *He* intervened when you saw my face." The Devil's expression soured. "I killed you."

I checked out my hands, which seemed normal to me. To make certain, I plucked at the fleshy bit between my thumb and finger. As expected, it hurt when I pinched myself. Then, to make sure I was truly all right, I shifted enough to cover my skin in fur. To my delight, my coat grew in at its plushest. "I don't feel dead. Am I a zombie, then?"

"You are not an undead."

"But if I'm dead, how else am I talking? I'd

say walking, but I seem to have lost the general use of my legs for the moment." The cat in me enjoyed being carried around, especially as I could rest my head against the Devil's chest whenever I wanted, which I did without any shame in my enjoyment of his warmth. I remained comfortable, but exhaustion clobbered me, and I yawned. "You can just dump me on the nearest soft surface. I'll sleep it off."

"The nearest soft surface is my bed, where you will rest. I will handle the matter of your brother while keeping a close and careful eye on you."

I could work with that, especially if he was in it, keeping me nice and toasty. To implement my plan to disrupt his plans, I grabbed hold of his suit jacket along with a handful of his shirt. "I've been told you're spoiled, so I am expecting a very comfortable bed." I yawned again and muttered a few curses over how I'd gone from wide awake to barely coherent. "Do they serve iced coffee in hell?"

"If coffee is what you want, coffee is what you shall have."

"Iced, and like the way they make it down the street from my house." I wouldn't tell him it was a rare treat. He might take over the entire shop, as he seemed like the kind to indulge in excess. "But don't kidnap any baristas or anything like that. If you give them a five dollar bill and ask for an iced coffee, they'll give you my iced coffee. They're usually below five dollars. Money is useful for things like that. If you give the right person money, they make problems go away, like my problem of not having iced coffee. My spots are to you like iced coffee is to me, I think."

"You underestimate my enjoyment of your spots," he growled.

"You underestimate my enjoyment of iced coffee."

"We shall see about that."

AS SO OFTEN HAPPENED IN my life, I lost. That I lost my hold on the Devil's suit, thus preventing him from leaving me alone, made my defeat all the worse. Somewhere along the way, I'd lost my clothes, too.

Waking up naked and alone in the Devil's bed needed to be classified as cruel and unusual punishment. I debated voicing my complaint as a feline yowl or getting out of bed, shapeshifting to my fully furred self, and making my displeasure known with my claws.

I needed to inform the Devil I had no problems with the idea of being naked and not alone in his bed, but he needed to take off his shirt for my enjoyment. I grumbled over my severe case of raging hormones, sat up, and searched the room for something to wear. While he had several dressers, if I wanted to wear something from them, I'd have to steal something of his.

I bet I'd swim in one of his dress shirts, and who needed pants when his shirt probably came down halfway to my knees? It would classify as gloriously indecent. If I found one of his ties, I would count as mostly dressed.

Rolling out of bed hurt, and while I spotted a bathrobe tossed onto one of the nearby armchairs, I ignored it in favor of the Devil's dressers, rummaging through his eclectic collection of apparel in search of a dress shirt. The first dresser included socks, underwear in a bewildering assortment of styles, colors, and fabrics, and his ties, which numbered in the hundreds. I claimed a silky scarlet one, which would contrast nicely with my fur, spots, and the white shirt I'd pilfer once I found them. On the top, I spotted a silver cross necklace, a choker accented with dark purple stones.

The thought of the Devil wearing the choker cracked me up, and when I found no evidence of ownership, I fastened it into place.

Finders keepers.

The second dresser contained more jeans than any one man needed. Huffing, I went to the walls, pawing at them in search of the magical closets that had to exist or I'd be storming his many hells again to fix the problem. After two rounds of the room, I discovered a button in the corner. When pressed, it popped open a door, which led into a massive closet filled with suit jackets, dress slacks, and dress shirts, all hung properly. A full-length mirror stood in one corner, and I bet the Devil spent a ridiculous amount of time admiring himself in front of it.

A quick investigation revealed he had a suit for every day of the year and some extra thrown in, and he had a shirt in every color. Sticking to my plan, I went with white, approving of his meticulous hanging, with the cuffs and collars properly settled, and every other button fixed into place to help make certain the shirt kept its shape. I checked the hanger, nodding my approval he hadn't used a cheap metal one, which had a tendency to destroy dress shirts given enough time.

As expected, the dress shirt hung halfway down my thighs, standing in for a rather short dress.

Wearing a tie transformed the shirt into rather indecent apparel, as it drew a great deal of attention to my breasts, which would end the shirt's days as suitable for the Devil's wear due to an inappropriate amount of fabric strain.

Oops.

He could afford a new shirt.

Satisfied with my choice of apparel, I cracked open the bedroom door and peeked through the gap to discover the Devil in his sitting room surrounded by a herd of succubi, all of whom had opted to wear slinky cocktail dresses designed to show off as much skin as possible.

I flattened my ears and my fur stood on end, but before I could do more than hiss at the sex demonesses surrounding the Devil, he stood, strode my way, opened the door, placed his hand over my eyes, and said, "Teach your tricks to the newcomer rather than trying to teach me tricks I taught you centuries ago. Also, do not join Darlene in raiding my closet for my clothes, as I do not have nearly enough shirts to sacrifice to your filthy ways."

The succubi giggled, and I clacked my teeth together, growling at the thought of them having successfully lured the naked Devil to his bed while I'd only accomplished getting naked.

"When would you like to resume our discussion?" a sultry voice asked.

"How long will it take for you to thoroughly educate your new friend? You should all have a turn with him."

The giggles intensified, and the same woman replied, "We'll take our time. Call us."

The Devil chuckled, and he didn't lower his hand from my eyes until the sounds from his sitting room quieted. "I see you found your way into my closet." His eyes drifted down to my chest. "I'm finding the sacrifice of my shirt to be perfectly acceptable."

I joined him in staring at my breasts, which stretched the shirt enough he could peek through the gaps with little trouble. Unfortunately for him, my fur and his tie did a good job of masking his view, and the shirt obscured most of my best spots. "I find the fit to be questionable, possibly scandalous."

"I find the fit to be quite attractive, possibly seductive."

"More seductive than that herd of succubi you just kicked out?"

"Considering I just kicked them out so I would not have to share you, yes. Also, they were dressed modestly for succubi."

"That was *modestly*?"

"Quite conservative, actually. They were attempting to prove they could be ladies rather than the little devils and demonesses they actually are."

"Why are lady devils just called devils, but demons and demonesses are gender separated?"

"Demons originate on the mortal coil, and they are often corrupted by human societies. Most demons don't even come to my hells; they live out their lives hiding among humans unless it is between emergences, in which case they're either here, slumbering, or struggling to survive." The Devil placed his hands on my shoulders, turned me around, and pushed me into his bedroom, closing the door behind him. "You'll technically classify as a demoness, although you'll have a more devilish nature. *He* has a shitty sense of humor, and *He* refuses to tell me what *He* did to your soul. I have been told I will have to figure it out. Then, because *He* is insufferable, *He* made a point of mentioning you will be in a delicate state for a while, and I should be gentle with you."

I sucked in a breath at the memory of his perfect chest, his battered clothes, and the flames sheathing his body. I shook my head so I wouldn't remember the rest, focusing on his face. On second thought, I shifted my stare to his chest, hidden beneath yet another suit. "You really do have perfect nipples. Why do you insist on hiding them?"

The Devil lifted a hand and rubbed at his temple. "My brothers have been enjoying ribbing me about your obsession with their chests and your utter disappointment and disapproval over their lack of nipples. I'm hiding them because they're so wonderful that women will inevitably fall over themselves to touch them, of course."

I needed to figure out how to use my spots to gain access to his chest without behaving like one of those women. "Well, if your brothers put some nipples on, they'd be as perfect as you. But no, they choose to not wear their nipples, thus marring their potential perfection. If you even think about removing your nipples, you will never get to touch another spot ever again."

"How do my nipples compare to your beloved iced coffee?"

"I don't know. Go buy me an iced coffee and give me a show, and I'll let you know."

The Devil disappeared in a cloud of brimstone, and I waved my hand in front of my face to make the stench dissipate faster. I opened the door and peeked into the sitting room to discover a succubus waiting, and unlike her fellow demonesses, she didn't wear a scrap of clothing.

No wonder men dreamed of being with a succubus. From the top of her head to her toes, she redefined sensual beauty.

"It's absolutely ridiculous how pretty you are," I informed her. "If I had half your beauty, I'd think about romping around naked, too. As I'm not nearly as pretty as you are, I stole a shirt and a tie so people wouldn't be struck blind."

She raised a brow. "I'm Phenexia. My father is Phenex, and I am his firstborn daughter. You're Darlene?"

"I'm Darlene, yes. I don't usually go running around wearing a man's shirt, but someone stole my clothes, so I figured turnabout was fair play. Since Lucifer dumped me in his room, well, I'm wearing his clothes."

"Expect that often. He tends to make the clothing of his infatuations mysteriously disappear. You'll get used to it, assuming you hold his attention long enough."

Oh boy. According to her tone, she expected me to be dumped out with the trash within a week. "Are you one of those idiots trying to convince him he should have a queen and bang him for the privilege? If so, I feel this strange need to inform you he's a pain in the ass, bossing him around is seriously annoying, and his devils aren't too clear on the concept of generalized obedience, so you'll be begging for a lot of frustration and little satisfaction. The only reason I took the place over for a while was for my brother. If you see Jonas, and he isn't a chipmunk, please slap him for me. After that, I don't care what else you do with the bastard, just don't kill him, because if you do, I'll be forced to kill you, and if I'm forced to kill you, His Most Sulfurous Majesty will likely whine. I'm really, really sick of the whining."

"Perhaps I should have acquired two coffees," the Devil said from behind me, and he reached around me, offering a large iced coffee from the cafe near my house. "Phenexia often assists in a secretarial role, as she enjoys hunting human men in an office environment. She also enjoys showing off her beauty, because she enjoys tormenting the other succubi. Your brother is fine, and he is not currently a chipmunk, although I have taken steps to enable him to use that form for any plans you might wish to make involving him. You can consider him to be a weaponized chipmunk now."

"How did you get that so quickly? You

were gone for maybe a minute." I took my coffee and sipped it, sighing that it was just how I liked it. "You weaponized my brother? And he's a shapeshifting chipmunk now? For the record, snow leopards are far superior to chipmunks, and I refuse to be outclassed by my wretch of a brother."

The Devil showed me his phone. "I called them when I first heard you pattering around in the bedroom to make sure it would be ready. As for your brother, he needs to be useful, and nobody expects a chipmunk to be capable of dismembering annoying mortals who might look at you the wrong way. Consider him an insurance policy, and his continued existence is directly tied to your general happiness. Right now, he is busy learning how to conduct himself, but you'll see him soon enough. Really, I tossed him to my succubi to occupy him for a while."

Damn. The Devil cheated in the best ways, although I didn't want to know what the succubi were doing with my brother. I took another sip of my coffee. "Phenexia isn't one of the stupid ones?"

"She's quite smart, she takes her interest in multiple partners to an extreme, and while she's a fun time, I disgust her with my unwillingness to share. I'm a selfish, greedy being, and she likes telling me that. Phenexia, please don't mind Darlene. I've learned she becomes very territorial. It's surely a feline thing. I have not yet earned sufficient spots, so I am striving to earn my way into her good favor."

"You're *earning* her spots?"

"One must have proper permission to indulge in perfection." The Devil took hold of my hand and showed the succubus the spot on my wrist. "This spot? This spot is merely one part of her perfection. So far, I have earned precisely five spots. She gives time limits on my indulgences, too. She is a most cruel mistress. I am grateful her time limits are usually measured in hours, although she has threatened an absurd ten minutes."

"And you abide by these rules?"

"I've the word of an archangel that there are seventeen spots alone on one of her elbows. I have done some careful calculations. I could spend several hours playing with the spots on her elbow alone. I will make worshipping her a masterpiece."

"Have you lost your mind?" the succubus asked, her tone a blend of incredulous and curious.

"I don't think so. I might lose my mind should she bar me from her spots. I'm between spots right now, and I find this to be an unacceptable situation."

"Dare I ask?"

"I have earned five spots," the Devil announced, and I rolled my eyes at the pride in his voice. Rather than join Phenexia in asking him if he'd lost his mind, I sipped my coffee. "She's pretty stingy with her spots. She will give me a new spot if she needs to keep me amused. She's trying to make me use a dirty word to earn more spots."

"Please or thank you?" Phenexia guessed.

The Devil made a show of shuddering.

"Please," I confirmed. "Spoken to one of his brothers. Where I can witness him using this word."

"You are downright evil. I like it. And your reason for taking over?"

"Some asshole turned my brother into a chipmunk, and no other divine would help me, so I had one choice: Lucifer. I figured Lucifer wouldn't just do what I wanted if I asked him nicely, so I recruited an archangel or two, came here, and took the place over." I frowned, sipping at my coffee. "I'm a little hazy on the details of getting here again or why I've taken over his bed, though."

"You were in poor health, and he wanted to attend to you personally. I can verify he used the please word to an archangel twice while you were indisposed. I am hoping notifying you of this will earn me some of his favor."

"There's a human you want. Who is this human, why are you asking me about this human, and what do you want?"

"Not precisely just a human," the succubus admitted.

I raised a brow. "You want to join a triad?"

"Yes."

The Devil sighed. "Haven't I dealt with

enough angels this week? What did I do to deserve this, Phenexia? Do you know what triads cause me? Trouble. Triads cause me a great deal of trouble. You'll end up seduced by an angel, and clever angels trap both of their partners for a minimum of thirty years. I don't want to lose my secretary for thirty years."

"If you pay me, I can still be your secretary. He isn't precisely wealthy, and I don't expect that to change." The succubus's expression turned wry. "He's frugal."

"You must be quite enamored with him for you to even consider tolerating a, may the heavens have mercy on you for I will not, frugal lifestyle." The Devil shrugged. "You know the rules. He better be ready to satisfy me *and* your father."

"Seriously? I'm not a child! I do not need you intimidating him."

"You most certainly are a child, and I most certainly will make certain he is aware you have multiple fatherly figures who will be keeping a very close eye on him. Since *He* won't show up, I'll stand in and make sure both you and that damned angel are properly chaperoned."

Phenexia raised her hand, rubbed her brow, and muttered curses. "Must you?"

"I absolutely must. It's a time-honored tradition. I have annoyed every triad to ever walk the Earth, and I do not plan on changing this now. Depending on the angel, I may be inclined to be a little more flexible. Which country is your human from? We will be, as always, meeting the baby shortly after birth."

"He's from India."

"Darlene, have you ever been to India?"

"What makes you think I've left America?"

"Right. Would you like to go to India?"

"So you can torture your succubus and an angel? Not particularly, although somebody has to make certain you behave and play nice with her gentleman and her angel. I support the idea we have to meet the baby. However, I thought India wasn't precisely a hotbed of Christianity."

"It's not. Triads are flexible. Love is blind, and angels, once they fall in love with a human, couldn't care less over the logistics of the human's religion. Angels do not begrudge the other religions. Surprisingly, angels are typically welcome among most pantheons."

"Doesn't that go against everything Christians believe?"

"Who said Christians had the right idea about *His* will?" the Devil countered. "Phenexia, you know full well I'm not going to bar you from joining a triad. I will complain bitterly my secretary will not be accessible for several decades. However, I'd like you to help Darlene adapt, so you may wish to lure your Indian gentleman to a location where it's tolerable for his wives to attend to day jobs, which will free up a few hours a day for you to attend to her. Considering how many of the other succubi have lost their minds because of *someone's* questionable suggestion, I'd rather you handle some of the finer points of her adaption."

My suggestion was absolutely not questionable, and I debated which spot I would bar him from enjoying until he recognized the error of his ways. I shot a glare his way and sipped my coffee.

I'd need another coffee if I wanted to hold any hope of enjoying a nice drink while enjoying the Devil showcasing his chest.

The succubus raised a brow. "You're planning on stealing her, then? While exotic enough, she's just a mortal."

Yeah, I definitely understood Phenexia's skepticism, especially after getting a good look at everything she offered.

Really, the Devil had some major malfunctions if he preferred my covered spots over her exposed beauty.

"For all eternity. Don't tell the other succubi that, however. Their posturing amuses me, and Darlene needs a good look at their pettiness, so she is aware of precisely what she's going to have to deal with."

I needed to call the Devil's brothers and have a talk with them about potential treatment plans for insanity.

Phenexia looked me over. "I need a raise if you think she's going to compete with succubi on a mission to become your queen. There's also the matter of her mortality."

"That problem is being addressed."

It was? I frowned, wondering just how he planned on addressing my mortality, although I'd done a fairly good job of avoiding death thus far.

"I'm really going to need a raise if we're going to have two converts making a mess of the place. Also, you're going to have a problem with the man upstairs."

"I've been told it's already been handled, and I resent I've been hoodwinked. I'll be notified of what's happening at a later time. I'm waiting for *His* leisure right now, and that annoys me."

"*He* always annoys you," Phenexia muttered.

"Yes, *He* does. And I particularly hate when I'm told to sit and wait patiently."

"So, about my raise," the succubus prompted.

"You would need to be paid to get a raise. You're not paid. You do secretarial work because you hate getting bored, and you expect to be spoiled in exchange for your work. You don't need to be paid because you get what you want without worrying about how you get it. Are you sure you're ready to deal with all those annoying responsibilities mortals have to deal with? Maybe I should have Darlene teach you what it means to be mortal. You'll have to play pretend at being mortal if you feel like seducing an angel and your human."

Phenexia thought about it. "Perhaps, but that doesn't address the issue of her competing with succubi."

"She doesn't need to compete. The winner has already been selected, and while they were posturing, she was nestled in my bed sleeping or rummaging through my closet. I'm talking about you, Darlene. Congratulations. I'm keeping you."

I considered going back to bed to see if a few hours restored the Devil to sanity. "Are you crazy? Also, you're skipping a few steps."

"Yes," he replied with zero evidence of shame. "I am absolutely crazy. I'm the Devil. I'm supposed to be crazy. You only have yourself to blame. You came into my home and took it over. I've just decided I'm accepting your offer of taking it over, so you've made the bed and you get to sleep in it." He pointed at his bedroom. "That specific bed. I'll be joining you in it often. Are the other steps important?"

I considered that, and careful not to lose hold of my drink, I pointed at a spot on the back of my left hand. "See that spot?"

"I do. It's lovely."

"That's a gateway spot, but to obtain the gateway spot, you need to talk to your brothers and use both please and thank you in the same discussion. Ask one of them to bring me another coffee and use those words. This one isn't going to last long enough for the show I was promised. The next spot you earn involves the missing steps."

"You're really going to make me use those dirty, foul words, aren't you?"

"The gateway spot must be conquered before you can gain access to any other spots, so yes. I am. The witnessing portion of this must still happen, too. While Phenexia may have witnessed you use the word please, I missed it, so it doesn't count."

Phenexia's brows rose. "I am both disturbed and seriously impressed."

"She's cruel." The Devil captured my left hand and kissed my knuckles, and while there were spots on my knuckles, he didn't pay them attention like he did when he was offered a spot for his enjoyment. "As you're one of my more sensible succubi, Phenexia, do take care to monitor them for idiocy before you leave to join your triad."

"I can do that. Will she need a suite prepared?"

"No. She'll be staying with me, and while I will open rooms for her use, her residence is within my bedroom."

As I could be an epic bitch, I concentrated and shifted, wincing at the flash of pain associated with banishing my fur and spots, leaving behind only my ears and tail. Overall, it went better than I expected, although my skin appeared paler than I thought it should be. Frowning, I freed my hand from the Devil's hold, inspecting my skin. "Hmm. That's not quite right."

"It's your untanned skin color," the Devil explained. "You're fine. You'll tan again should you sunbathe for a while. My brother warned me you'd be paler."

"Which brother?"

"Gabriel. Michael was summoned, so Gabriel got saddled with preventing a small apocalypse. To my disgust, Belial also helped with that."

While vague, I remembered Belial pinning a demon to an unfamiliar floor. I concentrated, and to my pleasure, I conjured the devil's name from my memories. "Alloces."

"Yes, him. Belial has handled his imprisonment, and against my general wishes, I am saving him for you to deal with. Belial is making a concoction to transform him and a few accomplices into fish for your amusement. I have also put in some orders for everything required for your trophy room."

"You should offer gloating time for the devils and demons who dislike Alloces when they please you, and let me put some thought into who gets to clean their habitats."

"Magic will handle cleaning their habitats. I have decided you will not have to do any cleaning to enjoy your trophies, although you can feed them at your pleasure—or not."

"I'll make them accept food from devils and demons they really hate. Also for my amusement."

The Devil chuckled. "If that's what you'd like. I am sure I can find volunteers to feed your fish."

"Make it clear if they cross me, I'll be feeding them to my fish, too. There's no reason I can't reward my pets with good behavior."

Phenexia giggled, and she covered her mouth. "She's rather vindictive for a mortal."

"That she is. It takes spirit to come storming my gates for some classic revenge. Her plans for revenge were thoroughly disrupted, so I will have to make that up to her for when she regroups and tries again. She is not the kind to give up until she's satisfied."

The succubus nodded. "I see. There's still the matter of the other succubi."

"I thought it was pretty obvious I've already made my decision. Darlene just likes being bossy and gave Belial instructions, and because Belial is one of the smarter devils around here, he did as told. That plus he enjoys chaos a little more than he should, and honestly? Watching the succubi all try to lock themselves in unholy matrimony is hilarious. You? You I can see tolerating monogamy for a chance to bang an angel and a human in a twisted threesome, but most of that lot? Greed is considered a sin for a reason, and while I'm a fond supporter of greed and general sin, they seem to have forgotten some key details about what it entails to be my wife."

Giggling, Phenexia nodded. "When Belial mentioned this insanity to me, I'll admit, I laughed. I didn't think any of them would actually consider it or compete with each other to get your attention. I opted against reminding them they'd hate being monogamous. You're about as bad as a triad. No, you're worse. Triads tend to fall apart after the mortal's death. You tend to have a lengthy attention span with a dislike of failure."

"You would think the succubi would have remembered those things, but no. So much fawning."

"I've noticed he doesn't like fawning. Really, he likes being pushed around, and you have to dole out his rewards in small increments, else he will become even more egotistical than he already is. I haven't known him long, and I've already figured this out. He's a simple man to manage."

"It disturbs me how accurately and quickly you have determined how you will manage him," the succubus admitted.

"He needs a lot of management. If you need a place to live, and you're willing to move your man and angel to America, it seems I have a new residence, so you can rent my house. Someone needs to take care of it, and it's not in a bad location. And a frugal man could probably support his two wives without them having to work. It wouldn't be easy, but it could be done. Your rent would basically be the maintenance costs, property taxes, and utilities."

Phenexia's eyes widened. "You would do that for me?"

"Well, do you think this lout is planning on letting me out of his bedroom anytime soon?" I asked, pointing at the Devil with my coffee. "I've the word of an archangel he's clingy, and I need someone to take care of my house, so we're all happy. It's a nice little house, and you can have a child or two comfortably. Or, at least, I was comfortable in it growing up. Don't ask my brother for his opinion. He'll complain because he's spoiled."

The Devil sighed. "You're a fixer. What have I brought into my home? I've been tricked."

I shrugged and sipped my coffee. "You're the one with the spot fetish. I'm just solving the problem of who will take care of my house when I'm here making sure you do what I say."

"I love her," the succubus announced. "If you let her get away, I will be very upset with you, Lucifer."

"I don't have to teach her how to teleport once she's properly converted. That should keep her where she belongs. I'm debating how to go about the proper conversion process, however." The Devil eyed me. "I might borrow some tricks from the unicorns. Their preferred method is quite entertaining, and I could take my time and do a very thorough job. If I keep her exhausted, she can't run away. I'll provide iced coffee so she's happy with her exhaustion, and I'll give her a comfortable place to lounge while admiring her fish."

"He means exhaust you in bed," the succubus announced. "Unicorns seduce their unconverted mates and continue to seduce them over a period of several years until their magic essentially infects their lover and transforms them into a unicorn. Sharing blood is also done, takes a shorter period of time, but generally is the least preferred method because unicorns could give incubi and succubi a run for their money. Lucifer specifically bars us from meddling with unicorns. They are a determined species, monogamous, and long-lived. The last time Lucifer had to rescue a succubus, the stallion tried to follow her back here, and the whining was significant."

"Is significant," the Devil corrected. "I kicked Isabelle out and told her she could come back in a thousand or so years, at the end of her unicorn's natural lifespan. I warned her not to flirt with a stallion. It's all on her that she went and fell in love with him, and well, once a stallion picks his mare, he's in it for life. Unicorns make angels look like beginners in the loyalty game. And when his lifespan does come to a close, I'm going to have to find her another unicorn, and do you have any idea how hard it is to find an available stallion? I'm going to have to intervene or deal with the crying, and I hate when succubi cry. So, they're now banned from engaging in any relationships with unicorns without permission."

"Which means you have a bunch of incubi and succubi hunting for a unicorn?" I guessed.

"They have not been successful, as unicorns are sneaky. But I'm doing good work with them. I've helped the standard unicorns, now I need to work on the cindercorns. They're critically endangered, and I really like the cindercorns."

"Cindercorns?"

"They're carnivorous fire-breathing unicorns. I'll have to do significant meddling to help them out."

"Aren't you the Devil? Why are you helping *unicorns*?"

"I really like unicorns," he announced. "I refuse to be ashamed of my love of unicorns and the glorious chaos they bring, especially when it's time for them to settle down. They're also important to the natural life cycle. Many unicorns, frankly spoken, are whores until it's time for them to settle down, then they take a sharp left turn into extreme monogamy. I warned Isabelle she would develop a severe case of monogamy if she toyed with a stallion, and she didn't listen to me. What would *I* know? I'm just nosy, worse than any one of their fathers, overbearing, and obviously deranged."

I needed more coffee, and I drank mine down, crossed his sitting room to the coffee table by the couches and armchairs, and set it down. "You are overbearing and obviously deranged."

"I absolutely am."

"Start with calling Gabriel and using your two filthy phrases to acquire me another iced coffee. Once my iced coffee is secured, I want that show I was promised."

"Did I promise a show?"

I didn't care if he'd promised a show or not. As the Lord of Lies, he surely understood the purpose of a lie, especially when the lie led me to enjoying a view of his perfect chest. "You absolutely did."

"Must I use those foul phrases?"

"You must if you want that spot. If you don't earn that spot, you can't earn the next spot."

"You're ruthless."

I shrugged. "You like it. Is there anything else about this lout I should know, Phenexia?"

"He has a voracious appetite once he decides to take someone to bed."

"I don't share," I reminded the Devil. "I don't care how voracious your appetite is. I will recruit your brothers, and we'll have an apocalypse in your bedroom if you test me."

"I'm going to test you because I like the look of jealousy on you, but as I don't share, either, I'll only do it explicitly to annoy you into attempting to create an apocalypse in our bedroom."

"Is he serious?" I regarded the succubus with interest. "Perhaps we should do an exchange of information."

"He's serious. We succubi don't tend to be too jealous outside of a triad or when there's a child under foot. We pick our partners for a variety of reasons, although he's a damned fine meal for one of us. He has more sexual energy than he knows what to do with, so should one of my sisters happen to land him permanently, he'll feed her very well. But that comes with the price of his rather ridiculous amount of endurance and enthusiasm."

"Why is that a problem? I have determined he is aware of what the word no means."

"But will you really want to say no when he's on a rampage?" Phenexia asked in an amused tone. "He's something else during a rampage, but that comes with a price. He cannot tolerate straying. And then he sulks for weeks when we stray. We're succubi. We're supposed to stray."

"Unless you're with a triad."

"Oh, the angels know we're going to try to stray. That's half the fun for them. They drag us home and keep us entertained. Incubi get more angels than us succubi, though. Human women tend to draw the attention of angels. That's a cultural thing. There just aren't as many men who have the purity of spirit and gentleness required to earn an angel's love. A pity, really. Incubi get the better hunts, too."

"Hunts?"

"Human women are typically repressed, so incubi have to work harder to warm their targets up—and it's far more satisfying when our mortal partners desire us of their own accord. It's a better feed. With Lucifer here, you won't have to worry about that. He comes prepackaged with more desire than he knows what to do with most days, so he sulks."

"He does seem to be very talented at sulking. At least he's pretty when he sulks."

"He really is. It's why we put up with him. The competition isn't really competition, so don't worry about them too much. In reality, they don't want to be picked because they know they'll be run ragged, lose their freedom to dally with any male to cross their path, and won't be able to have children in the future. That's a lot to lose to be a queen, especially for a succubus."

I already had a solution to that problem, and her name was Kanika. "They were in here in a pack."

"Well, yes. We hate to lose."

So did I. "Did he really say please twice?"

"He really did."

I considered Lucifer with interest. "You still have to use both filthy phrases to one of your brothers where I can witness it, but you will get two spots for doing it, for having demonstrated your ability to use filthy phrases in decent company."

"My brothers are hardly decent."

"They're archangels. They're decent."

"You are a most cruel and ruthless woman," the Devil complained, tapping at his odd cell phone. "But very well. I am expecting two excellent spots."

"All of my spots are excellent."

"And on that note, I'm going to leave before I witness something I'd rather not. Good luck, Darlene. You're going to need it. And don't let him trick you. There are simple solutions to even difficult problems, and your current problem is not a difficult one to solve."

## TWELVE

She's wearing my shirt and tie.

WHILE THE DEVIL dodged saying please or thank you, he managed to convince Gabriel to pay him a visit. The archangel appeared, and he held a black kitten in one hand and a white kitten in the other. Without a word, he handed me both animals, and I sat on the floor, put them on my lap, and joined them in purring.

"*He* sends his regards," Gabriel announced.

The Devil heaved a sigh. "Must I, Darlene?"

"You absolutely must. How badly do you want access to new spots?" The white kitten yawned, curled up on my leg, and closed its tiny eyes while the black kitten attacked my hand with a squeak. "Why do I have kittens? Gabriel? You brought kittens? Whose kittens are these? They're adorable."

"They're your kittens. The white one will return to the heavens with me to encourage you to bring Lucifer for visits, although I expect there will be much whining from your kitten upon separation."

I flattened my ears. "Can we bargain about that? I'll bring both kittens with me and make him come so I can keep the kittens. I've never had a kitten before." I hesitated, realizing I had two of the fluffy balls to care for. "Two kittens. I've never had one kitten, and now I have two kittens. I don't know how to take care of a kitten. Thank you. Please thank *Him* for me, too." I stared at the Devil. "That is how you use those filthy words to polite company who brought me kittens."

"Kittens?" Lucifer complained. "You brought her a pair of terrors? I'll be overrun with felines."

"*He* felt she could use some company, and they will help her adapt to her new home. The black kitten has a devilish nature, and the white kitten has an angelic nature. That way, we remain in balance, and considering Darlene's more balanced nature, it's fitting. They are long lived, and their age will reflect her needs, so some days, you will have playful kittens, other days, you will have older cats wishing to warm laps and keep quiet company. They are empathetic, although they will only be empathetic to members of your family unit. Even she has limits to how much she can adapt in such a short period of time, and the kittens will help her in the upcoming days. They also have a secondary form."

I perked at that, and while I wiggled my

fingers for the black kitten to play with, I straightened and asked, "What secondary form?"

"That of rather large predators. They're guardians, and *He* has made you their responsibility. How can I help you, Lucifer?"

The Devil heaved a sigh and bowed his head. "Are you really sure this is going to earn me a spot?"

"Good behavior is rewarded with spots, and I already said I'd give you two for performing this terribly straining and filthy task." I wanted to grin, but I forced myself to maintain a serious expression.

Muttering curses undermined the general idea of what I forced him to do, but the Devil finally sighed again and asked, "Would you please retrieve an iced coffee for Darlene? She drank her first one and requires another one so I can dance around at her whim." After shooting a glare at me, he added, "Thank you in advance."

Gabriel's laughter chimed, and he slapped his leg, bowing over with his wings spread wide, his feathers splayed. He shook from the force of his mirth, and I wondered if archangels could cry. If they could, he likely sobbed on account of the Devil being reduced to saying please and thank you. "You have been brought low by a woman, Lucifer."

"She's wearing my shirt and tie," he announced. "I am completely justified in my actions."

"Only because you took her clothes for them to be washed and mended. You could have used magic to do that, by the way."

Wait. The Devil did housework? There was a single man who could do housework without being told to, and he was also willing to retrieve coffee for me in the mornings? "You cleaned my clothes?"

His answer would determine just how hard I fought back against the succubi seeking his attention.

"Well, I wasn't going to throw them out. If you want to throw them out, I will not stop you, but I make no promises I will provide new clothes, as I'd prefer you wearing no clothes."

The succubi would surrender, or I would go on a campaign to rid the Devil's hells of them. I regarded his shirt and tie and shrugged. "Not a far leap with my current attire."

"I find your current attire to be quite vexing."

Gabriel moaned his laughter, went down to his knees, and beat the floor. "You haven't said thank you in over a thousand years. A woman wearing your shirt has done you in."

"I'd say look at her, but I'd rather you not."

"You can use please and thank you rather sarcastically there," I prompted.

The Devil sighed. "I'd say look at her, but I'd rather you not, please and thank you."

He needed to work on his sarcastic delivery of his pleases and thank yous, but he had the right general idea. "Don't mind him, Gabriel. Are you all right?"

The archangel continued to laugh, and he waved his hand in what I thought was a dismissal of my concern. Well, I hoped it was a dismissal of my concern, as I had no intention of rescuing him if he laughed himself to death.

"Don't mind him, Darlene." The Devil put his perfect shoe on his brother's arm and shoved him over. "She needs more coffee, and I'll destroy anyone who upsets her or fails to provide her coffee at her request."

"No one can say I didn't try. Also, if you do that, you'll bring the End of Days the first time I have to wait in line for coffee. If you create an apocalypse and remove my ability to obtain coffee, I will not be happy. Frankly? You idiots should put a complete stay on the End of Days, because if you eliminate Earth, you eliminate coffee, and whomever eliminates coffees dies at my hand."

"It doesn't work like that," the Devil replied.

"It does now." The white kitten opened its eyes, twisted its ears back, and hissed at Lucifer. "See? My kitten agrees with me. Are they boy kittens or girl kittens, Gabriel?"

"They are both girls. *He* figured my brother would like to be able to claim he has a harem. They do not yet have names, for they are yours, and you should have the naming of them."

I laughed at that. "Who knew? *He* has a sense of humor."

"Yes, he does. *He* made you, after all."

My mouth dropped open. "I'm going to feel that one for a while. I might need two iced coffees to recover."

"That was a pretty good one," the Devil admitted. "It's usually Michael coming up with those. Did Michael put you up to that, Gabriel?"

"That one was all me this time, although I will confess I have carried the burden of Michael's sense of humor in the past."

"Your brothers are amazing. They're amazing assholes, but they're still amazing, Lucifer."

"But they lack nipples," the Devil reminded me. "As such, they are inferior beings compared to me."

I sighed at the reminder of the archangel's utter lack of nipples. "It's a pretty severe flaw, but I'm willing to overlook such things when they bring me presents. I really like presents."

Gabriel, while he still laughed, recovered enough to stand. "I will bring you iced coffee in sufficient quantity to survive what my brother has in mind for you. I will also bring sustenance, as I suspect my brother has lengthy plans for your conversion."

"Conversion. Explain that. I've heard it several times already, and then he started in on unicorns, and things became confusing at that point."

Gabriel snorted another laugh. "Don't mind my brother. *He* is not the only one who created your Earth, and unicorns were Lucifer's first contribution to the mortal coil's many wonders. He has a fond spot in his heart for them. Before his fall, he was the Lord of the Morning, and little else captures the glory of the sun and its rise than a unicorn. As such, he is always out to protect his beloved children. At current, he only has one succubus sacrificed to their ways, although he'd cast them all out if they located stallions for themselves."

"I'm working on that," Lucifer announced. "I do have a plan. The standard unicorns will be fine, and there's hope enough for the cindercorns. I despair for some of the other species. Standards were my first creations, and I created the other unicorns to maintain the balance. The cindercorns developed in ways I did not expect, however."

"There are only a few left," Gabriel warned. "And their numbers dwindle yearly. Within thirty years, they will run the risk of extinction."

"I have recently tended to that garden."

Gabriel straightened, and something about his body language changed, a slight tensing that worried me. Then the archangel relaxed, and his laughter once again rang out. "You are a rascal. How did you pull that off?"

"The moon and the sun have always loved one another, and the moon's light is a reflection of her love for the sun. I merely made it so they would meet. How far ahead have you looked?"

"Far enough."

"Did I not choose wisely?"

"She will be magnificent, but your choice of humans for her parentage is worrisome."

"Sariel can handle all that she is and will become, I'm sure. And when he comes asking for my help with the rest of it, who else is better for the task?" The Devil rubbed his hands together. "Agares is well suited for the work as well. Ah, that reminds me. I'd like to get those two settled with a new wife. A seed will be required, and as I had the making of the last one, it's *His* turn."

Gabriel waved his hand. "*He* has no objections to you selecting the seed for them. They have done more of *His* work than yours, so it would be better balanced if you select the seed again. *He* will look the other way if you cultivate a non-human seed for them. Try not to break more rules than necessary. If you plant the seed now, the seed will be matured sufficiently for them at the end of their work on your current project."

"I could bend the rules a little without breaking them," the Devil murmured, and his expression turned distant. "It'll need to be a particularly troublesome seed for those two to unify again. But sweet and pure. Troublesome, sweet, and pure. The thought alone disgusts me. It was bad enough setting up my last scheme. The mix had to be just right for that seed to take root. Don't you know how long I've been cultivating that seed?"

"Yes. It was your first seed after your fall. I remember. I wondered when you would use it, but I never looked."

"*He* had the other seed needed for the project, and I've been scheming around his intentions to use it. It's not *my* fault he's slow. That seed of mine deserves only the best, and *He* kept refusing to give me the seed I wanted. It's *His* fault."

"Which seed?"

"The one Sariel's grandson has."

"Fitting. Your precious seed should be well protected then."

"Exactly. I'll have to continue meddling if I wish to preserve the balance. If I set my seed loose on him without properly tempering, they will not be a balanced coupling, and that will ruin my other plans. He's too innocent regarding his power, and she will be too aggressive for him to handle."

"Mortals have their freedoms, Lucifer," Gabriel said. "You cannot plan all things for them."

The Devil smirked. "That boy will make his mistakes, and I will make certain he makes the mistakes in such a way he's properly cultivated. He can't help his nature, and he needs to be matured in his powers before he gets his hands on her—or she gets her hands on him. She'd break him if he wasn't tempered first, and he needs the strength to handle her at her worst—and she will not be easy to handle even at her best. She is what she is, and I regret nothing of my meddling in the requirements for her existence. She is one of my jewels, and she will shine, you mark my words."

"Her father will be quite annoyed with you when he finds out."

"I know. Isn't it wonderful? He'll owe me, and he'll hate it. Anyway, I like her mother, and her mother is deserving of that seed. Despite how much I enjoy toying with him, I like her father as well, and *He* won't provide a seed, and the universe itself likely won't. The balance would be disturbed if it worked out any other way than this."

"You are truly a being of evil," Gabriel complained. "It is your disaster. Clean up after yourself this time, or Sariel will cry, and I cannot tolerate Sariel when he cries. It is most annoying."

"That's only because Sariel is delightfully twisted for an archangel and does *His* work on the mortal coil while seducing mortal women. He hasn't fallen because he's disgustingly honest about it and loyal to the death with the mortals he claims. And Agares is disgustingly pure for a devil. They're balanced, and they do balanced work on the mortal coil. But Sariel weakens. He's been on the mortal coil too long."

"*He* will attend to that, so don't fret. Our brother will have plenty of power for what you need him for to complete your plans."

I listened with interest, petting my kittens while marveling that the pair discussed *unicorns*. I'd grown up daydreaming about the stories I'd heard of them, but to learn they were *real* and the Devil had created them?

Life always found a way to become weirder than anticipated.

The Devil smirked. "Peeked, did you?"

"It disgusts me you have made their union almost inevitable."

"I like my unicorns, and I refuse to see them wiped out."

"All things end, Lucifer."

"But not my unicorns. They will be the last to fall even through the End of Days, you hear me? And they'll be my first in the next life. For as long as my seed exists, there will be unicorns."

"Lucifer."

"Not. My. Unicorns."

"Darlene, please address this problem," Gabriel requested.

"Wait. You're telling me unicorns are real, and that you want me to support *not* preventing their extinction? No. I'm with the Devil on this one. They're my unicorns now, and I will resent if anyone were to aid in their extinction. What species needs the most help?

You said the standard unicorns and these cindercorns will be okay?"

"Okay is a stretch, but they are not going to all die out, and they can convert members of their numbers. The qilin and kirin are secure enough. The qilin have established themselves with the Babylonians, and the kirin still roam the wilds of China, India, and Russia. There are still wild places left for them, and they have sufficient power of belief to sustain themselves."

"Power of belief?" I asked.

The Devil strode to the couch and thumped onto the leather surface, propping his feet onto the coffee table. "The kirin are much like succubi and incubi, in that they require energy to sustain themselves. I tied their existence to the belief in the higher powers, of goodness and protection, and the Chinese culture maintains many rituals suitable for sustaining them. Western cultures help as well, for little children who believe in any unicorn help sustain the kirin. The qilin are more like my standard unicorns, and feed in another manner."

"They're carnivores," Gabriel explained. "Scavengers, really. Standard unicorns shepherd souls from the battlefields of the world, disposing of abandoned bodies so that the Earth is not flooded with the spirits of the deceased. The qilin are much like them, but they're meant for the Eastern cultures. For all I dislike his methods, the unicorns all serve an important purpose for the mortal coil. I would argue that my brother's fall is among the greatest gifts *He* has given mankind, but I would also argue that *He* did all mortals justice cultivating Lucifer to be inclined to create unicorns. Only because of them is there magic, for their creation birthed mortal magic."

"Unicorns are the source of magic?"

"Not precisely." Gabriel picked up my empty coffee cup and held it up. "Until the creation of unicorns, the cup of magic was much like this, empty but for a few drops. Those drops were the requirements for life, gifts from the universe itself. The seeds Lucifer planted, which became unicorns, resulted in the first surge of magic mortals experienced. The cup filled, and it eventually overflowed. Once the power of their births faded, the cup became drained, and the wave ended. The cup then began to refill. Each emergence is the point when the cup overflows and magic spills out from the vessels meant to hold it. Depending on what is fueling the surge of magic, it can burn out quickly or last decades, centuries—or even a thousand or more years. The first emergence lasted several hundred years."

"And this emergence?"

"That would be telling."

I bet the Devil's shirt the archangel smiled a smug smile much like his brother. "Basically, I'm barely a ripple in the pond in terms of my lifespan. That's what you're saying."

"That is what conversion is for. My brother intends to finish what was started and keep you at his side until the End of Days and beyond. And do not ask about what was started. My brother would become distressed. *He* has handled the important work, and *He* has already arranged for the balance of it. You can have your temper tantrum over it later if you please, Lucifer."

The Devil sighed. "This is where I'm supposed to use filthy words again, isn't it?"

While I had no idea what they were talking about, I nodded my agreement. "Do it to *His* face. It won't hurt you."

"Are you sure?"

"Does losing access to my spots hurt you?"

"I'm already hurt you have made your fur disappear."

"They will stay disappeared for longer if you put up a fight about using your filthy words to show appropriate gratitude at the appropriate times. It's called manners, and I expect you to use them."

"You have some pretty harsh rules," the Devil complained, and I recognized his lies through his body language, which relaxed. "I can't help but notice you are lovely even without your spots. I need that coffee now, Gabriel. I think it's time to teach her precisely what she's getting into, and she needs her coffee to enjoy herself properly."

"I recommend you hang a sign on your door requesting you do not be disturbed. Remember, until you convert her, she is still technically mortal, and you need to take extra special care with her. However much it disgusts me to say this, for it means mortal men are beyond stupid for not desiring her for what she is, you are the first to take proper notice of her."

"Gabriel. You do realize I am the Devil, right?"

"You are the Devil, but you are also an idiot when it comes to matters requiring delicacy."

"I'm well aware of what I have to work with, and it makes claiming every spot that much more enjoyable. She resists *me*, Gabriel."

"Resist is not the word I would use."

I snorted at the archangel's rather blunt implication I had zero interest in resisting anything involving the Devil's perfect chest and a bed. "Should I have just worn the tie to send the appropriate message?"

"You wisely selected your attire for your purposes," the archangel assured me. "Just tell him to be gentle and keep in mind you'll tire easily. I will bring all of the things for your kittens along with your coffee, and I'll even provide the sign and perhaps warn the other residents they would be unwise to bother you at this point in time. Do not let him forget the mortal customs you enjoy, and I recommend you recruit one of the friendlier succubi with help with your attire. You can learn some interesting arts from them, although I suspect most of your lessons will be handled by Lucifer while he handles your person."

"If he ever hopes to count a single one of my spots in the future, he better be handling me along with my lessons."

The archangel laughed. "I'll bring your coffee and your kittens' supplies momentarily. Be patient until then."

I waited for the archangel to disappear before saying, "Are you capable of being patient?"

"I dislike it very much right now, although it wouldn't do to have you bereft of a cold drink while you enjoy a hot show."

The Lord of Lies told a great deal fewer falsehoods than I expected. "It surprises me he's not embarrassed by my untraditional attire."

"While he is not Sariel, he appreciates women as much as other archangels. When my brother is swayed by a mortal, I will be there, ready to indulge in mocking laughter. Should he fall for a mortal woman, I have the perfect incubus in mind. And should he fall for a mortal man, well, I'd have to put some serious thought into which succubus is partnered with her, as she'll have to swap to be more of a Gabriella for a while."

"Honestly, after witnessing his lack of nipples, learning he can be a she at will isn't even all that disturbing. But his lack of nipples? That's just horribly disturbing."

"You have a nipple fetish," the Devil informed me.

I shrugged. "I know what I like, and I like a perfect chest with equally perfect nipples. It just happens you possess the perfect chest with equally perfect nipples. I'm afraid you're just going to have to deal with it. I'm pretty sure my chest and my nipples are not nearly as lovely as yours."

"That is not a challenge you wish to issue to me, Darlene. I will spend hours proving you wrong."

"Talk, talk, talk. That's what the women say, that men are all talk about that. While Gabriel wasn't precisely lying, he left out the part about my general disinterest in a great deal of posturing for ten minutes with a chance of pregnancy. And yes, your brother told me you cannot have children. Something about your fall." I dismissed the issue with a huff and a wave of my hand. "If I want a baby, I'll steal an unwanted one from somewhere."

"Is it stealing if the child is unwanted?"

"I'm not sure. Is it?"

"I don't know. I've never stolen unwanted babies before."

"You're the Devil, and you've never stolen an unwanted baby? Wait. Have you ever stolen a baby?"

"I can't say that I have. I have a great deal of fun with mortals who steal babies when

they come to pay me a visit, however. I sometimes leave them stewing a little longer than I
should to make sure they've learned their
lesson before their next lives. When mortals
say there are special places in hell for certain
people? There truly are."

Huh. "That's good to know. Can I help
decorate?"

"Why would we decorate the dungeons
for them?"

"I meant with their blood, mostly."

"We can discuss your decoration plans
later. I have other plans for you right now."

Gabriel reappeared, and he held a tray
with four iced coffees, which he placed on the
coffee table. He disappeared, and when he
reappeared, he carried several bags from a pet
store. "Here is everything you require for
your kittens' care. Do set up their litter boxes
before you indulge, set out their beds so they
can catch up on sleep, and the instructions on
how to feed them is in a card in the bag along
with their toys. Enjoy yourselves, but try not
to enjoy yourselves too much."

Gabriel vanished, and the Devil chuckled,
rising to his feet. "Do take care of your kittens, my darling. I have exhaustive plans for
you, and it wouldn't do for us to be interrupted."

I eased the kittens off my lap and headed
for the bag, setting up everything with some
help from some note cards with directions in
the bag. The instant I put their black and

white cat beds down, the kittens crawled into them, flopped, and went to sleep.

"They're so cute," I whispered.

"Kittens are devilishly cute. Now come get your drink. It's time to make you purr."

# THIRTEEN

I'd found heaven located in the
depths of hell.

I SHOULD HAVE LISTENED to Gabriel. There
was a line between indulging and indulging
too much, and I'd flung myself across it
without any care of the consequences. I got
the show I'd wanted, enjoying two of my iced
coffees before the Devil decided he was finished behaving like a peacock and pounced to
claim his reward.

As promised, he made me purr. Then, as
he defined sin, he kept me purring until he
broke my purr motor and left me a quivering
mess. Long after I lost my voice, he carried
me to his bathtub, resumed his general explo-
rations, and wore me out until I could barely
keep my eyes open. Only then did he declare
himself satisfied, amusing himself with the
bubbles while I lounged in the warm water
and dozed.

I appreciated being able to use his perfect
chest as my pillow.

Somehow, I'd found heaven located in the depths of hell.

A knock at the bathroom door made the Devil sigh. "Is nothing sacred? What is it?"

I cracked open an eye. Phenexia entered, and she held two folded towels, which she placed on the vanity. "Your sitting room is infested with sleeping succubi. You forgot to dampen your aura."

"I didn't forget. I just didn't bother to do it. I am making a very important point. Have they seduced the entirety of my many hells yet?"

The succubus chuckled and shrugged. "Most of it. I would best describe that lot as jelly at the moment, for they're incapable of doing anything other than quiver and ooze across the floor. I wisely paid the mortal coil a visit upon your retirement for the evening, so I missed the general festivities. Belial wishes for me to inquire with your lady if she would like to be rescued now that you have worked through your hunger."

"That's because you're smart. She doesn't require anyone to rescue her, although I will be putting her to bed after she's soaked for a while longer. Have you successfully seduced your angel and human yet?"

She wrinkled her nose. "He's being stubborn, and she thinks I'm amusing. They're discussing the 'm' word. Apparently, I have to wait until we're properly wed, and the only reason his family is permitting it is because they believe angels are honorable partners and impeccable mothers, except I'm the one who'll be hauling our baby around during the pregnancy. That earned my welcome with the family, although they're not sure about me at all. I'm here because of that horrible word."

"It's an important word," I mumbled.

"You're still capable of talking? Tsk, tsk," the Devil replied, and he held me closer. "Speaking of the 'm' word, do make sure those succubi realize that winning their little game does involve that word, and it is not a vow they can break. If they want to give Darlene some entertainment, I am fine with that, but they need to keep their games tolerably civil. Influencing her at their leisure at opportune moments, for my enjoyment, is tolerable. They'd likely earn favor with me, especially as I'm rather enjoying this method of conversion. How long do you think it'll take? What sort of delightful creature will she become?"

"She'll become a succubus, of course. If you're converting her that way, there are limited options, and as she seems to be enjoying your attention, it would be the one route that would ensure she'd receive more of your attention. As she's not currently a succubus and cannot sustain herself through stealing your energy, you need to dry her off, either wrap her in a towel or dress her, take her into the sitting room or dining room, and feed her. After she's been fed, you can tuck her into your bed and hover while she rests. I need you to convince my father he has to play at being mortal, else I can't get married. Do you know what my father did when I asked?"

"He laughed at you."

"He laughed at me," she confirmed.

"Did you see the kittens?"

"They're on your bed. They hissed at the succubi stampede and invited themselves to your pillows. I checked on them before coming in here. They are Lady Darlene's kittens?"

"They're her kittens, a gift from *Him*."

"Oh. Oh, my. How unusual."

"*He* wishes for her to have companionship while I'm busy, and they'll be her guardians when she rests."

"Is she recovering well?"

I yawned, settled against the Devil's chest, and closed my eyes to resume my enjoyment of the bath.

"She's well enough. She was quite enamored with my chest, and she energetically pursued her interests. When I tried to pursue my interests, I got bitten."

"I'm sure you deserved it."

"She's very talented with her teeth."

"I'm sure she is. Would you like to be rescued, Darlene? Belial is concerned you might delay your revenge indefinitely if you remain a hostage in Lucifer's bedroom, and he has everything you require to bring ruination to the mortals responsible for your brother's plight."

I yawned and cuddled closer to the Devil. "Nap now, revenge in about eight hours. No rescuing, but tell Lucifer he needs to behave for a while."

"You need to behave for a while, Lucifer. She sounds horrible. What did you do to her?"

"I just made her purr! I like when she purrs."

"You are awful. I'll get her a drink and something to soothe her throat. You've established your territory, so behave yourself. Help her acquire revenge before you resume establishing your territory."

"But are you really sure I've established my territory?"

"There are exhausted succubi bodies all over your sitting room and some very happy incubi strutting around. I think you've made your point. I'm the only coherent female here, and the neighboring levels aren't in much better condition."

The Devil shrugged. "It's not my fault she's so lovely. I'm hoping I've earned at least a few spots with my performance. I'll bring her out in a few minutes and find appropriate sustenance for her. I'll also make sure the kittens are tended to. Please make it known they are not defenseless creatures, and they are not to be disturbed. I may or may not be inclined to replant any slain devils or demons who disturb her kittens."

"I will make certain the other denizens are aware the kittens are lethal kittens, and that you will have no mercy on any who disturb them or your lady."

"Good. Please ask Belial to come here so we can discuss the matters of revenge, and check on Jonas."

"Jonas is in a rather subdued state at this point in time."

"How many succubi got a hold of him?" The Devil snickered. "It's their fault for making it clear I had to establish my territory."

"He enjoyed the company of twins, and they're still quite tangled together at the moment. Perhaps you should have given him a chance to adapt before setting him loose?"

"The best way to learn is through experience. He's now somewhat experienced, content, and he'll have his other nurturing instincts turned on when he has two exhausted succubi to attend to. I can't have all the incubi being selfish fiends. Some of them need to be nurturing, or there'd be whining succubi when they wish to have children."

I didn't need to hear what my brother was up to, especially not if the Devil had transformed him into an incubus. "You turned my brother into an incubus?"

"I absolutely did. The other options would

have been more disastrous, as your brother has significant violent tendencies. Becoming an incubus will smooth those particular instincts out and orient him more towards reproduction. Having tired succubi around in his early development will flip on the markers that will make him more inclined to be delicate with women. I expect we'll be having a few more incidents like this before I'm confident he can be trained in other arts appropriate for his new species."

I did the math: the Devil plus a bed equaled delicious exhaustion with time spent soaking in his tub with bubbles—bubbles the Devil enjoyed as much as I did. As the formula produced acceptable results, I said, "You can train him properly and thoroughly after I've acquired my revenge. We need to get the abused family of those fuckers to a safe place, too."

"Yes, that is a situation I am monitoring. I will make certain your revenge accounts for them. You may not be able to personally handle that matter, but I have some excellent demons and devils who are able and willing to do the work."

"I don't care who handles it as long as it is handled."

"Let me get you something to eat so you can enjoy your nap while I make other arrangements."

"Don't you sleep?"

"Only with you. I'm the Devil, Darlene. I don't have to sleep unless I want to. I took a nap once. It lasted a hundred years. That was a nice nap, but for some reason, the fucking assholes in residence were cranky because the other devils had their way with the place for a while. I was asked to limit my naps to no more than nine hours after that."

"Have you?"

"For the most part." The Devil waved Phenexia away. "Off with you, you wicked temptress. You have an angel to seduce. I'll talk to your father, so go make sure you both have pretty dresses, and do at least try to convince your angel she can have breasts if she'd like for her wedding day."

"She doesn't need breasts."

"The angel has already gotten to you." Heaving a sigh, Lucifer shook his head. "I see it's too late. I'll go talk to your father about that awful 'm' word and make it clear he can only put up a minimal fuss. You can't dodge all of the fatherly disapproval. It's part of the package. You *are* his eldest daughter, so he's obligated to make a fuss. If your human's customs require the mother of the bride, I'll make an arrangement."

Phenexia nodded and retreated from the bathroom.

"What arrangement?"

"Her mother passed away a very long time ago, and her mother's seed is currently at rest. Unbeknownst to her and her father, I have the seed, and I intend to bargain with *Him* for a conversion so the seed can return to her father, who still mourns for his mortal wife."

"After so many years?"

"Phenex is an odd creation. He was made in the image of angels, but he is a devil in his nature. Oddly balanced, him. Back when humans were new, he fell in love with a mortal woman. Phenexia is their first immortal child and their first daughter. They had a mortal son together, for I did not have the right seed to give him. They had other children as well, but she eventually died from old age. Then, mortals were longer lived. He is a poet among other things, and he is not inclined to let his first love be followed by anyone. He loves science and grooms the mortals to develop their knowledge. My phone is part of Phenex's workings."

"Phenex sounds similar to phoenix. Why?"

"He is their father, that is why. His tears birthed the first phoenixes, for it was his wish for his wife to rise from the ashes of her long life. *He* saw beauty in Phenex's grief and made it immortal. Phenex's natural form is very similar to a phoenix as well, which was part of their creation."

"That's sad."

"Things will be different next time. I'm just deciding how best to plant his wife's seed so that she finds her way to my many hells where she belongs. Her mortality was what he loved about her when he first met her, so I will cultivate her seed in that fashion and have her converted, much like you will be converted."

"And my brother is being converted."

"Has been converted. I took the rougher route with him. A chipmunk's lifespan is not long, and I did not wish for your brother to age. It was only a little pain. Now, out you get. It's time to dry you off and make sure you have breakfast so you can enjoy your nap."

"Are you always so considerate?"

"No, and it's disgusting I've been reduced to this low level by a woman and her spots. And I haven't even claimed all of your spots yet. Mark my words, Darlene. I will claim every last spot. They're mine, and I will not share them with anyone else."

Shaking my head, I debated how best to extract myself from his embrace and the warm waters of the tub. "You're something else."

"Does that mean I can lay claim to all of your spots as soon as this revenge business is dealt with?"

"I'll think about it," I promised, wiggling out of the Devil's hold to escape the tempting tub and its sinful occupant. I grabbed a towel and went to work restoring myself to functionality. "Maybe I'll skip the nap and get right to work on the revenge. Who needs sleep when I can have coffee?"

"You're going to need a lot of coffee, then."

"Fetch," I ordered, wrapping my hair up in the first towel before covering myself with the second. "I need coffee, and I need coffee right now."

The Devil vanished.

"You could have put some clothes on first," I muttered. Somehow, I'd fallen prey to a sinfully sexy idiot with a spot fetish.

There were worse fates.

WEARING a towel wouldn't endear me to the succubi sprawled over the sitting room floor, the couches, the chairs, and even the Devil's desk, although I had no scruples with spilling the woman onto the floor. She landed on yet another succubus. The one flopped on his chair shared her fellow succubus's fate.

Beyond a few groans, they ignored my presence.

Maybe they wouldn't care about my towel apparel after all.

As there wasn't anywhere else for me, I sat on his desk and waited for the Devil to return, as I figured he'd sit on me if I took over his chair. It took longer than I expected, but he reappeared in the doorway of the bedroom wearing one of his black suits, stepped around the bodies, and brought me two iced coffees. "I figured two might get you started until we return to the mortal coil and I can get you more. I have plans to take you out for lunch, as I have decided it will be more enjoyable to feed you that way."

"While I'm wearing a towel?"

"There are temporary clothes for you in the bedroom. They are temporary, as I fully plan on destroying them when I get you home, as it appears you are not sufficiently tired yet. You can still talk and walk. I am hoping lunch and the foundation work for your revenge will make you easier to properly exhaust."

I could work with that, although I worried that he'd only have to show off his perfect chest to transform me into clay for him to mold for his enjoyment. I set the second coffee down and went to work drinking the first, gesturing to the unconscious succubi littering his floor with my free hand. "What's the deal with them?"

"I shamelessly influenced you to make certain you had appropriate exposure to my devilish energy, and I couldn't be bothered with being considerate towards them. They were strutting like they wanted to be my wife, and if they can't handle the excess energy, they can't handle the real deal. They probably wanted to either complain or be left alone to recover. I'm amused you're in better shape than they are, truth be told. Obviously, I need to step up my efforts next time. As I'm male, I typically influence females, although I can influence males at my leisure as well. Mostly, I was influencing you, and they got the excess from my efforts. I have plans to influence you as often as necessary for you to convert. There'll still be some pain for the initial part of the process, but I fully intend to have you thoroughly distracted during that time. Your brother did not enjoy such luxuries."

"Poor Jonas. Too bad. If he hadn't been an idiot, he wouldn't have been turned into a chipmunk, thus requiring such treatment. He survived, and that's all I care about."

"How does steak sound for a late lunch or early dinner? It is two in the afternoon where your home is."

I licked my lips at the thought of a steak, something I usually didn't get due to its cost. "You have my attention."

"If we wait until four, we can begin revenge through partaking of steak in a place your target and his underlings often visit. You might even have your first approach and second poisoning by the evening. They're pesky creatures, and they seem to prefer trying the same trick twice. They are under the impression you were careful to avoid being poisoned with their first experiments, as your general plans to acquire revenge were delayed."

"And one of the archangels likely purged the poison to keep you from additionally rampaging?" I guessed. "Alloces triggered enough of a rampage without you having additional reason to rampage."

"Yes," the Devil replied, his expression darkening.

"I feel you should know that your chest really is perfect."

He sighed and his body relaxed. "And you say I have a spot fetish. You're just out for my chest."

"I see no reason to be ashamed of my interest in your chest."

"Just as I see no reason to be ashamed of my desire to possess all of your spots."

"Revenge first, spots later. Have you picked where my fish will live?"

"As a matter of fact, yes. We've already set up for their stay. I'll show you."

I slid off the Devil's desk, retrieved my second coffee, and dodged fallen succubi on my way to the door. "And yes, I can still walk, and I wish to maintain my ability to walk on my own for the moment."

The Devil pouted. "Must you?"

"Yes. I don't want to drop my coffee."

He chuckled, beat me to the door, and opened it for me. "Do allow me to show you to your trophy room. I think you'll find it perfect for your special needs." At the sound of the door opening, my new kittens came running out of the bedroom, and they didn't care who they crawled over. They rubbed against our legs when they caught up with us.

I smiled at their antics, thrust a coffee to the Devil, and crouched to pet them both once I had a free hand. "Special needs?"

"I've noticed you require copious amounts of coffee, so there is a new coffee machine for you and an ice maker so you can indulge should I be unavailable to provide coffee for you."

I gave both kittens a final stroke before rising. "You have my attention."

"This way." The Devil led me down one of the infinite hallways of his home carrying my second coffee, and our kittens bounced along with us. "Your trophy room will also be one of your offices for when you need a little space and a change of environment. So far, I've picked three offices for you, and most of them are adjacent to mine."

"Why do you have so many offices?"

"I get bored after a while, so I switch offices to have a change of pace. You'll get it after the first decade of being in the same office."

"That's what redecorating is for."

"I just redecorate the new office right before I move into it. I cycle through them."

"You're weird."

The Devil laughed. "If weird is what you like, then I am pleased to be weird for you." Pausing at a door, he nodded to it. "This is one of my offices. There will be a connecting door installed, but for now, we'll have to come down the hall if you're in your trophy room. I was told I cannot just punch a hole through the wall."

"You would disturb my fish if you did that."

"I resent I cannot simply kill your new pet

fish. Alloces was moved into his new home while I was keeping you amused."

"I have my first fish?" I asked, and I hurried down the hall to the next door. "This one?"

He laughed. "Yes, that one."

I pushed open the door to discover a spacious room with floor to ceiling aquariums devouring space against most walls, with enough of a gap for a door to the Devil's office. A large desk occupied the center of the room, and it would allow me a view of all of the tanks from the leather chair. One corner, devoid of aquariums, held a stainless steel coffee maker and everything needed to make coffee for myself. To my delight, clear panes of glass created sections in the glass aquariums, and upon closer inspection, there were air gaps between each level and flaps so I could access the tanks, virtually invisible unless close to them. "This is incredible."

"In the cabinet beneath your coffee maker is a refrigerator so you won't have to venture far to get your milk or cream. I've been warned as you are a feline, I will have to invest in ridiculous amounts of milk for you."

Damn it. Jonas must have tattled on me. "My brother has been telling you things, hasn't he?"

"I've been lectured about your favorite foods, your milk obsession, your tendency to be stingy towards yourself, thus turning milk into a luxury, and your obsession with a good steak and fish. I found it rather amusing he was willing to face off against me while trying to defend your chastity."

"I hope you told him that I do not need or want my chastity protected."

"The succubi in attendance for that meeting laughed and informed him I was on your menu, and it would require a miracle for you to keep your hands off me. It was very difficult to keep from laughing at your brother's expression over that one, as the succubi were most displeased over your intense interest in my person. You were rather incoherent when I brought you in, and you were still tripping their triggers."

As I refused to be ashamed of my adoration of his chest, I shrugged, crossed the room to my desk, and discovered a fish bowl near the computer, which contained a bright red fish with long, flowing fins swimming by itself. I set my coffee down, bent over, and peered into the water.

The fish spread its fins and attempted to make itself look as big as possible, probably to intimidate me. All it accomplished was impressing me with its beauty. I pointed at it. "Is this Alloces?"

"Oh, no. That is a fish I spotted at the store when helping select your tanks and figuring out how to get them installed in here. He did that to *me*. At that point, I had to have him, so he's now our fish, but I have decided he'll stay in your office. He's a normal, mortal fish. I'm debating making him an immortal fish. He postured at *me*."

"Fish that are brave enough to show aggression to you is impressive, I take it?"

"My devilish nature often intimidates small animals. This is a consequence of my fall. All I do to this one, though? Piss him off. That's it. I just piss him off. And worse? He loves being pissed off at me. He is *so* proud of himself. So, I'll have to make sure I visit him daily so he doesn't become upset."

The Devil had a soft heart, and I couldn't even fault him for his reason for taking the fish home. "He's really pretty, like a swimming jewel."

"Alloces is over here, and I have to admit, he's been outclassed by a mortal fish." The Devil stepped to one of the tanks near the space meant for a door between our offices. "I thought you'd like to name the red fish."

"Ruby, because he really is like a little jewel. Is this bowl big enough for him? Does he need anything else?" I admired Ruby, who continued to show off his fins for me. He had a little plant in his glass house along with a rock he could lounge on at his leisure with sand filling the bottom. When inspecting the sand, I discovered two more fish, small, pale, and covered in dark spots. "Oh! There are two more in here. They look like finned snow leopards!"

"Those are catfish," the Devil announced proudly. "They're called Cory cats. The water will be magically filtered, and I took steps to make sure everyone gets along. If Ruby becomes lonely, the Cory cats can keep him company."

"Catfish for a cat." I purred, sipping my coffee and taking another few minutes to watch my new pets. "They're adorable."

"Your brother told me you enjoy aquariums, and you would appreciate some fish keeping you closer company. I may have gone overboard."

"Yeah, it really does look like you have done just that. How many tanks are in here? How did you get them in here and set up so quickly?"

"Sixty. I recruited devils and demons to do the work, and I offered them some incentives. I also may have used Alloces as an example, and I'd be much less likely to use the same punishment on those who keep you happy. It is amusing how many will volunteer under those circumstances. Add in a little magic, and it was done in a span of a few hours. There's an office next door that can be converted into another trophy room if you run out of space in here. Alloces is not a social fish, although he will happily breed with any female due to his devilish nature. I recommend against that, as his finned children would have the potential to be sentient, so he is best left alone. Should any sentients unexpectedly be born in your aquariums, they'll be your responsibility, so manage your residents carefully. And yes, I'll check on your residents to make sure you know should it happen—and figure out the best way to handle transforming them into a more appropriate shape. Alloces will fight to the death with other males of most species, so he gets solitary confinement."

I made a mental note to be particularly careful about who shared tanks with who—and to ask around about what would happen if a sentient happened to be conceived in one of my tanks. I turned my attention to the tank. A bright blue fish the size of my hand with proud fins swam in the clear water, darting among the bright coral. "Oh, that coral is pretty. He's kinda pretty, too. Okay, I won't lie, he's really pretty. What is he?"

"He is an angelfish. I decided he didn't get to be anything other than an angelfish. Belial and I had quite the argument over that, but I won."

I stared at the Devil. "You turned a devil into an *angel*fish?"

"He will remember how he is to behave when it comes to you in the future."

"You have issues," I informed the Devil.

"But worrying about how he will treat you in the future is not one of my issues. By the time I allow him out of his tank, he will know to walk around you with great caution and treat you with the respect you are owed. Should he not, I'll let you do your worst to him. By that point in time, I expect your worst will be a delight to behold." With a rather vicious grin, the Devil gestured to my collection of tanks. "You'll have a wonderful time finding new residents for your office."

I really would. "He's a lot prettier as a fish. Belial did him a favor."

Chuckling, the Devil wrapped an arm around me and guided me towards the door. "You'll have plenty of time to admire your new pets after I've taken you out for dinner and begun drawing attention to you from your most unwanted suitor."

"That Gallo asshole isn't precisely a suitor."

"He thinks he is."

"Rejected, and I don't even care if he's hot."

"I'm hotter."

"You're Satan. You're hotter by default. You live in the middle of a lava field, and you happen to have a perfect chest. It's hard to compete with perfection. Are you going to be needy?"

"I am a very jealous man. He has hurt you once, and he is willing to hurt you again."

"That has nothing to do with jealousy. Jealousy would be getting upset if I said hello to him. Also, my hello may be communicated with my fist or a knee to his groin."

"Jealousy is a good word. The other word is filthy."

I rolled my eyes and sipped my coffee, debating which word he took offense to. "Protective."

He made a show of shuddering. "Such a filthy, positive word."

"Overprotective is a negative. You can be overprotective, but if you're too overprotective, you may lose access to my spots until you're protective rather than overprotective."

"I don't like that rule."

"You weren't supposed to like it."

"Why must you make me say positive things? I have a reputation to maintain."

"Your reputation is thoroughly ruined. First, you tucked me into bed and provided iced coffee because you know I enjoy it."

"I have an ulterior motive involving sex."

"That does not change the fact you tucked me into bed and provided iced coffee."

"Cruel," he complained.

"You recruited your devils and demons to make sure I had a nice office with beautiful tanks solely because you understood it would make me happy. Your reputation is ruined. Completely destroyed."

"I am lowering your guard so you're enchanted and compelled to marry me."

I raised a brow. "My daddy would kick your ass if you even thought you'd despoil me without the intent to marry me. He was a pastor, after all. Granted, he would've been okay with you if you meant to marry me. He was surprisingly liberal on that front. He was even the one who gave me and Jonas the talk when we were little. He didn't trust ignorance to keep us safe. Of course, he was pretty religious before the emergence, and unfortunately, the emergence itself ultimately did him in. Magic challenged too many of his beliefs."

"Yes, I suspect your father would have been inclined to do his best to teach me what would happen if I abused his little girl in the slightest. And he would have pushed for me to hold off on despoiling you until after we were safely wed. I would have been forced to play mortal, being aware of his nature, but I clean up nicely. I would have even catered to his ideal image for what he wanted in a son-in-law."

I wondered what my father would have wanted in a man for me, but I decided against asking. Knowing wouldn't bring my father back, and I suspected I'd be happier in the dark. "See? You can use filthy words. I made you use two so far in this conversation." I grinned at him. "Will it upset you to know that I'm so undesirable among most men that I'm very much inclined to accept the posturing of the first serious man to cross my path with an interest in marriage? It's the ears and tail."

"I am upset because you're beautiful, and you should have been treated as among the most desirable of women. However, I am not upset over your inclination to accept the posturing of the first serious man to cross your path with an interest. However, I'm the Devil rather than just some mere man, so you will have to compromise on that front. You can even convince me to engage in mortal customs should they please you. While your family is small, mine is not, so you can have as elaborate a ceremony as you would like."

"I don't require a fancy ring, but I require a ring. You can get it out of a cereal box for all I care. You will also require a ring, which I will acquire for you as soon as I figure out your ring size and where to get the money. I'm pretty sure I've been fired by now."

"You've been hired as my wife. My brothers have taken care of that situation, and they have spoken to your employer, who is aware you are not feeling well and may not be returning to work. Michael wanted to handle the matter, but Gabriel took care of it, including finding someone deserving who needed the work to take over your position. You can always trust an angel to complicate things. Anyway, your interview was concluded in our bathtub, although it seems I need to create a more strenuous interview process. You're able to walk. You're also able to talk back. I've noticed you really enjoy talking back."

The Devil amused me. "I'm feeling pretty good now that I have coffee, and it's definitely helping my throat, which is a little sore. I'll survive."

"No comments on having been hired as my wife?"

I made a point of looking at my left hand. "Do you see a ring?"

"I see you are going to be stubborn about this."

"Absolutely. I don't require a fancy ring, but I require a ring. I will look into the money matter so I can acquire your ring."

"I can give you money."

"But then I didn't earn the money that bought the ring, and it's the effort that matters, not the price tag. I will earn your ring properly."

"I find myself strongly disliking the morals your parents instilled in you at an early age right now. You earning the ring equals a delay in acquiring the ring, and I wish to fully count your spots."

"Patience is a virtue for a reason. And anyway, mugging the asshole who tried to poison me counts as earning the money to acquire the ring. If he hadn't hurt my brother and poisoned me, you would not be in the situation where you must exercise your newfound patience, so that's a bonus."

"I'm conflicted. Am I supposed to use a filthy word in regards to this fucking asshole or not?"

"You can say your filthy words to his aquarium while I admire my trophy, and you can have your fun with him after I've grown bored with him as a trophy."

"That could take all eternity," he muttered.

"Well, you'll just have to be patient, then."

"You're using really filthy words again."

"I need to get changed into real clothes so you can take me out to dinner. We can discuss my use of really filthy words later."

"In bed?" the Devil asked in a hopeful tone.

Hell yes, but I wasn't going to let him think he'd won already. "We'll see," I lied.

"You're a terrible liar, Darlene."

I shrugged. "He who is still fully clothed doesn't get to say I'm a liar about resisting your advances."

"The instant I take my shirt off, it's game over for you, woman."

"And?"

Laughing, he guided me back to his sitting room with its herd of unconscious succubi. Phenexia waited, sitting on the Devil's desk, and she held up a bag of cough drops. "I got these for you if you need them later, Darlene. I also picked up a purse and put your things in it along with a bottle of water. Consider it my welcoming gift so you can get used to your home. I also acquired you a blanket, as I've noticed you felines do very much enjoy having soft, warm blankets on hand. Your dress for this evening is Carmella's contribution. It's waiting for you, out on your bed."

My kittens, who'd quietly followed me around, bounded to the bedroom, probably to leave a contribution of fur all over the dress. Oh, well. As it was something I would do, I would smile and wear their fur. "Carmella?"

The Devil chuckled, a rather wicked sound. "Carmella is one of the devils of greed and temptation, but rather than sexual temptation, she tends to favor other forms of sin. Theft is more her speed than lust, and she likes encouraging unsavory mortals to indulge in their greed in complicated schemes. She particularly loves when she can turn the greedy against the greedy. Planning the downfall of the greedy through temptation is her specialty."

I could think of a few people I'd enjoy pointing Carmella at. "I like her already. I hope this dress helps with the downfall of Gallo and his gang of fucking assholes."

"She's probably planning my downfall, as I'm exceptionally greedy," the Devil muttered.

Smiling at that thought, I claimed my second coffee from him and headed for the bedroom, careful to keep from stepping on the sleeping succubi. "Thank you, Phenexia."

"You're welcome."

The Devil grunted his displeasure over our use of filthy words, and I laughed.

## FOURTEEN

Sometimes, I was not a nice person.

CARMELLA HAD SELECTED A BLACK, floor-length gown for me, one with a startling conservative neckline, which was low enough I could wear the cross collar I'd pilfered from the Devil's dresser without making a scandalous statement. All in all, with a little work on my hair, I passed as pretty enough, and I wouldn't bring much shame to Lucifer when out in public with him.

He outclassed me, but I refused to care.

I'd seen his fury, and I understood its source. Maybe he outclassed me. Maybe I'd never meet his expectations. Maybe we'd be a lot like gasoline meeting fire down the road. Maybe I'd try to put his ass in my new fish tanks for annoying me. Maybe a lot of things might happen, but I understood a simple truth. For that one moment, he'd been consumed by passion for my sake.

I shivered at the memory and did my best to forget the moment he'd become blinded by his rage over what someone else had wanted to do.

To me.

Had I not known some of the fucking assholes destined for my aquarium tormented other victims, I might've been satisfied with setting Belial or one of the other devils loose on them. My knowledge barred me from taking the easy way out, however. At least one family deserved a better life, one free from the mafia's hateful and greedy clutches. The dress served several purposes. First, it would draw attention to me, with the intent of capturing the mafia's notice. Second, it would draw attention to me, with the intention of keeping the Devil's eye on me rather than some succubus.

I'd rather not have to go rummaging through Belial's things and transform his demonesses into fish for my tanks. I would, too.

Sometimes, I was not a nice person, and I had zero intention of playing fair. Until I obtained my goals, which included laying a claim on the Devil and securing revenge for my brother's transformation into a chipmunk, I would redefine what it meant to be ruthless.

Any other day, I would have disliked wearing heels, but the black stilettos served several purposes. They did wonderful things for my legs, put me closer to eye level with the Devil, and offered me the illusion of power with an added bonus of being easily converted into weapons.

The kittens curled up on the bed for a nap, and I emerged from the bedroom armed with my new purse. The Devil sat at his desk, an elbow resting on it while he propped his chin up and observed his whining succubi sprawled on the floor and complaining at him about his cruel mistreatments of their persons.

As they amused him, I decided to leave it be unless one of them tried to paw at him, at which point I would discover if I could use a stiletto to sever hands from wrists. "Enjoying yourself?"

"I've been told I should keep my influencing to myself."

"But why?" I tilted my head, puzzled over why anyone would want to skip the influencing for whatever the hell women got without a hefty dose of devilish affection tossed in. "I had no idea heaven could be found in hell, but here we are."

"They're tired."

"That's not your problem."

"Why aren't you at all tired? This is not right. You should be an exhausted puddle resting in my bed so I can indulge in tucking you in and sneaking peeks at you while I do it. I obviously didn't influence you enough, and I find this both elating and disturbing."

"May you have better luck next time," I

replied. "Am I over dressed, under dressed, or sufficiently dressed?"

"You're making me question taking you out for dinner by wearing that dress." The Devil looked me over. "I'm either going to have to recant tearing you out of that dress or I'll need to buy several more of them so you can have one at all times while I methodically tear the other ones off of you. I'm going to have to thank Carmella. I had no idea she was so talented at dressing you. I'm going to have to ask her to help you with your wardrobe. You're perfectly dressed, and I'm going to have issues holding my temper when Gallo gets a good look at you."

As turnabout was fair play, I took my time admiring his suit. "We want to catch his attention so we can be involved with making him disappear under mysterious circumstances."

"I have succubi. I'm not afraid to use them."

"That would not be very satisfying for me, Lucifer."

He scowled.

I smiled.

"You're going to be obstinate about this, aren't you? I could take you to a different steakhouse. Perhaps on the other side of America? Or I could wine you and dine you somewhere exotic. I can show you the world. Then I can unleash the legions, they can deal with Gallo, and we'll have a great time where he cannot come close to you."

"Showing me the world doesn't win me revenge or help the victimized family members gain a better life. I'm sorry, Lucifer. You're just going to have to do good deeds in an evil way. You'll cope somehow. I'll turn around if you have to handle him in a gruesomely violent fashion, however. That said, I would really like to put him in one of my tanks, perhaps next to Alloces?"

"If I tell you no, you're going to put up a fight about this, aren't you?"

"Absolutely. I'll just ask your brothers and Belial to help me do it if you won't."

He narrowed his eyes. "I demand spots."

"You can demand all you want, but that doesn't mean you're getting them."

The Devil grunted his frustration, wrinkled his nose, and straightened, shooting a glare at me. "You were so docile in the tub, and your ears are really cute when wet. So is your tail."

The spot obsessed freak might do me in if he kept it up—or I might be inclined to shred his nice suit to gain access to his chest. I bet he would heal scratch marks in record time. "You can earn some docility through good performance after dinner and mayhem. Also, I will resent if I'm poisoned again, so we'll have to do something about that part of things. That headache was not my idea of a good time."

"Your spots. I require them."

"And I require new fish. And?"

The Devil screamed his frustration, startling the collection of succubi whining all over the sitting room floor. "Please."

Excellent. I'd trained the Devil to use a new word. "Better. You may have a new spot once we're home from dinner and finished with creating mayhem and gathering at least one new fish for my tanks. You'll have to wait until my fish is settled in his or her new home, however. I'll also need some fish that enjoy being together, because single fish look sad."

"They're supposed to look sad. It's a punishment!"

"The catfish are cute together."

"I have no objections taking you to stores to pick new mortal fish for your enjoyment."

"My next fish I will be picking out in person, and they will be fucking assholes who get a taste of their own fucking medicine. Am I clear? And if I'm not, allow me to clarify the situation: I'll bite your fucking hands off if you try to touch a damned spot until I personally see to those fucking assholes!"

The door into the sitting room opened, and a taller, tanner version of my brother stepped into the room, and I turned my ears back and hissed. "And you're a fucking asshole, too! I should put you in a tank for a year and claw that pretty face just so you learn your lesson."

The Devil got up, strode to my side, and wrapped his arms around my waist, lifting me off my feet. "Somebody needs dinner, and then she needs a nap. Once she's had her nap, then she can be coddled in disgustingly sweet fashions. But somebody needs a nap."

I struggled and kicked my feet in protest of losing my ability to go claw at my brother's face. "You made him prettier!"

My brother raised a brow. "Should I come back later?"

"That's quite all right, Jonas. She's just tired. Unlike my succubi, she resisted taking a nap, so she's tired, cranky, and hungry. You were correct about her enjoyment of fish, so thank you for that tip. I'll require you for our trip out, as she seems determined to handle her business. Your first task will be to play as a chipmunk in her home, and as soon as she is only tired and cranky, you'll direct us to the first of our targets. We'll see Belial on our way out."

"What about them?" Jonas asked, gesturing to the succubi littering the floor.

"They'll be fine. Once the incubi stop strutting around, they'll drag them off somewhere. They should be happy with me right now, but no. They're all whining." The Devil shrugged. "Well, the ones coherent enough to whine. And even those seem to have resumed napping. Really, what are they even trying to do?"

"Why are you asking me?" Jonas asked.

"That's a damned good question. I really don't know. You're so wet behind the ears you disgust me, and if I didn't need you as security for Darlene and to maintain appearances, I'd just leave you here to stay out of trouble."

Jonas shrugged. "I can't say I didn't earn that."

"Who are you and what have you done with my brother?" I demanded.

"Darlene," he complained.

"That's better. Do that some more. My brother whines and causes me trouble. He does not accept responsibility for his stupidity. You need to act normally, or I might not be able to cope with too much change at one time."

My brother stared at me as though I'd lost my mind.

I crossed my arms over my chest, grunting at the pressure of the Devil keeping me off my feet so I wouldn't kick my brother with my weaponized shoes. "Seriously? You think I'm nuts for wanting you to behave normally? I should stab you with my shoes! Come here and take your stabbing like a man or whatever the fuck you are now."

"Well," the Devil began, and then he set me down, although he kept a firm hold on my waist. After a long moment of silence and a sigh, he continued, "I believe he is startled because you're openly more aggressive than he is used to. I'm just turned on because it's sexy watching you want to kill someone. I don't want to take you to dinner now. I want to seduce you."

"I need dinner," I growled. "After I'm done eating dinner, I need to kill my brother. Wait. I can't kill him. Damn it."

"I find your irritation very attractive."

"Jonas, tell him what I do when I'm hungry."

"If she doesn't bite, she cries," my brother reported. "And nothing is scarier than my sister crying because she's hungry and is too angry she's hungry to handle her hunger problem, and once she's that hungry, she becomes emotionally unstable and inclined to kill people. I recommend offering her something to eat and stay quiet until she's eaten enough she is no longer unstable."

"Is that true, Darlene?" the Devil whispered in my ear. "I have trouble believing you cry over anything."

"It's ugly crying, I splotch, and if I'm wearing fur, it falls out from stress and I end up patchy. Nothing upsets me more than patchy fur. I lose spots when I'm patchy. Entire spots, just gone right along with my fur. I resemble a mangey mutt when I'm patchy due to stress shedding."

"Unacceptable. I will not stand the loss of even a single spot."

"My fur grows back."

"Still not acceptable."

For fuck's sake. "Just get your ass on the

move so I can have dinner, give me a baseball bat, and point me at one of the fucking assholes."

"Baseball bat? Why do you want a baseball bat?" the Devil asked.

"I'll just fucking beat them and you can then make them fish and I'll nurse them back to health in my tanks. Look, I'm hungry, and you promised me steak."

The Devil grinned at me, rested his hands on my shoulders, and pushed me towards the door. "Then let us be on our way. It won't take long to get what we need from Belial. Jonas will just have to deal with the sting when I force his transformation as he has yet to learn how to control it himself."

"This is going to suck," my brother predicted.

"Oh, you have no idea how right you are," the Devil promised.

BELIAL GAVE the Devil a bag and a box along with a stern warning to be careful with the contents, as they were among his most potent. Without waiting for an acknowledgment, he vanished in a plume of vile-smelling smoke. With that portion of our plan completed, we addressed the matter of my brother and deceiving any idiots who might check in on my home to see what was going on.

I suspected the Devil made Jonas's transformation as painful as possible to remind me of the various sins of those I meant to crush under my pretty heel. My chipmunk of a brother whined and waved a furry paw at the Devil, and I carried him around on my shoulder. Teleporting to my home left me dizzy and with a headache, and I frowned.

"Your body has been under a lot of strain, and I'm not as gentle with teleporting as my brothers." The Devil scooped my brother off my shoulder and put him in his cage on my coffee table.

"How did you know?"

"I cheated and checked, but only because I was expecting it to have some adverse consequences. We will be traveling to dinner in style, and I requested a tray of appetizers to tide you over until we arrive. I'd rather not teleport you again right now, so we'll be taking a limousine. It will also make a statement when we arrive. I've had various demons and devils spread some whispers around to streamline our work."

"Think a baseball bat will fit under my dress?"

"Alas, no. Jonas, you will be able to transform yourself back to a humanoid form with a little concentration or if you're startled or injured. Be aware you will take on a more demonic appearance unless you're focusing on your human form. At that point, you may as well employ your natural weapons and handle the problem directly. Do try not to kill any of the mortals, as I would like to claim them for your sister's trophy room. You may bring them to the brink of death and teach their souls why it is not wise to cross me."

My brother bobbed his head and settled into his rodent paradise, and he pointed at the TV while squeaking.

As I loved my brother most of the time, I turned it onto his favorite channel rather than mine.

Someone knocked at the door, and the Devil offered his arm. "That would be our driver. With your leave, I will administer Belial's concoctions. He has a sense of humor, and he often tricks those who use his wares. I can handle anything he throws my way, including amusing additions I might not prefer."

"Additions?"

"He might, for example, decide I should have a tail and ears the match of yours, or he might attempt to stain your fur a rather obnoxious color."

I linked my arm with his. "If he dyes my fur, I will make my revenge so elaborate your many hells discuss will it for all eternity."

The Devil frowned, thought about it for a minute, and shrugged. "It is a good thing I am who I am, as I find this thought tempting. You would feud for all eternity and turn my many hells into a battleground for your pranking. It could be most amusing."

"Don't you even dare think about setting that disaster up, Lucifer."

"Oh, I'm thinking about it. I do hate getting bored."

Right. I should have known. "If you help with any action that dyes my fur in any shade without my permission, I will be banning you from any spots for a period of one year per every minute my fur is the wrong color."

"I see you have a very deep line in the sand on this issue."

"Not only will you be banned from touching any spots, I will dye my fur black so you can't see them, either."

"Please marry me."

I raised a brow at that and laughed at how my cruel removal of my spots for his enjoyment could result in the Devil liking it to such an extreme he'd make such a request. "You can try again with a ring and on bent knee. Only then will I consider giving you an answer."

"You're really going to make me kneel."

"I absolutely am going to make you kneel, and if you're slow about it, I'll help Belial go through the interested succubi and set up interviews." I'd also contemplate killing them all or adding them to my tanks.

"So ruthless," he murmured, and he took me to the door. True to his warning, a limousine waited in front of my house.

The driver, who appeared human enough but wore a suit the perfect match of the Devil's, bowed and gestured to the vehicle. "Everything is as you requested, sir."

"Excellent. Thank you."

"That earned you a spot," I informed the Devil. "Good behavior is rewarded."

The driver smirked and headed for the limousine. When we reached the black car, Lucifer opened and closed the door for me before circling the vehicle to join me. A bottle of champagne and a tray of cheese, crackers, various meats, and seafood waited for our attention. I eyed the clams and shrimp, licking my lips.

"A man should aspire for his woman to look at him like you are looking at your appetizers." The Devil snagged the champagne bottle and opened it, and while it made a startling bang, he somehow kept a hold on the cork. He poured a glass and offered it to me. "As you refused to adhere to my plans and take a nap, I do not have as much information on Gallo and his operations as I would like, although I have handled some of the work. His wife—"

"He's after me when he already has a wife?" I growled, flattening my ears. Taking the glass, I took a single sip before snagging a chilled clam, still in its shell and garnished with a dab of cocktail sauce and a sprinkling of green onion. I made it disappear into my stomach with a happy purr, setting the empty shell down. "This guy is a class act, isn't he?"

"Yes. Upon securing your person, his plan

is to murder his wife so you can take her place. He has poisoned her like he had you poisoned, and she's already lost a significant portion of her memories. Should his plans go unimpeded, she will die by the morning."

The more I learned about Gallo, the more I wanted to bash his brains in and decorate the entirety of New York with his pulverized remains. "What a nice gentleman. What is best for her?"

Before meeting the Devil and his brothers, I would have been inclined to save her and to hell with the consequences. I'd learned a lot in a short period of time, and a future in a different life might truly be the better option than continuing a life of misery and un-happiness.

"She has a strong spirit."

"That doesn't tell me anything." I snagged another clam, and unlike the first, I took my time savoring it. "What is best for her?"

"It's not that simple. Every choice has a thousand consequences or more. Every word you speak can trigger a cascade of change. A life is an endless chain of consequences and possibilities. What is best for her may not be what is best for many. At what point do you assign such a value to her life and her percep-tion of it? If what is best for her hurts many, which is the greater sin? Ending one person's misery when they can struggle through and do great good or evil because of their suffer-ing? Right now, mercy would be to end her suffering—but in five years, she could spawn many new beginnings that make her life a priceless treasure. What is best for her evolves with every breath."

I thought about it, snagging a shrimp and nibbling on it. "That headache is pretty miserable."

"It is. Right now, she suffers. But I can't help you decide what is best for her. Life is an ever-changing path, and everything can become new with but a single word. For example, if you were to accept me as your husband, there would be great change. If you tell me no, there will also be great change and even more sulking on my part. Be responsible. You wouldn't want to make me sulk."

Several shrimp and another clam fell to my appetite before I grinned and pointed the shell at him. "I already told you what you needed to do to get an answer out of me."

"At least you're not making me ask your brother for permission."

"He'd say no, and I would be forced to put him in one of my tanks for shitty behavior. He doesn't get to dictate who I may or may not wed, if you please—and even if you don't please."

"But would you have made me ask your father?"

"Absolutely. My father was the best despite everything, thank you."

"Well, of course. He raised you to be as you are, after all."

I blinked and stared at the Devil. "What?"

"You are a product of your parents and their upbringing of you. From your first breath, they molded you. You are as you are because of their actions. Had you a different father, you would not be who you are today. Humans are imperfect, and that is part of what makes them interesting. But your father and mother had a hand in every part of your life, and I find myself disgustingly appreciative of that in this moment."

"That doesn't explain how Jonas turned out."

"He's male."

I frowned. "What? I mean, yes. He is my brother rather than my sister."

"Men are often raised differently from women in religious environments. Your brother grew up feeling a certain amount of entitlement due to his position as a preacher's son. You grew up with the burden of expectations. That is how two humans could produce two children on entirely different behavioral spectrums. It was all in their care with your upbringing. Jonas did not have the same upbringing as you despite the fact that you share parents. He spent all of his life being told he should expect certain things, and that became the seeds of greed, sin, and treachery. You spent all of your life being cultivated to be a responsible wife and mother with a splash of the crueler realities of mortal life. Jonas will learn quickly how to become self-reliant, for I am not as kind as your parents were in their mortal life. You are not meant to be his mother, and I will put my foot down if I must. Or put him in one of your tanks in time out until he learns to be self-sufficient. And I have plans on how I'll handle you should you fall prey to those old habits."

"What plans?"

"Test me and find out. We'll both enjoy it, that much I can promise."

Ugh. All the Devil had to do to make me enjoy myself was take his damned shirt off. "I can't tell if I'm supposed to be falling prey to these old habits or not."

The Devil thought about it, and he claimed one of the clams for himself. "You know, I'm not sure, either. I seem to have created a dilemma."

"You have created a dilemma all right, you ate one of the clams!" I grabbed another one, eyeing the last one left on the tray. I set my Champagne down and claimed the last one, too. "Mine."

"But they're good," the Devil complained, and he focused on the clam in my left hand. "I'll be really good to you if you share that with me."

I translated his offer to involve a bedroom and the removal of his shirt, but as I was not a fool, I asked, "But will you show off your perfect chest for me should I give this to you?"

"Maybe."

I raised a brow and lifted the clam to escort it on its adventure to my stomach where it belonged.

"Yes."

I grinned, turned my hand, and held out the shell in his direction. "Talk dirty to me."

"Please."

There was something inherently sexual about feeding a clam to him, and I regretted I had an entire dinner and securement of revenge between me and my date with his chest. "I am expecting a very nice reward for sharing that with you."

His smirk promised trouble. "Don't you worry about a thing. I have rewarding you penned in after dinner and a rather entertaining after-dinner show."

## FIFTEEN

How can a wine be mysterious?

THE DEVIL TOOK me to a fancy restaurant deep in the heart of Manhattan, the kind of place I didn't even bother dreaming about going to. A single look at the menu taught me a very important lesson.

A bottle of wine could cost more than the safety and security of a baby.

I couldn't understand why. Unsure of how to ask, I pointed at the bottle and showed it to him, unable to keep my puzzlement from showing.

"Status," he replied, and he pointed at a much cheaper bottle, something I could afford if I skimped for a week or two. "This vintage tastes better to me, honestly, and it partners with a lot more things. That bottle you're looking at is purchased when someone has a point to make and doesn't care how much money he drinks away to make that point. Is it worth that much? Sure, to those who wish to make that point, but in so many cases, more expensive doesn't mean it's actually better."

Huh. The Devil could be practical. "Which one is your favorite?"

His finger slid up several items to a bottle of wine not much more expensive than the one he'd initially showcased. "This one is a little sweeter, and it's full of mystery. I like mysterious things."

"How can a wine be mysterious?"

"Obviously, I will have to teach you." He flagged down a waiter and pointed at the two cheaper bottles of wine and requested both of them. Once the waiter left, he used the wine menu to point somewhere behind me. "Gallo just arrived with several of his right-hand men. It seems my demons and devils have done their work well."

"How do you know?"

"I'm cheating."

Ah. I wondered what sort of things men like Gallo thought about when going to a fancy restaurant knowing his wife slowly died. "How is his wife doing?"

"Your concern for her condition will eat you alive, won't it?"

"Probably," I admitted.

The Devil reached into his suit jacket, dialed a number, and held his cell phone to his ear. "Belial, I require you to handle the matter we discussed earlier. I recommend you inquire with Michael for how best to treat her. Darlene is disturbed, and she will not enjoy the rest of tonight's activities unless it is addressed. You may as well implement the rest of our plans. I have visual verification the more dangerous elements are occupied. Make the guest quarters in my home comfortable until proper placement can be made, and take extra care with any younglings. Recruit the succubi to handle them as needed. Yes, we're being a charity tonight. Treat it like Halloween or something, and you're dressing up as angels or some nonsense like that. Turn it into a game. Whomever makes the best performance gets treats instead of tricks with an added benefit of pleasing Darlene. Also, I'm going to need fresh clams for my feline, and the kitchen can get creative with their preparation, just remember she's not quite as adventurous as the average devil yet. Also acquire any other feline appropriate treats she might enjoy."

I giggled at that, turning my attention to the actual menu while my stomach gurgled complaints over its mostly empty state. When the Devil hung up, I pointed at one of the steaks on the menu, which cost more than I tended to spend in an entire week on groceries. "Is this one good?"

He checked my choice, nodded, and eyed the rest of the menu, pointing at an appetizer of lobster bisque. "I bet some lobster cooked in cream will make my little kitty purr."

I bet it would, too. "They have cocktail shrimp, too."

"Yours for the taking as well." After a moment of consideration, he pointed at something on the menu. "You should round out your seafood conquests with their smoked salmon before enjoying your steak."

"What are you having?"

"Steak, steak, and more steak. I might have a potato for variety, but I enjoy steak very much."

Since he'd picked for me, I pointed at the salads. "And a salad. We should both have a salad so we're pretending we're eating healthily."

"We don't have to eat healthily."

"But salads taste good, especially when they're slathered with creamy dressings and bacon. There's bacon on these salads, Lucifer. There's egg and cheese, too."

"You're going to make me eat a salad, aren't you?"

"The salad will help me pretend I'm not indulging in an act of gluttony. What are the fucking assholes doing?"

"Gallo has positioned himself so he has a good view of you. He has no idea what to make of me, as I do not match the type of people your brother would associate with, and he's convinced you would only associate with people your brother knows. I am dressed too well, and he is confused about where you acquired your apparel."

"That is so bizarre. Why?"

"From what I can glean from his surface

thoughts, he had been cultivating Jonas to serve as one of his underlings, but Jonas was proving resistant to some of his more ruthless schemes, so he removed the problem. Apparently, he'd noticed you earlier than your brother's transformation into a chipmunk. His treatment of your brother was to test you more than anything."

"Listening to people's thoughts is a rather convenient ability, isn't it?" It was well enough I couldn't hear Gallo's thoughts, as it would likely result in me trying to throw the entire damned table at him.

"He wants to strip you out of your dress, and I find this to be very irritating." The Devil sighed, shook his head, and glared at the menu. "I'll get us the mixed appetizer platter, too. If we have leftovers, so be it."

"You want to strip me out of my dress, too," I reminded him.

"Yes, but I wish to do so in a mutually beneficial fashion, and when I'm finished with you, I would tuck you into my bed and continue to shower you with affection. He does not have any good will towards you, and he is only concerned with himself. He is a most selfish human being. He disgusts me, really."

I needed to get my hands on a weapon, occupy the Devil with some task, and take the bastard out. "What a creep. Are you sure I can't beat him to a near-death state with a baseball bat?"

"You would kill him, and then you would become annoyed you are bereft of a new fish for your trophy room. You will be more satisfied should you keep him alive."

"But I'm very motivated to kill him right now."

He chuckled and closed his menu. "That you are. I will have to call Belial again. It appears he intends to grab your brother and use him as leverage after making certain you are poisoned this time. He also plans on poisoning me, although with the intent of getting rid of me, who he rightly views as competition."

"Can't he at least try to be creative?"

"His poison is quite creative, truth be told. He does deserve credit for its manufacture."

"Can the credit be my foot inserted into his ass, heel first?"

The Devil considered my question, his eyes narrowing. "I'm intrigued. Would you be wearing that dress while you're giving him credit?"

"It would be a shame if I were to get blood on this dress. I'd probably need to wear something else. This dress is really nice, and I don't want to destroy it."

"Magic can remove blood from fabrics, and your dress would emerge from its bloody debut intact."

"Will my brother be all right?"

"I will ask Belial to keep a watch on the situation and help teach your brother how best to defend himself." The Devil glowered at his phone, muttered a few curses, and dialed. "These humans are annoying idiots. There will be some who wish to bring harm to my new pet. Take care of them and move them into Darlene's trophy room. Yes, you may handle the matter personally, and don't feel a need to hold back. I tire of this nonsense." He returned his phone to his pocket. "Some days, I regret having delved a little too far into the future, but I couldn't bear to be caught with one of those most annoying bricks mortals are currently using for portable phones. Tell your fellow humans to hurry up and design more sophisticated things. It's most annoying having to trick the humans into believing I'm using their backwater technology."

I bet. "Yours is pretty convenient."

"I'm very spoiled, so I need convenience, and I need my convenience to be elegant."

"Belial won't mind watching Jonas?"

"Not at all, and it solves some problems. We'll take care of the idiots at the other table, and I'm debating conjuring you a baseball bat."

"You can do that?"

"Of course."

Before I could ask what else had riled the Devil up about Gallo and his lowlife thugs, the waiter brought both bottles of wine and opened them, going through some odd dance with the Devil to make certain both were acceptable before taking our order. Lucifer made a few additional requests, and to my fascination and delight, he did so in a different language. My eyes widened at the waiter's lack of reaction, bowing at the Devil's requests. "I will attend to this immediately, sir."

"Okay, that was really neat. What language was that?"

"An extinct language, truth be told. The people who once spoke it lived in Africa, although they're long gone. I used a little magic to make sure he understood my request, as I wished to preserve the secret for your enjoyment."

"You can just start talking dead languages to people with the expectation of them understanding you?"

"I've been doing it all night long, and I've been manipulating you to do the same, all so Gallo can't overhear us. He believes we're speaking some South American language, apparently, for he understands Italian and Swedish and we make no sense to him. When I spoke to Belial, I used a devilish language. That one I'll teach you properly, as you'll need it."

"What is the fucking asshole thinking about now?"

"He's generally frustrated, as I ordered most of our meal in English, and he couldn't catch my last request. To his perception, I lowered my voice in a more controversial manner. He has the poison with him in his pocket, and he's debating how to make the most use of it. His companions also have doses of it with them. I find them foolish, carrying such a thing in something as fragile as a glass bottle in their pockets. They are just smart enough to be dangerous."

"What does he think about you?"

"I annoy him because I'm in the way of what he wants."

"Well, that's certainly true. Is he going to interrupt our dinner?"

"No. He likes this restaurant and doesn't want to risk being unable to return, so he's biding his time. His current plan is to wait until we're finished and follow us out, approaching and poisoning us when we're on the street. Once the poison kicks in, he wants to claim you. He will have me followed and dealt with at the earliest opportunity."

Well, at least my dinner would be safe, and if he did screw up my dinner, I would turn my chair into a lethal weapon. "That's not going to work out as he's expecting."

"I do find that to be very amusing. I have plans to make you my equal on the survivability front."

"Through conversion."

"I'll enjoy it immensely, and I will endeavor to make certain you enjoy it as much as I do." The Devil smirked. "Of course, all I have to do to catch your attention is unbutton my shirt. I have you figured out."

Busted. "I refuse to be ashamed of my interest in your chest."

"And I refuse to be ashamed of my interest in your spots. We are well matched in that regard. I'm far more generous about my chest than you are about your spots. You should be more generous with your spots. I'd very much appreciate them."

"You might kill your succubi if I let you play with all my spots at one time. I've seen what you can do with only access to my ears and tail."

"I wouldn't kill them. They'd just be excessively satisfied and whine over having been thoroughly exercised. The incubi will love me. I'm just spreading the joy. They'll be fine. They're just very well fed and need to digest. Both succubi and incubi feed off sexual energy, and you bring out the best in me. Once I have you fully converted, you'll be well tended, that much I can promise. I'm greedy and selfish, after all."

He was the Lord of Lies, and I raised a brow, wondering who he was trying to convince with that load of drivel. "Yes, you're so terribly greedy and selfish."

"Is that sarcasm I'm hearing, my darling?"

"Perhaps."

He chuckled. "Most would not be so bold with me."

"I have what you want, and as such, I get to be as bold with you as I want. Anyway, you like it."

"I like it very much."

"If I can't have a baseball bat, can I break my chair over his head and beat him that way?"

Lucifer coughed and covered his mouth. "First, I fail to tire you out. Then, because that was not bad enough, I have not fed you sufficiently to control your murderous instincts. If the thought of you beating some foolish mortal to a near-death state while wearing that dress wasn't so damned attractive, I might be concerned. But it's very attractive, and I regret I can't encourage you to do just that. A little wine may help take the edge off." Reaching for the bottle of his preferred wine, he poured some for me and offered me the glass. "One of the perks of being my companion is your newfound ability to drink as much as you want without concern over becoming too drunk. I find the idea of abusing magic for my enjoyment amusing, and keeping you pleasantly intoxicated without being fully impaired is my idea of a good time. Lowered inhibitions and all."

"Does that come with a reduced chance of hangover?"

"Absolutely."

"How have you stayed single for this long?" I sniffed the wine and took a careful sip of it, finding it to be a little sweet and complex in its underlying flavors. "You're right. This is a good wine."

"I'm always right."

"Are you going to try to sell me the Golden Gate next?"

"Do you want it?"

"No. What would I do with a bridge?"

"Fling men like Gallo off the side, I suspect."

"I don't need to own the bridge to do that. Can I change my mind about keeping that fucking asshole alive? He pisses me off. Just knowing he's behind me, plotting to turn me into his pet, really, really pisses me off."

"Smooth your fur, kitty. He's not going to do anything to you. I'll see to that."

"I don't want you to see to that. I want to beat him to death with my chair. He was going to do *what* to my brother?"

"Use him to lure you out and then kill him," the Devil replied.

"Giving a long and pretty life in my tanks is too good of a fate for that fucker."

"I see your brother was not exaggerating over your mood when you become hungry. Please don't venture into the crying portion of your hunger. I'm sure our appetizers will be here soon. I'm now concerned we didn't order enough."

I considered how much I'd eaten in the limousine, which boiled down to the entire damned tray with only a few tidbits going to the Devil, which I'd fed to him by hand. "I'm a little hungry."

"A little?"

My stomach complained, and I sighed. "Maybe a lot hungry."

"You're definitely starving. If you really want to kill him, I won't stop you. After all, it's not really a party until the bodies start hitting the floor, and a dead man can't come back to bother you later."

I found the way the Devil phrased his statement to be rather amusing. "Not haunt?"

"Ghosts are serious business, and they're as persistent as they are annoying. I try not to deal with ghosts unless it's absolutely necessary. While some of them are harmless, others are not. Ghosts happen for a reason, and the last thing you want is an angry ghost haunting you. They're typically stuck, and any sensible being will be cranky about that. Souls are typically shepherded to their next destination quickly. That's why I created unicorns, to help make certain that process was not interrupted. There are other shepherds, of course, but I'm particularly fond of my unicorns."

"Why do I have the feeling your unicorns are not sunshine and rainbows like the legends claim?"

"Well, where would be the fun in that?"

"You are the reason you fell," I informed him.

He laughed and shrugged. "What can I say? *He* made me this way for a reason."

Something about the Devil's words bothered me, but before I could think long on it, the waiter brought our appetizers, and I focused on what was important: filling my hungering stomach and keeping a close eye on Lucifer so he—and his perfect chest—couldn't escape me.

LUCIFER REGALED me with ancient stories of love-sick men and the women doomed to put up with them. I couldn't remember the last time I'd laughed so hard, especially after he waxed on and on about one of his misadventures, where he'd done his best to seduce a tribeswoman to be met with utter failure. Having his heart ripped out of his chest hadn't been enough to deter him, but since the first time hadn't been enough to teach him a lesson, she'd sacrificed him ten more times before he'd gotten the message and returned to his many hells to sulk.

"What happened to her?"

"Well, I tried to claim her soul, but one of my brothers slapped my wrist and told me no. I have been complaining ever since. She told me no!"

I smiled at that. "I tell you no frequently, too."

"She really meant it. You just like telling me no because it riles me up. Then you get me to tell you yes, so you get to do whatever you want with me. It's disgusting, really. I've been brought low by you and your wretchedly perfect spots."

The Devil, I decided, thoroughly represented modern men. "How traumatic for you, lusting for spots you don't have permission to play with yet."

He sat straighter, regarding me through narrowed eyes. "The magic word of that statement is yet."

"The magic words are actually please and thank you, but yet is a positive possibility for you." I licked my lips and considered how best to finish my steak, which defied all my expectations for a steak. Had I even been eating beef before this restaurant?

My steaks at home, while a rare treat, couldn't compare.

"I would very much like for you to look at me like you're looking at that steak."

I'd get there soon enough, once my stomach was convinced starvation wasn't around the corner. "Honestly, I've never been so hungry in my entire life. You obviously did something wicked with me for me to be this hungry."

"For about twelve hours, yes, I had my wicked way with you. It's the start of the conversion process. You're hungry because your body is beginning to adapt to exposure to so much devilish energy, which I delighted in subjecting you to. You also delighted in being subjected to it. I'll just have to make certain my home has plenty of food for you to enjoy.

Once you're converted, your diet will be mostly energy, although you'll still hunger for regular food as well."

"Is regular food an actual part of your diet?"

"It's not mandatory, if that's what you mean, but I do enjoy it. I'm a spoiled creature and enjoy good food and even better dessert. Once you have your murderous tendencies satisfied, I intend on enjoying you for dessert."

"How is Gallo doing? And my brother?"

"Belial will take care of your brother, although with those two, I expect there to be bodies along with a few new pet fish for your collection. I have decided one of Gallo's companions will not be surviving today."

"Oh?"

"I do not wish to discuss what he wants to do to you."

Ah. Right. As I hadn't been born yesterday, I could read between the lines. "He's keeping company with an asshole who wants to poison me in order to coerce me into marrying him after he kills off his wife. Were you expecting anything different?"

"I was not precisely expecting anything different, but you will be *my* wife, and I take great offense over what he has planned for *my* wife."

Oh, boy. "You don't get to call me your wife until you get on bent knee with a ring, and even then, there needs to be a wedding," I reminded him, and as he was being pushy and overprotective, I added, "You will bend your knee in front of witnesses consisting of your more notable demons and devils. My brother is my only family, so he absolutely better be present for the wedding, or I will be very offended. As for the reason your demons and devils need to witness, you have to make it clear that they'll be making a poor decision should they cross me."

"I feel strangely cornered yet intrigued and aroused by your disgustingly reasonable requests."

Aroused? Had the Devil been dropped on his head as a baby repeatedly? After a moment of consideration, I realized he was an idiot who liked when I bossed him around. "Well, you are the Devil, and you have this expectation that people should grovel at your feet because you're big, bad, and scary. I just find you sexy as hell, so it's entirely possible I'm too intellectually deficient to be scared of you, so I boss you around instead. Because you have ridiculous expectations, this is attractive to you."

"You're too smart to be scared of me, as you have evaluated the situation and have come to the conclusion that I am not a threat to you, thus you have no reason to be scared. I'm very appreciative you find me sexy as hell, as this is a good indication I can pursue being sexy as hell for your enjoyment as soon as we finish with our after-dinner show tonight."

"I will let you kill the one you don't like if you let me kill the one I don't like. Then you can teach me how to best welcome fucking assholes to your dungeons. Hey, how long does it take to make some badass leathers? I bet I'd rock leather."

"Being the Devil has its perks, and I'm sure I could acquire some leathers for you to wear while you're educating our newest fucking assholes in our dungeons. What color would you like your leathers to be?"

I pointed at the collar I'd pilfered from his dresser. "It needs to look good with this. I've claimed this as mine."

"I put it there so you could steal it at your leisure. Such a lovely throat deserves to be adorned with jewels. If you had not helped yourself to it, I would have enjoyed pinning you and making you like my adornment of your person."

Some equations were easier to solve than others, and I liked the Devil's wicked ways. "I will make sure to leave it out so you are forced to indulge when you've been particularly good."

"I really like reward systems, as I enjoy being rewarded for my behavior." The Devil smirked, and he stared at something behind me. "Gallo has no idea what we're discussing, but he recognizes your tone as seductive, and he does not like that at all. He feels quite entitled to your company."

"How am I doing on the seduction front?"

"I am highly annoyed we have things to do before you can successfully seduce me."

"Will you at least try to contain yourself, so your succubi don't whine?"

"No."

I raised a brow. "No?"

"You deserve my best, so the succubi will just have to whine, as restraining myself means you do not get my best. I'm a perfectionist, my darling, and you'll just have to get used to it."

There were worse ways to go, including being poisoned by a fucking asshole. "I'm going to require a full demonstration of your prowess, and what I should look out for if you're not giving me your best."

"But I only want to give you my best."

"You're going to be stubborn over this, aren't you?"

"Absolutely. But maybe if you beg me, I'll make some sacrifices for the sake of tormenting you until you understand the mistakes you're attempting to make."

"So, basically, you would be extending your seduction of my person? I am not seeing the problem here. Isn't more for longer better? You can give me linked demonstrations of your enthusiasm for a full experience."

"I suppose it isn't neglectful if I am showcasing the various ways in which lesser men would frustrate you."

"Exactly."

"I haven't even converted you yet, and

you're demonstrating you're quite capable of being a naughty kitty."

"I have, through careful consideration of my situation, determined naughty kitties are rewarded."

"My naughty little kitty is definitely going to be rewarded."

I purred. "That's my cue to finish my steak so we can get onto the evening entertainment."

## SIXTEEN

They believed victory was within their grasp.

When the Devil asked for the bill, the waiter brought back a small dessert box along with the receipt. Curiosity ate away at me, but Lucifer guarded the box with great care, keeping it out of my reach so I couldn't peek. When the limousine picked us up, the box went with the driver, who promised to guard it.

The Devil toyed with me, and something delicious likely lurked within that box, and after having sampled several of the restaurant's desserts, I would do a lot of things to gain access to the treat waiting within.

The Devil didn't have to cheat to lure Gallo and his accomplices to a secondary location. Any other day, I would've viewed being taken to a secluded and dark stretch of woods to be creepy at best and downright terrifying at worst. In a way, I almost felt badly for the quartet of idiots following us.

They believed victory was within their grasp.

"They are waiting for us to be distracted before paying us a visit. They are planning to use their poison on us, as they have the antidote and won't have to worry about me at all within a few hours." The Devil shook his head, wrapped his arm around my waist, and pulled me closer to him. "Should all go as they plan, you'll be poisoned, but it will be addressed quickly."

"Before I get another one of those headaches type of quickly, or I should be bracing for a terrible few hours type of quickly?"

"You will not get another headache from their poison."

I decided if I wouldn't be inconvenienced with a headache, I didn't care if I was poisoned again. Eliminating the main culprit would be sufficient, and if I suffered through some more poisoning, it would be a small price to pay. However, I'd found a very nice silver lining to having been poisoned, one I wanted to experience again. "Can we have a repeat of the part where I got to sit on your lap and use your chest as a pillow without the headache? Being honest, I liked that part."

"My darling, you're going to run out of juice at some point. When you do, I will be pleased to serve as your pillow. Frankly, I have no idea how you're still on your feet and so energetic for that matter. I've been waiting for you to pass out all night long. I was hoping you'd pass out so I could have handled this without worrying how you'd complicate matters, but no. You're stubborn. Well, I have some news for you. You're mine, and they're not going to live long enough to apply what they're about to learn."

Maybe I'd taken over the Devil's hell, but somehow, I'd allowed him to perceive ownership of my person. Worse, I couldn't think of a single reason to refuse him. "You're being possessive again."

"Yes, I am."

"Why?"

Chuckling, the Devil tucked me against his side. "Because I said so."

"That's your justification for most things, isn't it?"

"You will have a wonderful time attempting to curtail my bad behavior, but I will reward you well for your frustrations. And on the days I come into your office, influence you to abandon whatever work you were doing, and take you wherever I feel like, I will say it's because I felt like it, and I will be above reprimand."

I spent a moment wondering where I might get devil repellent, if he had an off switch, if I actually wanted to make use of an off switch, and how I'd cope with my new lot in life, flitting from seduction to seduction with some meaningful work mixed in. "At least you admit you're going to be frustrating."

"You enjoy making your life as orderly as

possible and planning for every contingency. I have minions to handle the contingencies, except they enjoy screwing things up to annoy me. My poor hells are going to be turned upside down once you really get started taking them over and situating everything to your liking. I'm not going to have to declare you to be my queen. You're going to show up, start knocking heads together, and create your own authority. And because I am who I am, I'll enjoy it immensely."

I could see myself doing just that. "What are the idiots thinking?"

"The fucking assholes are annoyed over how affectionate I'm being with you, as my close proximity makes it difficult for them to administer the dose of toxin appropriately. They don't want to kill you outright, and while they don't care if they kill me outright, there's too much of a chance of them lethally dosing you. I'm enjoying vexing them just from holding you close."

"So, basically, we have to separate a little when we want to lure them out?"

"Yes."

That would be easy enough. "I'm ready for my bat now, Lucifer. My personal freedoms have been infringed upon, and I wish to take my temper out on the source of my problems."

"Please just pass out and go to sleep so I can indulge in wholesome violence without worrying about you being caught in the middle."

Was he joking? Why would I miss out on the opportunity to beat the asshole responsible for transforming my brother into a chipmunk? "No. That said, that was a good use of your filthy words. I will think about rewarding you with a spot for using it appropriately."

"What does it say about me that I'm falling prey to your system of behavioral adjustment?"

"I have what you want, and you have learned you can easily get what you want with minor behavioral adjustments. You win a spot, I win not being annoyed by your lack of manners."

"I don't have to always display these wretched manners, do I?"

"Of course not. I do not expect you to use decent manners with those fucking assholes stalking us. Do any of them get off easy?"

"What do you mean?"

"Are they all as bad as Gallo?"

The Devil frowned. "The one, perhaps, is not completely unsalvageable. He is in a situation similar to what your brother faced prior to his stint as an obnoxious rodent, although he finds you disturbingly attractive. I resent that. I'm the only one allowed to find you to be attractive."

"You absolutely are not the only one allowed."

"I am absolutely the only one allowed."

"No, you're not."

"Why the hell not?"

"I like when people think I'm pretty rather than diseased."

"You're not diseased," he growled.

"Tell that to the rest of society. The CDC is still not really clear on how I can shapeshift without having a nasty disease."

"Lycanthropy is hardly a nasty disease. Obviously, I am going to have to work on this. I'll have to let some of my randy incubi loose for a while, spread some love, debunk the prejudice against lycanthropes, and make life a little more pleasant for shapeshifters, so you, my future wife, can enjoy your visits to your mortal home. I will repeat myself so I'm clear: lycanthropy is hardly a nasty disease."

"To most it is."

"They're wrong," the Devil declared. "Idiocy is a far nastier disease, and it seems modern mortals are plagued with it."

"I don't see why you're getting all offended over this. I just like when people think I'm pretty rather than diseased."

"You're not pretty. You're beautiful. And all of those beautiful spots are mine."

I needed to have a long talk with the Devil's brothers about his tendencies, inquire about if he needed therapy, and what my role in the Devil's therapy might be. "Can I have a baseball bat, please? I would very much like to beat these assholes with it. Please separate the one I'm not allowed to beat."

"That will inevitably result in you being poisoned again, and I really would rather you not be poisoned again."

"Protective tendencies are rewarded, overprotective tendencies are not rewarded. You are venturing into overprotective tendencies territory."

"Protecting you from a nasty case of poisoning is hardly being overprotective."

"You already said I'd be poisoned anyway. I'm fine with this. I want a bat, Lucifer, not excuses."

"If I provide a bat, will you marry me?"

I narrowed my eyes at the proposal, weighed the traditional on bent knee with a ring versus no bent knee, a baseball bat, and carnage, and I found the ring to be rather overrated, although I'd figure out how to get the bastard on his knees at a later time. "Very well. If you provide a baseball bat, I will consent to your general proposal, but I'll get you on your knees one way or another, even if I have to break your legs with my new bat to make it happen. Make it a good bat, and should I break my new bat on one of their skulls, you'll have to fix it. It'll also need space in my trophy room when I'm finished with it, but it must be accessible so I can use it again if needed."

"I will have a stand installed for your new bat by your desk so it is easily reached,

should you need it." The Devil held out his
hand, and bat fashioned of a pale wood mate-
rialized and hung in the air until he took hold
of it. "As I have conjured a bat for you, you
are now secured as my future wife. I will be
very upset with you should you get even a
single bruise in this venture, so walk lightly
and hit hard."

I took the bat, and the wood's weight startled me, although I somehow kept my hold on
it. The heft would go a long way to making
sure I inflicted lethal damage. "What kind of
wood is this?"

"The kind that won't break when you
smash it against that fucking asshole's head.
After taking a few moments to consider the
situation, I'm rather turned on by your approach to handling this situation. That, plus
you've given your word you'll marry me in
exchange for that bat. Also, that is what we
consider to be a bargain, Mrs. Lucifer."

"I haven't married you yet."

"Ah, but you bargained with me for that
bat. Now you have to marry me. It's a done
deal. I just caught you at the ideal moment.
But, as a consolation for you having been
tricked into bargaining with me, later
tonight, I will give you the contents of the
box you were drooling over when the waiter
brought my receipt."

I licked my lips. "That was a carry out box,
the kind they usually use for desserts. And
the desserts were delicious. That box must

contain good things. There wasn't anything bad there. I liked everything."

The Devil chuckled. "You can enjoy the contents of the box for having been cruelly deceived into marrying me. But should you suffer a single bruise, I will be forced to punish you."

As I'd already come to the conclusion the Devil's idea of punishment involved extending my enjoyment of his bed and attention, I debated if I wanted to get a bruise to enjoy being punished or if I would be better rewarded for emerging unscathed.

"This shouldn't be difficult, my darling."

I shrugged. "It's your fault. You talk about punishing me, and the only thing I can think of as a punishment just means I get to enjoy more of you, and well, I have zero evidence you'd actually *punish* me, because you'll make me like it. I'm not sure if I'm rewarded better for being bruised or emerging unscathed. This is a real problem."

The Devil's brows furrowed, and after a moment, he also shrugged. "You're right. That was really an unfair choice to give you. Your punishment, should you become bruised, will involve being taken to bed, tucked in, and I will restrain myself from enjoying your person for at least a few days as a reminder of why you should take care and avoid becoming bruised. How long does it take for you to heal a bruise? Obviously, I'll have to withhold any strenuous activities until your bruise heals."

I stared at him with wide eyes. "That's not a punishment. That's just cruel."

"Well, I am the Devil. I have an entire arsenal of cruel and unusual ways to punish people. And, of course, because I am who I am, I will very much enjoy your general frustrations, knowing I am the object of your desire. Absolutely delicious. I'll be examining you closely for bruises, so do be careful. It would be absolutely a shame if I needed to pamper you until you heal. I might even have to do so while forgetting to put my shirt on."

His commentary didn't help me come to a decision about whether I wanted to be rewarded or punished. I firmed my grip on my bat, whirled out of his hold, and marched in the direction of my unknowing prey, as I needed to unload a great deal of hurt in as little time as possible so I could get to the reward or punishment stage of my day.

What could I say? I was a simple woman with simple needs.

I CAUGHT the quartet by surprise, and I went for the general source of my frustration with a hiss, my tail fluffed and my ears turned back. As dead men couldn't bruise me, I went for Gallo like I meant it, wound up like my daddy had taught me as a little girl, and treated his head like a ball. To my disappointment, I lacked the physical strength required to knock his asshole head clear off, but he dropped like a rock, sprayed a satisfying amount of blood, and twitched and convulsed on the ground.

One down, two to go, and the jury was still out on the last one of the lot.

One of Gallo's buddies threw a glass vial in my face, which broke on my hard head and covered me with white powder.

"And that would be the poison," the Devil announced, striding up without a care in the world.

What an asshole, but he was a very handsome asshole, and I would view him as my reward for doing a good deed in a rather evil way. "Thank you, but I had that figured out on my own." As I interpreted poison to the face as a damned good excuse to continue my murder spree, I held my bat in my right hand, flexed my left hand, and transformed enough to give myself a nice set of sharp claws, perfect for tearing apart idiots who thought they could interfere with *my* family.

I made it half a step before the Devil caught me around the waist, picked me up, and pinned me against him. I howled my fury over his intervention, and as I couldn't reach the fuckers to beat the life out of them, I kicked my shoes off in their general direction, missing with both of them. When that failed to rid the poor Earth of their filth, I flung my bat, which they also dodged.

"You have a piece of glass sticking out of your head, my darling. And while I do quite love unicorns, I do not wish for my wife to imitate them using broken glass. I'm afraid this goes beyond mere bruising."

"If it doesn't bruise it doesn't count."

"It will bruise spectacularly. You have the broken ruins of a glass vial sticking out of your forehead. You're also doused in poison."

"Look, we already talked about this. They were going to kill my brother."

"Yes, yes, my darling, they were. Your brother is fine. You're not fine. You're imitating a unicorn when you should not be imitating a unicorn."

"Why are you stopping me from murdering them? You're being an asshole. Let me down so I can finish what I started."

"Darlene," the Devil chided.

"You're the fucking Devil. Why are you stopping me? You like when people sin. Let me go add some corpses to my rap sheet so I can earn my place in hell, damn it!"

The mafia thugs, who wore more than a little of their boss's blood, gaped at us.

"Darlene, you have a piece of glass sticking out of your forehead. Your playdate with death has been postponed on account of your decision to pretend you're a unicorn."

"It's not like I did it on purpose. It doesn't

hurt. Let me at them. You gave me that bat, and I want to use it."

The Devil sighed. "Excuse me, gentlemen. My wife is a little upset your former friend thought he could hurt a part of her family, and she becomes quite unreasonable when it comes to her family."

"I haven't married you yet, you kill-stealing asshole."

"But you will. Settle down so I can remove your horn."

"Just leave the fucking thing there so I can get to beating them to death. You like unicorns. You should be happy I'm honoring their spirit through the accidental growth of a horn." Struggling did me no good, and I grunted at the strength of his hold on me.

"No. You'll injure yourself further."

Why the hell was the Devil trying to stop me? I hissed and snarled, but I couldn't wiggle out of his damned hold on me. "Why are you being like this?"

"I thought it was obvious. You've hurt yourself, and if I allow you to continue your rampage, you'll hurt yourself further. As I've come to the conclusion I do quite love you, this means I have to stop your rampage before you do something I regret, which does include hurting yourself further. If these gentlemen are wise, they will reconsider their life choices, sit down, and wait for you to calm down so you can issue a more appropriate punishment for their misdeeds."

Two decided to run, and the youngest of the lot sat down, crossed his legs, and waited patiently.

Shifting his hold on me to free a hand, the Devil snapped his fingers. Two devils, not even bothering to take on a human form, popped into being in a dark cloud of smoke, which stank of brimstone and molten metal. While I recognized Belial, his grotesque form reminded me of a tomato crushed under foot with hooked tentacles and sharp protrusions glistening under an eerie yellow glow emanating from his quivering flesh.

Crushed tomatoes with hooked tentacles and spikes would be a lot less horrifying without Belial's face added to the mix.

The other devil vaguely resembled a six-legged dog with burning flesh and spines for fur, and to my relief, it lacked a humanoid face.

Whatever. I'd deal with Belial's form another time, preferably after consuming a great deal of alcohol. "You're the one with the head injury, Lucifer."

"Why do you say that?"

"You claim you love me, but you won't let me kill them," I complained. "Wouldn't love be letting me kill them?"

"No. Now stop squirming so I can remove that damned glass shard out of your head without adding to your injuries."

As there were two devils stalking *my* prey, and even I couldn't justify killing someone who'd sat down and shut up when given an option to save his skin, I limited my protests to bitter cursing, minimal wiggling, and kicking my feet.

It wasn't as if the Devil, who had a fucking steel beam for an arm, was going to let me loose until he felt like it. He reached for my face, and I barely felt him pluck the shard out of my forehead.

When I looked at it, the rounded end of the vial could be mistaken for a very odd horn. Blood dripped from the broken end, which had held the stopper once upon a time. "How did that even happen?"

"Good question." The Devil lowered me to the ground, and I regretted having kicked my shoes off. As though aware I might join the fray, he kept a firm hold on me. "Remember, the one that sat down is in a similar situation to your brother's, and you could possibly re-form him with sufficient training. Of course, I wouldn't release him into society without some education, but he's not unsalvageable."

"Why are you wanting me to salvage him?" I stretched my leg, doing my best to reach my bat with my toes. The Devil picked me up, moved me safely out of reach of any-thing I might use as a weapon, and set me down. "Will you stop that? I could have reached that if not for you."

"You would regret beating him later."

"Are you sure?"

"I'm positive."

"Are you really, really sure?"

"My darling, you're more bloodthirsty than most of my devils. You need a nap. Just take a nap already so I can attend to your forehead, tuck you in, and evaluate how long you get to be punished for daring to be injured."

"It's not my fault Gallo's asshole friend threw glass at my face. I should be rewarded for taking him out in one hit. I let the fucker off lightly."

"You really did," said the man who'd been smart enough to sit his ass down. "I'm sorry. I owe him money, and he threatened to go after my little sister." He regarded the body of the deceased loan shark. "Owed him money. Do I still owe money to a corpse?"

As Gallo had no morals or scruples, I was unsurprised. "Let me beat the fucker again."

"He's already dead, and he'll be awaiting for your attention in the darkest pit of my many hells, so you'll have plenty of time to learn your art on him."

I narrowed my eyes. "Promise?"

"Of course. I'm still not letting you go, though. You, my darling, are truly cranky. Should I let you go right now, you might destroy the world, and the End of Days is not scheduled for this moment."

For a spiky, crushed tomato with a tentacle problem, Belial could pounce with the best of them, and he landed on his victim, who screamed. The man's cries didn't last long, and to my dismay, Belial came rolling over with one of my mother's vases held in a tentacle.

Inside, a bright purple, blue, green, and yellow fish flopped and splashed in barely enough water to cover it. "Oh, he's pretty."

"He's a Mandarin dragonet, just as promised" Belial announced, and he presented me with my prize.

When given a choice between admiring my new fish and indulging in violence, admiring my new pet became my top priority. "Oh, he's really pretty, but he's not as pretty as Ruby."

"Is any fish prettier than Ruby?" the Devil asked in an amused tone.

"Well, no. But he's pretty enough. He will not bring shame to my trophy room."

The dog bounded over, and he had one of my mother's vases in his mouth, and a tiny red and orange lion fish bounced and thumped in the jar, most of its water spilled out. I took it, and suspecting my second fish would die if I didn't get it into some water, I held the lion fish out to the Devil. "I don't think that's enough water."

Lucifer snapped his fingers, and water splashed into both vases. I grunted, clutching the glass to my chest so I wouldn't drop them. "There. Maybe that will keep you amused. Belial, please inquire with Michael or Gabriel regarding my wife's attempt to transform herself into a unicorn. While she put in a valiant effort, they are more accustomed to checking on a human's health, and she seems to have taken temporary leave of her senses. I *thought* feeding her would contain the beast, but it turns out feeding her has created a rather amusing monster oblivious to pain. Frankly, she's a menace, and I find this to be delightful."

The crushed tomato with spikes and tentacles vanished, as did his hellish canine companion.

"You're the Devil, aren't you?" the seated mafia member asked, and he paled to a rather sickly grayish tone.

"What gave me away? Was it my good looks?"

The man pointed at the Devil's head, and I regarded Lucifer with interest. When I hadn't been paying attention, he'd sprouted curved horns and had sheathed his head in fire. The horns amused me, as they peeked out of his hair, long enough to be seen while maintaining a hint of mystery. I scowled, as holding my new fish prevented me from being able to get my hands on him and discover if the flames had any heat. "You're pretty," I informed him. "I don't want to compete with a bunch of succubi to have you. They're prettier than I am."

"You're absolutely prettier than they are, and they also lack your spots and your determination to ruthlessly use your spots against me. And anyway, I already declared you're my wife, so you don't have to worry about any competition. Of course, I might look from time to time, but only because I want you to punish me."

I could think of a lot of ways I could enjoy punishing the Devil. "You haven't married me yet."

"Ah, but you bargained with me for a bat, which I gave you. You're now as good as married to me."

"That wasn't really all that bright, lady," the sole survivor of the quartet of mafia thugs announced.

As he was right, I sighed and nodded my head. Blood dripped down my face, and I frowned, unable to deal with it while my hands were full of fish. "What are we supposed to do with him?"

The Devil laughed and kissed my cheek. "As you're determined to earn your proper place in hell, kidnap him for a time, train him on how to be a proper minion of yours, and release him back into the wilds when you have given him an assignment. This one is more useful to you alive, and while he is misguided, he has not strayed too far. He's redeemable, and he has family."

"You're lucky the Devil likes you," I informed the survivor. "Fetch my bat and my shoes, and you're lucky I can't stand the thought of having anyone work for me without pay, so you'll even get a decent salary, even if I have to mug the Devil to make it happen."

"I'm not paid," the Devil complained.

"Yes, you are."

"I am? I haven't received a paycheck."

"You're paid in access to my spots, so be quiet before you take a pay deduction for poor behavior."

The Devil clacked his teeth together in his hurry to shut up or lose access to my spots.

I rolled my eyes. "Just take us to my office so I can put my new fish in their tanks and take care of my stupid head. I'd rather not bleed to death today."

The Devil sighed. "That implies you're willing to bleed to death another day. I'd really rather you not bleed to death at all."

As I couldn't argue with him, I shrugged. "You're right. What's next?"

"I'm going to take you home, tend to your forehead, and tuck you into bed. I'll then make certain your new pets are settled and pay our latest resident a visit to give him a taste of his future. It will be a most bitter brew. I'd say you can watch, but some things a man has to attend to on his own, and I am very displeased over what he had planned for my wife."

"I had no idea you were married," my new minion admitted.

"He hasn't married me yet, I just foolishly signed away my marital status to the Devil for a bat and a body." I regarded the body with a frown. "I hadn't planned on how to dispose of the body."

"You don't dispose of it. His victims deserve closure, and his body will provide that. The only person to witness your rather brutal and effective act is now on your team if he knows what's good for him."

"He deserved it. That said, you may want to deal with that powder he threw at you. It'll make you very sick. He has the antidote in his pocket."

"Oh, no," the Devil replied with a wicked smile. "I'm leaving the antidote for the police to find. It does more good where it's at. Darlene, I'll handle your care personally, and it wouldn't do if I robbed you of being able to nestle your pretty head against my chest."

I purred. "It really wouldn't do at all. Chop, chop, Lucifer. I don't have all day."

## SEVENTEEN

You just want to steal your brother's
thunder.

I COULD FEEL Gabriel's regard the instant we appeared in the Devil's bedroom. "You are a menace to yourself, Darlene."

As I couldn't argue with him, I nodded. "I'm poisoned, and my audition to become a unicorn flunked. Now I have a headache, but I think it's from my failed audition to be a unicorn rather than the poison."

With the archangel to keep me company, the Devil teleported out of the bedroom and took my pet fish and my new minion with him.

"Yes, I see your head is bleeding rather severely. Why did you audition to become a unicorn, and what did you use for this audition?"

"It was a glass vial that held the poison, and one of Gallo's asshole buddies threw it at my face. His aim? Honestly, it was pretty good. Belial got ahold of Gallo's asshole buddy, and some dog devil got the other one.

I got Gallo, though. I just about knocked his head clean off with a bat. Unfortunately, I seem to have bargained away my marital status because I'm stupid and really wanted that bat. Apparently, I have received the gift of a minion, however, because I can't just kill some guy who decided to do as told unlike his buddies." I pointed at the pale wood bat, which the Devil had cleaned when teleporting it to his bedroom. Our bedroom. "That bat is trouble, and the Devil made me do it."

The archangel took hold of my chin in one hand, lifted my head, and touched my forehead with the other. His chuckle relaxed me. "My brother is quite good at tricking mortals. He has no shame, and he was quite motivated to get you to bargain with him. Of course, from what I can tell, he truly was not expecting you to remain awake and feisty for so long, so he is worrying himself more than necessary."

A soothing warmth spread across my face. I sighed and closed my eyes. "That feels good."

"I have limited your ability to feel pain for a while, as the blend of poison and trauma would leave you with a rather severe headache quite soon. Lucifer could have handled this himself, but he is less practiced than I am, and his power tends to come bundled with a price of pain. He does not wish for you to endure any more discomfort than necessary. I am also better at eradicating irritating toxins from mortals. I feel my brother has begun addressing the issue of your mortality, but for some reason I cannot fathom, he has not finished the process. I do not wish to peek, for my brother often thinks lewd thoughts, and I would need to purify my soul."

I laughed at the idea of an archangel trying to detox himself from his brother's perversions. "I have noticed he is a fan of being naughty. He likes unicorns a little too much, and he feels a need to compete with his creations. I'm not going to fall over dead, am I?"

"You will not fall over dead. The injury from your unconventional horn will cause you some pain for a few days, but it is no big matter. There was minimal damage done to your skull, and the conversion process will help you heal. There are benefits to a gradual conversion, although you will find life a little easier when you are the queen over all other succubi and they do not feel they can challenge you. The groundwork has been laid already."

"You just want to steal your brother's thunder." I wouldn't begrudge the archangel's rivalry with the Devil.

The Devil had a disturbing tendency to make such things enjoyable.

"I absolutely do wish to steal my brother's thunder. He will mind his own business for years while making sure you have full control over your new powers. Physically, you are heavily fatigued and require rest. Completing the conversion process is simple. Truthfully, he's done most of the work, so he can claim full credit for your conversion. I would just be giving you a nudge so your body finalizes the changes to your genetics, which would take place over the next two or three days if I do not give additional nudges. I suspect my brother intends for you to rest for the next few days anyway, so he won't notice if you finish the process on your own. It's also why you're so easily provoked right now. You have quite a lot of devilish energy coursing through you. My brother can be quite determined and enthusiastic when he wishes to be."

No kidding. "Anything I should know about that?"

"When your conversion is over, you will be very interested in my brother, and you will become rather violent towards men who are not my brother. Your brother will mostly be safe from you, as in you'll permit him in your space, but you would be wise to entertain my brother for a few days before you interact with other men. That is a little gift from *Him*, so your new nature does not create problems you do not want. It does not hurt you are naturally inclined towards monogamy, much like my brother." Gabriel tilted my head to the side, and I wondered what he stared at and why—and how beings without heads looked at anything at all.

"So, you're saying I'll get to lounge around and rest in bed for a few days, after which I'll lounge around in bed but I won't be resting for a few more days after that?"

"Precisely."

"Can we just get this show on the road? I don't need to undergo any form of conversion to have a healthy interest in this plan, Gabriel."

"I am aware. You fell for my brother's wicked ways the moment you saw him. It took him but a few moments longer, upon realization you had stormed his home, for him to become unreasonable about his interest in you. There. I have done my part. The rest is in your hands. Try not to tire my brother out too much when you grow into your wings. Do make him take you flying, too —and make sure he teaches you how to land rather than insist on foolishness, including catching you instead merely so he can carry you around, as he enjoys doing that." Gabriel took a step away from me and waved his hand, which removed evidence I'd dripped blood everywhere.

I touched my face to discover if I wanted to rid myself of caking blood and poison residue, I'd have to go take a bath. "You would think the Devil would be far more of a cold-hearted creature," I admitted. "But he's warm."

"You have forced him to show you his best, and you have made him love every moment of it. As I do enjoy spying on my brother, and he is very focused on you rather than on me, he is currently in your trophy room explaining to your new minion his role in your life, which is as a bodyguard, mortal minion, and so on. I expect that one will undergo a conversion the instant *He* has need or want of a new angel. That one is more of a victim of circumstance rather than malicious, although you will find him suitable for some of your future schemes. I recommend you assign him as a hidden custodian and guardian."

"For Kanika?"

"Yes. There will be times my brother might wish to have information on her due to a bargain he has struck. Using your latest acquisition to track her activities, especially as she grows older, would be beneficial. You can also ensure she has work when she needs it through him or another one of your minions. It will keep your temper appeased if you are able to help from the background."

It amused me the archangel had decided to go with the term minion as well. "You're quite the meddler, aren't you?"

"I have my moments. Kanika will find me and my brothers to be most annoying. She will not be sure what to think about you at first, but you will find her to be most affectionate once she comes to the conclusion you are the sole bastion of sanity in my brother's many hells. Her rivalry with Lucifer will be a thing of beauty."

After having done a stint as a glass-vial unicorn, I hardly considered myself to be sane. "What is the bat made out of? Lucifer wouldn't tell me."

"It is made from the heartwood of the Tree of Life," the archangel replied. "He picked only the best for you. *He* also has some of the heartwood from that tree, although *He* waits to make use of it. *He* finds my brother's choice of wood most amusing. Your bat is a most potent weapon, and *He* finds it appropriate to be in your hands."

"Oh. Where are my kittens?" I checked the sitting room and the bedroom before peeking under the bed in search of my kittens. "They're usually in here, on our pillows."

"Do not fret. They are playing out in the lava fields, hunting demons and devils who have taken on the shape of mice. They learn how to be your protectors, and the demons and devils seek my brother's favor while enjoying the game. Really, it is disgustingly cordial here as of late. And do not worry. Mere lava will not hurt them."

"Except for that herd of succubi wanting my man," I corrected. "That won't be very cordial if they keep it up!"

"Conversion will resolve that problem, and you can carry around your bat to persuade them against making any moves on Lucifer. And anyway, you have bargained to marry him, so you will be wed—and my brother? He is not a patient being on this subject. He will not accept anything but your union with him at the earliest opportunity. Should you have those you wish to be in attendance, you should write it down and leave it where my brother can find it. Be aware he will likely kidnap anyone on the list, as he will not tolerate anything interfering with your happiness."

"If I put you and Michael on the list, will he kidnap you?"

"He would absolutely try, but we would consent to his kidnapping, so it would not be a kidnapping, for we would consent to attend."

I wandered to the desk in the sitting room and rummaged through it until I found a piece of paper and pen, and with the inclusion of the two archangels, my list of names went up to three. "I still haven't named my kittens."

"I am sure you'll find good names for them both, but if you wish to annoy my brother, you would name them after him—with their names misspelled. He hates that, and your feuding over their names would last until the end of days."

I laughed at the thought of someone spelling the Devil's name wrong. "That's so amusing."

"I thought you would appreciate that. Do not feel you need to name them immediately.

They know you cherish them even when you take your time, and they will appreciate the games you play with your future husband. Go clean up, as the sight of you ~~wearing~~ so much blood will ultimately distress my brother. I will go make certain he contains most of his impulses in the meantime. Rest well, Darlene."

I fully intended to.

TRUE TO GABRIEL'S WORD, I hibernated for several days before I woke up refreshed and in dire need of attention from the Devil. My brother made the mistake of trying to delay me from my mission, and rather than twist him into a pretzel, I set my kittens loose on him. To all appearances, a newly converted incubus should have had the advantage over two fluffy bundles of joy, but following a single pounce from my pets, my brother fled.

That left me with another problem: Belial. I lashed my tail and hissed at the devil, who regarded me with interest. When hissing didn't drive him off, I graduated to trans-forming my hands so I had nice, sharp claws to work with.

Belial only looked human, and if he couldn't handle being clawed up by a cat, he wasn't worthy of the Devil's regard.

"You woke up in a mood," Belial observed. "You also woke up quite hungry, I see."

"Where is he?"

"Lucifer is doing his best to convince some stubborn succubi he is unavailable for their enjoyment. You should put your wings, fur, and spots on so you can help him convince them you are the queen of his roost. He is in the great hall, and he has been sulking because you have been in poor health. There have been too many archangels in this place, all confirming you were merely tired and recovering. You woke once, but you limited your coherency to coming in here, crawling onto Lucifer's lap, and resuming your sleep. That tamed him, as he took that to mean you were recovering as promised, so he has ventured out of these rooms today. He will be pleased when you focus your attention on him."

"Well, if he'd been in bed where he belonged, I wouldn't have had to crawl onto his lap."

"You are most correct. Your brother and I were assigned to stand guard, as I have zero interest in you as a partner of that nature, nor do I wish for my soul to be ruined irrevocably. That is what Lucifer will do to any who cross him on this matter. Your brother was selected to stand guard, as you would not kill him without provocation."

I couldn't remember where the great hall was or if I'd seen it yet. "I don't know how to put on my wings. I have wings?"

"You're matured enough to be able to

manifest your wings," Belial confirmed. "Shapeshift as you would to become your furry yet human self, but focus on your desire. Your wings are tied with your need to hunt sexual energy. Lucifer will satisfy you, but displaying your wings will be a sign you hunger and hunt. Calm succubi hide their wings, and should they hunger too much, their wings will manifest. When you are well fed, you will be able to manifest them at your will, but a hungry succubus showing her wings is not to be trifled with."

"And that herd after him? They showed their wings," I growled.

"They are all fed well, so they are posturing and wish to remind those around them they are desirable. I have taken the liberty of bringing clothes suitable for your wings, and Lucifer has paid no attention to it, as most attire meant to accommodate tails also accommodates wings."

"He is easily tricked, I see."

"At times." Belial stood, entered the bedroom, and opened the closet door, pulling out a red, slinky dress. "I recommend this dress. It is one of Lucifer's favorites, and he is eager to see you in it, although he is unclear why you would want a dress capable of accommodating wings when his campaign to finish converting you is delayed temporarily. The archangels are quite smug about it. They hope Lucifer will learn to peek more and enjoy being surprised a little less."

"Don't ask for miracles. That way, you will not be disappointed."

Belial's laughter had a wicked, dark edge to it. "How right you are. Make yourself pretty, put on your wings, fur, and spots, and I will guide you to the great hall."

I retreated to the bathroom, closed the door, and stripped out of the silky pajamas the Devil had likely acquired for me. I'd have to thank him for that, as I enjoyed the feel of silk on my skin. Following Belial's instructions, I discovered I did have wings, and unlike the other succubi I'd seen, they were feathered. Conversion had done wonders for my coat, which came in thick and plush, and my new wings offered the Devil hundreds upon hundreds of new spots for him to become acquainted with.

Sliding into the dress took some work, especially when learning how to cope with wings, which were larger than I expected, ridiculously fluffy, and had a tendency to bang into everything.

After I caught the Devil, lured him into our bedroom, and had my way with him, I'd demand lessons on how to control my wings. When I no longer threatened to knock everything off the walls and nearby surfaces, I'd badger him into teaching me how to fly.

Satisfied with my plan for the rest of my week, I hunted for my collar, which was no longer on the dresser where it typically lived when I wasn't wearing it. "Belial? Where's my collar?"

"Lucifer is feeling needy, so he is carrying it around since he can't just drag you all over the residence without waking you."

What a cretin, stealing my collar after I'd stolen it from him. I emerged from the bathroom, checked the closet, and debated the problem of shoes. While I'd been sleeping, someone had converted the Devil's closet to have space for things meant for me, and a ridiculous number of sandals, heels, and leather boots waited for my use.

Belial joined me, and he selected a pair of black boots with a two inch stiletto heel. "These would do an admirable job of drawing Lucifer's attention. He is quite eager to see you wear these."

I bet. I took the boots, sat on the edge of the bed, and pulled them on and lost a ridiculous amount of time lacing them up. "He's going to have to reward me spectacularly every time I wear these."

"I am sure he'll attend to your every need." Belial gestured towards the door. "If you are ready?"

I nodded, and on my way, I snagged my baseball bat, laughing over the new addition of a pretty white bow tied around the handle. "The bow is a nice touch."

"That is Michael's contribution, as he feels you deserve a bow on your present. Gabriel magicked the bow so it will never become dirty, so you can keep it for however long you like."

"I love it. It adds such a feminine touch to my new weapon." To my delight, the bow was made of satin. "I'll have to thank them."

"As Lucifer has 'invited' them to stay for the next two or so weeks, you can thank them in the great hall. *He* even paid a short visit to make sure his archangels and his fallen son would not cause too much trouble. That startled most of the residents, as *He* does not visit often. Your kittens did an excellent job of containing Lucifer, as they took over his lap and slept, thus invoking the new sacred rule of the household."

"Don't disturb the sleeping kittens?" I guessed.

"You are most correct. You are the most prized of the sleeping kittens, but your kittens come a close second. It amuses me that two young felines prevented a premature End of Days."

"Well, Lucifer has a reputation, and he likes to argue with his father. Even I have figured that out."

"I wouldn't say he likes it. It is simply his nature."

"Well, there's nothing wrong with him as he is." I tested the boots to make certain I wouldn't fall on my ass and humiliate myself, purring my satisfaction over their comfort and fit. "Everything else has been okay?"

"For the most part. The succubi are

testing Lucifer's patience, so if you could establish your territory, we would all be appreciative."

"I'm just going to threaten to beat them to death if they don't get their hands off my man and keep them off, I hope you are aware of this."

"I believe Lucifer is hopeful for this sort of demonstration, as he finds your more violent tendencies to be quite attractive."

"Lucifer is demented."

"Well, he is who he is."

"All right. I'm ready." I debated how best to carry my bat, and over my shoulder and ready to make good use of it appealed the most. Had I been a little wiser, I would have located leathers rather than a dress to fully establish I didn't need to look pretty to kick ass, take names, and defend my turf.

With a startling pop, Gabriel and Michael manifested in the doorway. I smacked Belial with a wing, yelped at the unexpected pain, and sighed over my newfound clumsiness. "How do you handle these damned things?"

"Carefully," Gabriel replied. "Tucking them close to your back will help keep them out of the way, although it will take some practice. Your wings are lovely, and my brother will appreciate so many new spots for him to enjoy. How are you feeling?"

"I am feeling like I have to beat a bunch of bitches for going near my man, and I need my man to come to bed where he belongs."

Gabriel circled me, and he stroked his hands over my wings. "Excellent. Your wings have developed well."

"They're not leathery like the other succubi."

"Your wings are a reflection of your nature. Consider your spots to be evidence you are a naughty little angel."

I twisted around to regard my wings, which needed to be classified as furry, feathered weapons. "According to the density of my spots on my feathers, I'm a particularly naughty little angel who will enjoy beating the other succubi if they don't leave Lucifer alone."

"You will not need to beat the other succubi. You just need to show up, lure Lucifer off to your lair with a single come hither, and they will understand they have been outclassed. Your property is quite safe, and he has been defending himself from their advances without issue."

I huffed at the thought of him needing to defend himself from any advances other than mine.

"She woke up quite hungry and more than a little grouchy," Belial stated.

"She will be a little less aggressive after Lucifer properly attends to her, I am sure."

Michael chuckled and he held out his arm to me. "As I do enjoy vexing my brother, it would be my honor to escort you."

Turnabout was fair play, and if Lucifer

couldn't get his succubi to keep their hands off him, I'd accept his brother's courtesy with a smirk. "Thank you, Michael."

"She's totally using you to annoy Lucifer," Belial muttered.

"I know. It is so amusing. Lucifer will be delighted, for she is feeling well enough to shoot back over his failure to be present when she woke up in dire need of attention. This is for the better anyway, as us delivering her to our brother will send messages to the demons and devils in attendance. Right now is not an ideal time for us to be bickering, and it is better for us to be more allies than foes for the moment."

Belial stilled. "Mortal or divine?"

"A bit of this, a bit of that," the archangel replied.

I grinned. "That is masterfully vague and somewhat terrifying. Please take me to Lucifer, as I'll inevitably get lost in this maze if I try to find him myself."

Both archangels laughed, and Belial led the way. Michael and Gabriel offered tips on feather care, adjusting to hauling around big, heavy wings, and how to annoy most succubi, who often wished they could manifest feathered wings but couldn't unless they hunted a male boasting feathered wings.

"Ha! Succubi are attracted to angels because they can have feathers for a while, then?"

Gabriel snorted and Michael shrugged.

"It's a solid theory," Belial replied in an amused tone. "I can't think of another reason why a succubus or incubus would otherwise desire an angel of all things."

"It is complicated," Michael stated, and according to his tone, he had no intention of explaining it to me.

Whatever. My fallen angel had everything I needed and wanted. "Maybe if you had nipples, you wouldn't need an incubus or a succubus to get naughty."

While Belial snickered, I suspected I tested the patience of both archangels.

"What? It's true. Have you looked at Lucifer's nipples?"

A faint pop behind me warned me I'd drawn attention from someone capable of teleporting, and I managed to smack both archangels with my wings.

The Devil snickered, and he took hold of my wings to hold me in place. A few tugs and a push later, and Lucifer managed to settle my wings closer to my back so I wouldn't murder his brothers with them. "Look at all of those pretty spots, all for me. However, I can't help but notice two filthy archangels put their hands on you."

"Hardly. They have no nipples, Lucifer. We've talked about this before. I need perfect nipples. You have perfect nipples, and they do not. They're just keeping me from killing anyone with these wings, and I have no idea

where the great hall is, where you're supposed to be."

"I went to check on you to find my bed
devoid of my woman."

"I got dressed, put on some boots, and
grabbed my bat, and now I need to teach
some succubi you're mine."

"She woke up rather irritable and possessive," Belial announced. "Once she has
claimed her territory, she will be much easier
to please. I would not deter her from laying
her claim. That is how you end up unhappy
and on your couch."

"I noticed you've brought your bat with
you. I would rather not have to plant new
succubi seeds today, so please keep all
demonstrations and claims non-lethal."

"Fine. I won't kill anyone unless they pro-
voke me. If I hit a table with the bat, would
the bat or the table win?"

"The bat," Lucifer, Gabriel, and Michael
chorused.

"I need a table I can sacrifice on the altar
of territory claiming."

"I needed a new head table anyway. You
can help me pick the new one as penance for
breaking the old one." Lucifer scowled at
Michael. "Just break the table I'm sitting at
when you arrive. I will find this very entertaining. However, I do not find my brother's
handling of your person to be entertaining at
all."

The archangel laughed and refused to budge or let go of my arm.

"Just go back to the great hall, Lucifer. I'll be along as soon as these louts show me how to get there."

"Is there a reason you can't teleport her?" Lucifer asked. "It's a rather lengthy walk."

"Yes," Michael replied. "It involves her consuming too much energy before you've had time to properly teach her to feed. We would be pleased to help you with teaching her how to teleport, but you have work to do before she is ready. She's also eager to try her wings for flying, although she may be a challenge to teach on that front."

"Very well. I'll be waiting in the great hall. Don't tarry. I want to see their expressions when they see her beautiful wings. Feathered for my enjoyment. With spots."

Lucifer vanished.

I rolled my eyes. "He possibly needs therapy for his spot obsession. No, he definitely needs therapy for his spot obsession. Can one of you teach me how to ban all these spots when he's being naughty?"

Gabriel snickered and said, "As a matter of fact, yes."

The little things in life helped. "Excellent."

THE GREAT HALL lived up to its name, and I stopped counting tables after ten, flattened my ears at the presence of at least a hundred succubi, and considered making good use of my bat at the sight of hundreds of devils and demons filling the space and annoying me with hissing chatter. On the far end of the room, its ceiling vaulted and painted much like his entry, waited Lucifer at a table barely big enough for two, which he'd claimed all for himself.

Hell. No.

I firmed my grip on the bat, joined the devilish congregation in hissing, and marched towards the Devil, ready to make it clear he'd be adding a table suitable for two to use comfortably or I'd be beating him to a near-death state with it. I regretted agreeing to keep my confrontations non-lethal.

The sight of so many succubi dressed to seduce pissed me off enough I considered beating them with my wings like a demented, spotted Canadian goose on a mission of murder.

Why wasn't I allowed to kill them all?

To my utter disgust, the succubi backed out of my reach.

With a ringing laugh, Michael patted my arm before releasing me. "When you swing your bat, spread your wings out to their full length. It will help you balance and keep you from falling."

I nodded, and without the archangel holding me back, I marched at a rather brisk pace, got a good hold on my bat with both hands, and went to town on the offensive table I wouldn't fit at even if I wanted to. True to the archangel's claim, spreading my wings did help me keep my balance. The bat cracked into the table with hand-numbing force, and the dark wood cracked under the force of my blow. Snarling curses I hadn't completely destroyed it in one hit, I smacked it a second time, which cracked the table in half.

Lucifer raised a brow and eyed his former table. "That was three inches thick, my darling."

Well, that explained why it had taken two hits to finish it off. I regarded my bat with newfound respect.

I couldn't find even a scuff on it. "What do you think you're doing?"

"I am holding an audience, or I had been until you took offense to my table. What did my table do to you?"

"It's not big enough for two." I straightened, thumped my bat to my shoulder, and pointed at my wings. "You see these?"

"I do."

"That shitty table wasn't big enough for two."

The Devil leaned back in his seat and took his time looking me over. "It would have been plenty big enough for two if you were to sit on my lap."

Silence fell over the great hall, and I doubted any of the gathered demons or devils breathed. "I'd just knock the damned table over with these wings. I did you a favor getting rid of it."

"You would, and I would find this amusing, especially as you'd be sitting on my lap. Did you come all this way to tell me my table is too small?"

I needed to think about his offer of sitting on his lap for the rest of my life, as that would put me in close proximity with his chest. I took a moment to consider his question, and I shook my head. "No. I just opted to use your table as a way of demonstrating what will happen to anyone who crosses me, especially if she tries to get onto your lap. Your lap is mine, as is the rest of you. Are we clear?"

Lucifer chuckled. "That's not how you ask nicely, Darlene."

I stared at him. "You want me to ask nicely? Hitting the table rather than one of them *was* asking nicely. I could have just waited and hit the first succubus to try to get on your lap, in your pants, or even flirt with you. Taking my general annoyances out on the table was being really nice." I grunted and flexed my hand, debating what I could hit next. "Is this audience necessary, how long will it be, and can you be finished with it now? Please and thank you. I'm done with being nice."

Lucifer rose to his feet, and while I'd put on my fur coat and had a new pair of wings, he still dwarfed me while masquerading as a human. "The audience is absolutely necessary, and my succubi have been most helpful."

I flattened my ears and lashed my tail. "Helpful?"

All growling did was make him smile, and he prowled closer. He touched my cheek, ran his fingers through my fur, and nudged at my wings until I lowered them and tucked them against my back. "Take a few breaths," he ordered.

I obeyed, although I muttered a few curses. After a few breaths, I relaxed, and some of the tension plaguing me eased.

"You're hungry, you want me for breakfast, lunch, and dinner, and you're perceiving a lot of threats nearby in the form of other succubi. I think you have sufficiently established you'll bash heads in should they interfere with your current meal plan, which has dramatically changed since yesterday. Better?"

Focusing on my breathing helped, and after a few moments, I stretched my wings, gave a shake, and nodded. "I'm bad with my wings."

"You'll get used to them. They usually come in smaller and grow over time, but you've had a great deal of exposure to devilish and angelic energy lately. You'll adjust." The Devil took hold of my bat, and while I tightened my grip on it, he still managed to pull it out of my hand. While I scowled over being robbed, he tossed my weapon to

Gabriel, who caught it and tucked it under his arm.

"My bat," I complained.

Lucifer smiled. "I'd rather you not beat me with that right now." Reaching into his pocket, he pulled out my collar and fastened it around my throat. "There. Now you're perfect."

"You need your head examined if you think I'm perfect."

He laughed, captured my hands in his, and raised them to his lips, kissing each of my knuckles in turn. "Beauty is in the eyes of the beholder, as is perfection. You are perfect beauty in my eyes, although I can't help but notice I have meddlesome brothers who changed my plans for me."

The archangels' chiming laughter echoed in the great hall.

Before I could turn to face them, the Devil squeezed my hands and forced my attention back to him. He got down on one knee and smiled as though there were no other place he'd rather be.

My fur stood on end, and my awareness of hundreds of eyes focused on me froze me in place. My breath did me no good stuck in my throat, but I couldn't manage to even swallow.

"From the moment I saw you, daring to storm *my* gates and make demands of me, taunting me with those perfect, precious spots of yours, I knew one thing: you would be mine. You came right into my house, made yourself at home, and went about your plans to conquer, all unaware you'd become my prey."

"Liar," Michael coughed. "She knew precisely what she was getting herself into."

Despite myself, I laughed because it was true.

"That made tricking her into bargaining with me all the sweeter," the Devil confessed, and his smile widened. "You accepted the bargain, so you have to pay up, Darlene, but as I'd really like to explore your new spots at my leisure, I will use those filthy words you like so much. I won't even ask you to be the queen of my hells unless you wish to, although I'd find it very entertaining and attractive were you to help me handle business, punish the fucking assholes you so dislike, and otherwise make things here disgustingly orderly. I might be forced to have you keep matters with those asshole archangels civil. I do not approve of how much they like you. To sweeten the deal in your favor, I am planning on giving you your first fucking asshole, to do with as you please, and any training you might require to best handle his punishments, as part of your wedding present. As promised, here are the filthy words meant for you and only you: please marry me."

It was a good thing my fur hid my skin, as it felt like my cheeks could put lobsters and tomatoes to shame. While I had stipulated a bent knee and the use of filthy words, I hadn't expected him to do so in front of a rather large audience. I'd demanded witnesses, but I hadn't expected such a public declaration.

As always, he took things too far.

A simple yes didn't seem like enough. I spluttered, my face burned hotter, and I blurted, "Are you insane?"

He grinned. "When it comes to you, I absolutely am. Jealousy is beautiful on you, and you've been so jealous lately." The Devil kissed my hands again, and he stroked his thumbs over my fur. "Conveniently, I even captured two archangels solely so they could bear witness and confirm the truth when I tell you that I love you. As I'm the Devil, I'll stalk you to the ends of the universe if I must."

I pricked my ears forward at the thought of running just so the Devil could catch me. After his first lesson on what he did to his woman, I would run to be captured, and I'd enjoy every moment of it. "Promise?"

Laughing, he nodded. "As often as my naughty little kitty would like, but it's your fault when you get what you asked for."

Yes, it was. "Well, as I have been a very naughty little kitten lately and have earned my prolonged stay in your hells, it makes a great deal of sense to marry you," I teased. "But you better make this worth my while."

The Devil rose to his feet, smirked, and grabbed hold of my waist and tossed me over his shoulder. I squealed his name and grabbed hold of his suit jacket. My wings did an admirable job of getting in the way without doing anything useful, like batting Lucifer in the head.

Once he had a good grip on my legs, he bounced me onto his shoulder, gave a dark chuckle, and carted me across his great hall while a bunch of stunned demons and devils stared at us.

"Lucifer, you wretch!" Struggling did no good, as he had a firm hold on me and my wings served as effective shackles, weighing enough I couldn't wiggle upright even if I wanted to. "How is this making it worth my while?"

"You'll find out as soon as I get you to my bed where you belong. When I'm done with you, you won't even be able to purr."

Hallelujah and amen.

Dear readers,

I hope you enjoyed A Chip on Her Shoulder! This was one hell of a fun ride.

Keep reading for a list of my upcoming releases and a rough sample of Outfoxed. Please forgive the clutter, as the furred portion of the management opted to steal imperfect words for your amusement.

~R.J. Blain

## About R.J. Blain

Want to hear from the author when a new book releases? You can sign up at her website (thesneakykittycritic.com). Please note this newsletter is operated by the Furred & Frond Management. Expect to be sassed by a cat. (With guest features of other animals, including dogs.)

A complete list of books written by RJ and her various pen names is available at https://books2read.com/rl/The-Fantasy-Worlds-of-RJ-Blain.

RJ BLAIN suffers from a Moleskine journal obsession, a pen fixation, and a terrible tendency to pun without warning.

When she isn't playing pretend, she likes to think she's a cartographer and a sumi-e painter.

In her spare time, she daydreams about being a spy. Should that fail, her contingency plan involves tying her best of enemies to spinning wheels and quoting James Bond villains until she is satisfied.

RJ also writes as Susan Copperfield and Bernadette Franklin. Visit RJ and her pets (the Management) at thesneakykittycritic.com.

CPSIA information can be obtained
at www.ICGtesting.com
Printed in the USA
LVHW030050100921
697457LV00008B/1247

9 781649 640048